MORE THAN WORDS

A LOVE STORY

MIA SHERIDAN

piatkus

PIATKUS

First published in the US in 2018 by Forever, an imprint of Grand Central Publishing
First published in Great Britain in 2018 by Piatkus

5 7 9 10 8 6 4

A CIP catalogue record for this book
is available from the British Library.

ISBN 978-0-349-41916-9

Printed and bound in Great Britain by
Clays Ltd, Elcograf S.p.A.

Papers used by Piatkus are from well-managed forests
and other responsible sources.

Piatkus
An imprint of
Little, Brown Book Group
Carmelite House
50 Victoria Embankment
London EC4Y 0DZ

An Hachette UK Company
www.hachette.co.uk

www.littlebrown.co.uk

MORE THAN WORDS

This book is dedicated to Judy,
for helping me see the feathers.

MORE THAN WORDS

PROLOGUE

JESSICA—ELEVEN YEARS OLD

"The night was dark and…" I took a tentative step forward, the dry summer grass crunching softly beneath my feet. *Stormy?* No, it wasn't even misty. I squinted at the pale sliver of moon overhead. It wasn't even really dark yet, the evening sky just beginning to take on a deeper twilight blue. A dog barked somewhere in the distance, and then it grew quiet again, my footsteps echoing around me as if I were the only person alive in this strange, treacherous land. "Lonely," I finally decided, whispering the word. I squared my shoulders, summoning courage. "The night was…*dim* and lonely, and yet the princess continued on her journey, believing with all her heart that the prince wasn't far behind and that he'd rescue her. All she had to do was hold on to hope."

I kept walking, my breath hitching as my pulse sped up. I'd

never walked this far from home before, and nothing looked familiar. *Where am I?* As the sky turned gray, lights suddenly blinked on up ahead, and I moved toward them as if they were a beacon, a guide. "The stars glittered in the sky, and the princess followed the brightest ones, sure they would lead her to safety and"—my stomach growled, louder than the soft rise and fall of the cricket song in the evening air—"food."

A slope stood between me and the glowing lights—what I could now see were streetlamps—and I began making my way up slowly. I clutched my book in one hand, using my other hand to balance myself on the steepest sections. "The princess was tired from her journey, and yet she gathered her strength and scaled the cliffs, knowing that she would be able to see where she was from higher ground. Perhaps she'd spot the prince, galloping toward her on his trusty steed."

The lights were very close, and when I reached the top of the incline and emerged through some bushes, I was standing in front of a set of train tracks. I let out a harsh exhale, looking one way and then the other, turning around to survey the land below. Looking down the slope in front me, I could just make out the edge of the golf course that backed up to a wide field. I sighed in relief now that I had my bearings. My house was in a neighborhood on the other side of the golf course. How could I have been so caught up in my own fantasy that I hadn't realized how far I'd walked?

I should head home now that I know which way to go.

I stood for a moment looking in the direction of my house, hearing the echoes of my mother's tears, my father's annoyed voice, and the slamming door telling me my little brother had gone next door to spend the night at his friend Kyle's house. *I don't want to be there.* It'd be hours before they noticed I was gone anyway. If they noticed at all.

I turned back toward the tracks. There was a lone boxcar sitting still and silent a short distance away, and I eyed it curiously, shifting my weight from one foot to the other, a strange fluttering in my chest. "The princess spotted the caves up ahead," I murmured, "and was drawn to them for some reason she couldn't explain." *Fate.*

I walked slowly through the gravel, stepping over the first set of tracks and moving toward the boxcar. The sound of the crickets from the field below grew faint, and the night seemed suddenly quieter and more still, as if the entire world were holding its breath. My heart began beating faster again in anticipation of...something. I touched the side of the boxcar, the metal cool and smooth beneath my fingertips as I trailed my hand along it, moving toward the wide blackness of the open door. My whisper was a bare breath of sound. "The caves were dark, and yet the princess was brave. She would stop here for a while and wait for the prince to catch up with her. He was very close now. She could *feel* it."

Pausing at the edge of the open door, I leaned my head slowly inside, my breath catching and my eyes widening. A boy sat leaning against the far wall, his long legs stretched out before him and crossed at the ankles, his eyes shut. My heart galloped in my chest. *Who is he?* One of the streetlamps cast a glow into the shadowy interior, enough for me to see that the boy's lip was bloody and his eye swollen. I stared, noting the way the boy's dark hair fell over his forehead as if he were too exhausted to move it back. His face was bruised, his eyes shut, and I thought there might be tear tracks on his cheeks, and yet, even so, he was the handsomest boy I had ever seen in my whole life. He was a prince. A...broken prince. My mind spun. *The princess thought* she'd *been waiting for the prince and yet...and yet, she'd had it all backward. The prince had survived battle and crawled to the dark cave nearby to hide, where he'd been waiting...to be rescued by* her.

The boy opened his eyes, which were shiny with tears. He started slightly as he spotted me, his hands curling into fists. But then he blinked the tears away, his brow furrowing and his hands relaxing as he sat up straight.

I pulled myself into the boxcar and stood in front of him, my knees weak with the unexpectedness of finding him. "I'm here to save you," I said in a rush of words.

I felt the blush rising in my cheeks when I realized I'd said the words out loud. He didn't know what I'd been playing, and I suddenly realized how strange and awkward I must seem. I'd been far too involved in my own made-up world. Although...clearly he *did* need saving. Maybe not by a pretend princess, but by *someone* anyway.

The boy's dark eyebrows rose as his gaze moved down my body and then back up to my face. He laughed a small laugh that ended in a sigh. "Oh yeah? Then I'm screwed," he muttered.

Well. I put my hands on my hips, the sympathy I'd felt a moment before turning into irritation. Maybe I *was* strange and awkward, but I didn't deserve to be laughed at. "I'm stronger than I look," I declared, drawing myself up to my full height. I was the fifth-tallest girl in my class.

The boy smirked and ran a hand through his hair, moving it off his forehead. "I'm sure. What are you doing here? Don't you know little girls shouldn't be wandering around train tracks alone at night?"

I stepped farther inside, looking around at the graffiti sprayed all over the walls. There were several pieces of writing on the wall nearest me, and I leaned in to read them. "Better not to read those," the boy said. I turned to him questioningly. "Probably not for kids." He raised an eyebrow. *Probably?* As if he hadn't read them himself. Right.

I cleared my throat, deciding to take his advice anyway. For now. I figured they must be dirty sayings. I'd come back another time and read them when I was alone. Maybe I'd memorize them, too, just because. "You don't look that much older than I am," I said. In truth, I couldn't really tell. If I had to guess, I'd say he was a middle school kid, although there was something about his expression—or maybe his eyes—that made him seem older.

"Yeah, well, I'm a guy, and I know how to protect myself."

I considered his bruised face, thinking there was at least one person he'd had some trouble protecting himself from. "Hmm. How old are you anyway?"

He frowned at me for a moment, as if he wasn't going to answer. "Twelve."

I smiled. "I'm eleven and a half. My name's Jessica Creswell." I kneeled and put my hands on my thighs.

He studied me for a minute, as if he wasn't sure what to think of me. I glanced away, biting my lip, feeling suddenly insecure. I knew I wasn't the prettiest girl. My hair and eyes were both a plain, boring light brown, I had a scattering of freckles over my nose and cheeks that I'd tried to scrub away with lemon juice, which hadn't worked, and I was pitifully skinny. The girls at my snobby French school never stopped reminding me how knobby my knees were or how the stupid cowlick at the front of my head had a mind of its own. I'd smoothed it down with my mom's hair gel, but it had resisted, standing straight up in a stiff spike. *Hopeless.*

"What are you doing here, Jessica Creswell?"

I sat back on my butt, drawing my knees up in a more comfortable position, and leaned on the wall next to the one he was sitting against. "I sorta got lost. But now I know where I am. I know how to get back home."

"Then you should do that. Go home."

I pressed my lips together, frowning at the thought of home.

The corners of his eyes tightened as he watched me, making me feel nervous again. "Don't you like your home, Jessie?"

Jessie. My heart fluttered at the sound of this handsome boy calling me by a nickname. No one had ever called me Jessie before. I liked it. "I...not really. My mom and dad fight a lot." I wasn't sure why I said it, especially to a stranger, but there was something dim and dreamy about the inside of the boxcar, something that felt unreal, as if my pretend game were coming to life around me in some small way. As if what was said here couldn't go any farther.

He sighed again, looking off behind me. "Yeah," he said, as if he understood. I started to ask him if his mom and dad fought a lot, too, but he nodded to the book I'd placed next to me on the floor.

"What's that?"

"*King Arthur and His Knights of the Round Table.*"

He tilted his head. "You like fairy tales, Jessie?"

I nodded slowly. I thought about my parents, about how my mom was always dragging us to hotels and restaurants and to my dad's office after hours, where we'd find him with his girlfriends. I thought about how my brother had been so young when we'd first started finding my father that Johnny's eyes would always light up, and he'd say in this big, happy voice, "Hi, Daddy!" And our dad would cringe, the girlfriend of the moment would either seem to shrink or look shocked, and inside I would want to die of embarrassment. And then my mom would sob and throw a fit, and sometimes my daddy would come home with us, but mostly he would shut the door or drive away, or leave us standing there.

Johnny was nine now and had enough sense to be as embarrassed as me when we found our dad with one of his girlfriends.

My mom was always crying and wailing, and my dad was always making promises that nobody believed. *Not even him*, I thought. And Johnny and I just tried to disappear into the background.

Fairy tales helped me believe that not every man was like my daddy. Fairy tales helped me disappear into worlds where princes were loyal and honest and where princesses were strong and brave.

"Yes. Fairy tales, adventures. Someday I'm going to go on the grandest adventure of all—I'm going to live in Paris, have a French boyfriend who writes me the most beautiful love letters *ever*, and I'm going to eat French chocolate all day long."

"Sounds like you'll be fat."

I shrugged. "Maybe. If I want to be."

The boy chuckled softly, and butterflies fluttered in my tummy. He was even more handsome when he smiled. Although, really looking at him now, I saw that his clothes were worn, his sweatshirt a little too small, and the sole of one shoe was coming loose. He was obviously poor, and the knowledge made tenderness well up in my chest.

"You didn't tell me your name," I said softly, scooting closer.

He eyed me for a second but then shrugged. "Callen."

"Calvin?"

"No, Callen. No v."

I repeated it, liking the way it sounded. "Callen." I paused. "Did you get in a fight?" I asked, my eyes moving from his cut lip to his reddened eye.

"Yeah."

"Who'd you get in a fight with?"

He looked away for a second and then back at me. "Just a bully."

I nodded slowly. "Oh. Well, I hope you can stay away from him from now on."

He let out a laugh that was mostly breath. "No, Jessie, I can't stay away from this bully, but it's okay. I don't mind the bruises."

I frowned, not understanding how anyone could be okay with getting hit in the face. I opened my mouth to say something, when Callen reached forward and picked up my book, looking at the picture on the front cover. He turned it over and began reading the synopsis on the back. "You read French?" I asked, surprised.

His eyes flew to mine, and his expression did something funny. "No. I was wondering what language this is."

I nodded, scooting even closer, leaning my back against the same wall as him. "Want me to read it to you? I can translate. I go to a French school, and we're only supposed to read books in French."

"A French school?"

I nodded. "Every subject is taught in French. It helps kids become fluent."

"Huh," he said, tilting his head, studying me. "So you can eventually move to Paris and get fat."

I grinned. "Yup."

He smiled back, causing those butterflies to take flight again. "Sure, Princess Jessie. Read to me."

* * *

I walked through the neighborhoods, across the golf course and the field, and up the embankment to the train tracks every day that summer.

When Callen was there, I would read to him, or we would go on adventures together. He acted as if he were only doing it for my benefit, but he smiled more than usual when we were traveling into volcanoes in the Realm of the Merciless Vales or picking magical herbs in the Ever Fields.

"I don't want you staying here by yourself, Jessie," he said one afternoon when I told him I'd been there alone the day before. "You never know who else might be hanging around the train tracks."

"I've never seen anyone here except you."

"Yeah, well"—he glanced down the tracks to a turn, where the rails disappeared behind a grove of trees—"the people who hang around the railroad tracks usually stay half a mile that way because the old train cars are hidden by the trees and brush, but you never know."

He was a head taller than I was when we were standing, and I peered up at him, noticing the bruise under his jaw. "But how will I know when you're going to be here?"

He put his hands in his pockets and turned to me. "I'm not really someone you should be hanging around, either."

My heart dropped, and I was suddenly scared he was going to send me away, tell me he didn't want to meet me there anymore. "You're wrong," I insisted. "You're the most wonderful person I ever met."

"Jessie." It was more breath than word, though I was sure I'd heard my name on his soft exhale. He met my eyes and smiled at me, softly, sweetly, and he suddenly looked younger than he was. He sighed, looking off into the distance. Maybe toward where he lived, though I couldn't be sure. Whatever he saw in his mind's eye made his smile slip. When his eyes moved back to mine, he asked, "Can you meet Tuesdays and Thursdays at seven o'clock?"

That was after dinner, when my dad left for an "unexpected" business meeting that we all knew was really some woman waiting in a hotel room for him and my mom opened a bottle of wine and cried now that we were too old to be dragged all over town without putting up a fight. "Yes, I can meet you then. And Saturdays at three?"

He was quiet for a moment, and then he gave me a crooked smile that made my heart do a somersault. "And Saturdays at three."

* * *

One cold autumn day a year after we'd first met, we sat close together in the boxcar, my breath pluming in the air as I read to Callen from the French version of *The Adventures of Robin Hood*. I paused when he reached forward and pulled the edge of a piece of paper out of my backpack. He studied it for a moment, his gaze moving over the page before his eyes flew to mine. "What is this?"

I set the book down, tilting my head as I turned to face him. "My piano music."

He looked back to the paper and held it toward me, pointing at the first note. "These are notes."

"Yes," I said, frowning. "Haven't you ever seen music?"

"Not written out like this." There was something odd in his voice, and he was talking fast. He pointed at the first note. "This one?"

"Um, that's an *E*."

"An *E*?" he asked, bunching up his brow. "The letter *E*?"

I shook my head. "Well, yes, like the letter, but, um, a note. A different, er…language, I guess." I smiled, but he was still wearing an intense look of concentration as he turned back to the music, his brow smoothing after a moment. He pointed at another E and then another. "These are all *E*s."

I nodded, confused about his excitement. In the year I'd known him, I'd only ever witnessed two emotions: sullen or kinda happy. I had a moment of irrational jealousy over his sudden enthusiasm. "Yes."

He nodded, a jerky movement of his head. I could see his pulse thrumming quickly under the smooth, tanned skin of his throat. "What's this?"

I glanced down at what he was pointing at. "That's the treble clef. It tells you the pitch and key of the notes on that line."

His brow furrowed, and I rushed to explain further. "Pitch and key are…the highness and lowness of notes."

He nodded again, his eyes wide and shining with something I didn't know how to name. It was *more* than excitement. It was…disbelief. Was he that excited to be reading in a different language? I noticed the way he hummed when we were playing. He'd put music to our games—slow, dark, and creepy when we were hunting for a villain, light and happy when we were running through a meadow of magical, talking bluebells. Sometimes I'd look at him and smile at some particular melody and he'd glance at me in surprise, as if he didn't even know the music was anywhere except inside him. He looked up and our eyes met, causing a tremor of delight to move down my spine. "Will you bring me more?"

"More music?"

"Yes."

"O-okay. I, um, I have a keyboard, too. I could bring it? It has a carry case."

"Yes," he breathed. He grabbed my hand and squeezed it, and another small thrill went through me at his touch. I suddenly felt shy but glad to have given him something that obviously brought him happiness. I wanted to give him more. I wanted him to direct those clear gray eyes at me again and see them bright with joy.

So, two days later, I ran through the field and over the tracks, the keyboard case clutched in my hand and excitement filling my chest. I taught Callen which notes were which as his eyes lit with that same wonder. I'd never been very good at the piano, but I'd learned the basics, and I gave those to Callen along with the keyboard that had been in my closet unused for so long I'd almost forgotten about it.

He took to music like a fish takes to water, and I was amazed that in only a couple of months he was far better than I'd ever be, even though we had a Schimmel baby grand that I sat at each week, practicing for what felt like hours and hours, but in reality was only thirty minutes.

He showed up one day later that year looking angry, his face bruised, and sat down heavily, leaning his head against the wall. "Will you read to me today, Jessie?"

I nodded, taking the book I was in the middle of out of my backpack. "Sure." I started *The Three Musketeers*, pausing and glancing up at him after I'd read a few paragraphs. His expression had settled into sadness and his eyes were closed. I gathered my courage. "Is it your dad who hits you?" I asked softly.

His eyes opened, but he didn't turn his head toward me. He was silent for so long, I wondered if he'd answer me at all, and my heart began beating faster, scared that he would be angry with me and leave instead. "Yeah."

My heart squeezed, and I released the breath I'd held in my throat.

He looked at me, his gaze moving over my face. "I can handle the hitting. It's...it's the words that...Anyway..."

I desperately wanted to ask him to say more, but I wasn't sure how. I cleared my throat. "My dad isn't a good man either." I whispered it as if there were someone close by I was trying to prevent from hearing the truth. Maybe myself. I'd known it for a long time, as long as I could remember actually, but somehow saying it out loud made it an unavoidable truth. I'd never be able to pretend again. My father was weak and selfish, and he didn't love us enough, if he even loved us at all.

Callen reached out and took my hand in his, and my eyes darted to our interlaced fingers, mine small and pale and his tanned and calloused and so much larger than my own. I kept my eyes on our joined hands and swallowed before continuing. "But the worst part is that my mom can't stop loving him. No matter how much he makes her cry, she keeps coming back for more. I just...I don't know how one person has that many tears."

When I raised my eyes to his, he was staring at me. I felt self-conscious, even though he'd told me a secret, too, and I bit my lip and looked away. "Is that why you like fairy tales so much, Jessie?" His voice was soft, laced with something tender, but the question made me feel more exposed. He squeezed my hand gently. I wanted to pull away and I wanted to get closer, and the feelings running through my body were new and confusing, thrilling and scary.

"We haven't played those games for a while now," I answered, shaking my head. Instead of going on adventures, I read aloud or did homework, and Callen played the keyboard, his brow furrowed in concentration, creating partial melodies that were so beautiful they made my heart trip over itself. Music that often faded away into nothing, as if the loveliness had slipped right through his fingers, or he didn't know where to take it.

His full lips tilted up. "Sometimes I miss playing make-believe."

I grinned. "You do?"

"Yeah. You made me feel like a hero."

"You are," I breathed. "To me, you are."

He shook his head. "No, Jessie. I'm no hero. God, I can't even..."

"What? What does he say you can't do?" I asked, feeling fierce and protective, knowing it was his father who put that haunted look in his eyes.

Callen laughed, but there was no humor in the sound. "He only tells the truth."

"No! I'd like to go to your house and give your father a piece of my—"

"Don't you dare." The words were sharp and icy, and I stared at him, my cheeks flushing and my eyes filling with tears. Callen had never spoken so harshly to me before.

"I...I wouldn't do anything that—"

He leaned forward so suddenly, I let out a gasp, and then his lips were on mine, soft and warm, and a shimmery heat moved through my body. I paused, uncertain, for I'd never been kissed before, not even close. I had clunky braces on my teeth, and I had no idea what to do.

Callen gripped my hand more tightly and used his other hand to cup the back of my head as he pulled me even closer and rubbed his lips softly—slowly—over mine. I let out a tiny breath, and he hesitantly moved his tongue along my parted lips, causing me to instinctively open them.

He jolted as if surprised, and I opened my eyes to find that his were open, too. For a few moments we stared at each other close up, our eyes wide, and I was dimly aware that my heart was slamming in my chest, before he once again closed his lids. He tilted his head and pressed his tongue inside my mouth—just barely—and I closed my eyes, meeting the very tip of his tongue with the tip of mine, touching and then retreating. A cascade of feeling sparked inside me: excitement, nervousness, joy, and fear. Callen nibbled softly at my lips, and I sighed in wonder at the physical sensation, loving the taste of his mouth, the way he smelled up close like this—cinnamon, and salt, and some sort of soap. Like a boy. *Like my prince.*

When he pulled away, I felt dazed and half-asleep, floating in some other world. I blinked, bringing myself back to the moment, and smiled shyly at him. He gave me a crooked smile in return. "No one makes me feel like you, Princess Jessie. No one ever will."

It was the only time he ever kissed me.

Callen never came back to the train tracks after that day. I went every Tuesday, Thursday, and Saturday, hoping desperately he'd be there again. I didn't know where to begin to look for him. Santa Lucinda, the city in Northern California where we lived, was far too big, and I didn't even know his last name.

The only thing I had to remember him by was a string of hand-drawn musical notes written on a torn piece of paper I'd found in the corner of our boxcar.

As I waited week after week, I racked my brain for a reason why he had disappeared. Had I done something wrong? Had he hated kissing me? Had he felt ashamed? Had his father done something terrible to him? I felt desperate for answers I had no way to get.

Finally, one Tuesday evening in late summer, after an entire year of hoping he'd return, I sat alone in the doorway of our boxcar and said a silent farewell to my vanished hero—my broken prince—wiped a tear from my cheek, and never returned.

PART ONE

One life is all we have and we live it as we believe in living it. But to sacrifice what you are and to live without belief, that is a fate more terrible than dying.

—*Joan of Arc*

CHAPTER ONE

Ten Years Later

CALLEN

I threw back the shot of tequila and grimaced as it burned down my throat. Tequila was not my drink of choice, but my agent had ordered a round and I could hardly refuse. Well, I could have. I could do whatever the fuck I wanted. But why turn down perfectly good alcohol?

I brought the slice of lime to my lips and sank my teeth into it, the sour bite of the fruit soothing the lingering burn of the tequila. The room blurred slightly before coming back into focus. I'd already had too much to drink, but I felt warm and comfortably numb, and I leaned back in my chair, enjoying the familiar sensation. *Too familiar recently*, a small voice said before I tuned it out.

The chatter at my table was mere background noise, and I

looked around the bar, my eyes snagging on the brunette cocktail waitress standing at a table nearby, a tray in her hand. She placed a glass of wine in front of an older man, and her eyes darted over to me, widened when she saw I was staring at her, and then moved quickly away. My heart jumped, a buzz of electricity shooting down my spine, and I frowned, surprised by my reaction. The girl stood straight, said something to the couple at the table that made them smile, and then turned and walked away, not looking at me again. I watched as she moved toward the bar, entranced for some reason I couldn't quite pinpoint. She was pretty, but not exactly my type. I tended toward tall, willowy blondes...didn't I? For a minute I was confused by my own thought. Suddenly I couldn't remember *what* I liked. I couldn't remember actually having any preferences at all other than *available*.

I massaged my temples, feeling a headache coming on, still unable to tear my eyes away from the girl. She definitely *wasn't* willowy. Nor was she blond. She was neither short nor tall, average height, her hair in a messy ponytail, no makeup as far as I could tell, wearing an unflattering uniform, and I...God, I couldn't stop staring at her.

"Where have you gone?" Charlène, the latest tall, willowy blonde purred, leaning close to my ear and running her hand along the inside of my thigh. Her French accent was strong, but not as strong as her cloying perfume.

I shot her a lazy smile. "I'm right here, baby."

"But your mind is not." Her hand moved farther up my thigh, stopping just before she got to my crotch, and I twitched in my pants. My mind might not be on Charlène, but my body was paying attention.

I tore my eyes from the girl, who now leaned over the bar,

talking to the bartender, and returned my attention to Charlène. The contrast between the simple, clean prettiness of the girl I'd been staring at and Charlène's sophisticated beauty struck me, and I was surprised that I wanted to look away from Charlène and back to the cocktail waitress. I resisted the temptation, my eyes moving downward as Charlène crossed her legs and the split in her black evening gown fell open, revealing smooth, tanned thighs.

I raised my eyes from her legs and smiled, turning toward her and focusing back on our conversation. She wasn't going to let me fuck her later if I didn't put in at least minimal effort.

"Did you see this?" Charlène asked, handing me her phone. I recognized the logo of a gossip website she had pulled up that featured a photo of the two of us from earlier that night at the award banquet where I'd met her. "Look what they called you," she said, laughing softly and pointing at the caption beneath the picture.

I brought it closer and smiled wryly as I handed it back. "I've been called worse."

"I'd have thought you'd like that one."

You don't even know me. How the fuck would you know what I like? I looked around the lounge, feeling suddenly claustrophobic. *Idiot. Dimwit. Moron.* "Sure," I murmured.

Charlène sighed, smoothing her hair back. "You are strange, Callen Hayes. Any man would love to be called the Sexiest Man in Music."

The male server who had been bringing us drinks suddenly appeared with another round, placing a shot of something amber in front of each of us, and I was grateful for the interruption. "Jesus, more?" my agent, Larry, asked, though he didn't hesitate to pick his up, sniffing it and smiling appreciatively. There was a smear of white powder on the side of his nostril from his recent trip to the bathroom, and I considered letting him know in some subtle way but decided against it. No one here cared.

"It's not every day a new classical composer wins the Poirier Award," Larry's wife, Annette, said, shooting me a tight smile that was closer to a sneer. She gave Charlène a frosty look and then raised her glass. "To Callen, who is...*très bon* at *everything* he does." She gave me a suggestive smile and then raised her glass and threw the shot back, her long, elegant throat moving as she swallowed. I glanced at Larry, but he was laughing at something the guy next to him was saying.

I raised an eyebrow and nodded at Annette, throwing my own shot back, loosening the bow tie at my throat and attempting to take a full breath for the first time in what felt like hours. Dinner had been tedious, the award ceremony had been boring, and sitting here with these fawning, superficial people was completely tiresome. The catch was: *I* was one of them. *No better.* Fuck, I wanted nothing more than to ditch them all and go back to my hotel room alone. But the thought both lured me and filled me with clawing terror. I needed to start the new compositions I'd been hired to write, and so far I hadn't come up with a single note.

I pushed the fears away as best as I could, the alcohol aiding in that effort. The same way sex would later. At least long enough to shut the words out—*his* words. Long enough to get something on paper. *Please, God.* But God had never answered me before, and I didn't figure he would now. No, I'd have to do what I could to quiet the demons myself. Just as I always had.

Long enough to let the music play.

Three years ago I'd sold a composition I'd written to a small French indie film studio that had used it for one of their movie's theme songs. The piece had gained so much popularity that a larger film studio in Hollywood hired me to write several songs for a movie they were producing—a movie that became a blockbuster hit. Close on the heels of that success, I put out an album of compositions to more critical acclaim, and then a second that received only lukewarm reviews, but even so, I'd suddenly found myself a sort of celebrity, with people snapping pictures of me in restaurants and on the street and being offered interviews on high-profile networks. It had been a fast and furious whirlwind, and I hadn't always reacted well to the constant invasion of privacy.

As it turned out, that only made me more sought after, news-wise, as the "bad-boy composer." They thought they had me pegged as some sort of dark creative who sat alone in his apartment, tearing at his hair and scrawling notes on paper in a mad frenzy before hopping into bed with three supermodels who simultaneously indulged my wicked sexual appetites. Which, actually, wasn't completely off the mark. Although recently the music scrawling part had eluded me while the wicked sex had not.

The sex and alcohol *had* once offered the mind-numbing blankness that allowed the notes to take shape and form. I was able to lock myself away and write for days and days—weeks sometimes—whereas now I was lucky to get a few good hours of creativity. Which was unfortunate, considering I'd signed a contract to write a soundtrack and was expected to deliver something ingenious to the largest studio in Hollywood for a movie slated to come out the following year. I needed to produce something great, something that wouldn't give the critics cause to say my talent was slipping and my initial success was nothing more than a fluke. Of course, that pressure was my own, but it was weighty nonetheless.

"So, Callen, what's next now that you're an international sensation?" the guy who'd been talking to Larry a moment before asked.

I shot him a look. *International sensation?* For the love of Christ. Who talked like that? Yes, I'd won a damn award, and I was proud of it. But why did everyone around me always sound like they were interviewing me for some article?

"Grégoire's with *Le Célébrité*," Larry said, nodding to the man, who had his phone out and was aiming it at Charlène's hand still on my thigh. I glanced at her, and she was shooting the reporter a pouty smile, knowing damn well he was taking our picture for his French tabloid.

I stood, jostling Charlène, who let out a high-pitched sound of annoyance. "Next up is the john."

"It's called the 'loo' here in France," Annette offered.

I ignored her, looking at the reporter who'd infiltrated our group. Not that it would have taken any effort. Half the time I had no idea who the people hanging around me were. "Do you want to come along and see if you can get a picture of my dick while I'm pissing?"

The reporter appeared to consider that briefly before shaking his head. I made a disgusted sound in the back of my throat, teetered momentarily, and walked toward the dark hallway at the back of the bar.

Jesus. I'm drunk. Too drunk.

I felt my phone vibrate in my pocket and fumbled with it for a minute as it snagged on a thread. I finally pulled it out, squinting at Nick's picture just as my voice mail picked up, causing his smiling face to blink away. He was probably calling to congratulate me on the award. I paused in the hallway, watching my phone until it indicated I had a voice mail. When I pressed play, Nick's familiar voice filled my ear.

Hey, buddy, I just saw online that you won that award. Nice fucking job. I'm proud of you, man. <pause> Take care of yourself, okay, Cal? And call me when you can.

I returned my phone to my pocket, vowing to call him later, knowing he'd be disappointed in me if he could see me stumbling around drunk in a dark hallway to escape the shallow people surrounding me. People I'd made a bigger part of my life than him, my closest friend and the only person I could truly trust.

This is not you, Cal, he'd say. Only it was. It was.

I tried a door but saw that it was a utility closet filled with shelves of cleaning supplies and paper products. I pulled the door shut, looking for another door or a sign with a picture that would indicate where the damn bathroom was but didn't see anything. I turned the corner and spotted a door at the end of the hall and stepped through. I was on an empty outdoor patio that was either closed for the season or the night. I started to turn back but decided to take a moment to shut out the fake laughter and the idle chitchat, just to *breathe*.

Take care of yourself, okay, Cal?

Why did that seem like such an impossible task lately? I walked to the chest-high wall that surrounded the rooftop patio and put my elbows on it, bending my neck forward and raking my hands through my hair as I pulled cool air in through my nose. I felt better, a little less drunk, a little less…angry, annoyed. Who knew what the fuck I was feeling anymore? It'd been so long since I'd stopped to really consider it. I only knew that I wasn't happy.

I heard a noise behind me and turned around to see the

brunette waitress standing in the doorway, the door closing slowly behind her. Her eyes were wide and her lips parted in surprise, as if she hadn't expected to find anyone out here. When the door hit her butt, she let out a small gasp as it propelled her forward.

For a second we just stared at each other across the deck. I tried my damnedest not to sway on my feet.

"I...ah...sorry. I think I took a wrong turn." I raised my arm, making a movement that indicated the outdoor patio and that it wasn't where I'd meant to end up. I hoped she spoke English. My French wasn't very good. Actually, it was awful.

She opened her mouth to speak, but then seemed to change her mind. She stared at me for another moment before saying softly, "I'm here to save you."

I frowned, leaning back against the wall as something raced through my mind, something I tried to grasp, but it eluded me. She bit at her lip and fidgeted, and I realized she must have been making a joke. She was obviously shy, and I'd just made her feel uncomfortable. I smiled and then chuckled softly, raising one brow. "I appreciate that, but I think I'm beyond saving, sweetheart."

She let out a breath, and instead of looking relieved that the awkward moment had passed, she looked...disappointed. "Didn't you see the sign?" She nodded toward the door.

Yes, I had seen the sign. "I don't read French."

Her lips tipped up. "It's in both English and French."

"I must not have noticed." Her brows came in slightly, and I moved toward her slowly, drawn to her in some inexplicable way.

She didn't move, didn't flinch, didn't even really look surprised, and when I stepped up to her, she tipped her head back to look at me. The disappointed expression was gone, and now she looked soft and sort of breathless. Expectant.

"You're American," I said, realizing suddenly she hadn't had any trace of an accent when she'd spoken. She only nodded.

My eyes moved over her face, and from up close like this she was more than merely pretty. Her skin was smooth and creamy, and I could see a very light dusting of freckles across her nose. I wanted to kiss those freckles, each and every one, to touch them with my tongue and know if they tasted like innocence. I almost laughed at myself. *Innocence.* When had innocence ever been appealing to me anyway?

Her large hazel eyes widened, framed by dark, sweeping lashes. Her upper lip was fuller than the bottom and turned downward in a way that gave her a natural pout. Christ, from where I'd sat watching her earlier, I hadn't been able to see how soft and tempting her mouth was. I very suddenly needed to feel those pink, parted lips on my mouth, on my skin, more than I needed anything else on the face of the earth.

I leaned in, expecting her to stop me at any moment, but she didn't. My lips met hers, and she let out a whimpering sound that shot straight to my cock. I hardened as I swept my tongue between her lips, tasting her, exploring. Her tongue met mine shyly, tentatively, and though she was obviously unskilled, her kiss set fire to my blood in a way no one else's had in a very long time, maybe ever. God, she tasted so damn sweet, so fresh and pure.

My cock swelled and pressed against my zipper, causing me to groan and move against her, to pull her closer and thread my fingers into the back of her hair. I felt her ponytail come loose as her hair spilled over my hands, the faint scent of her shampoo filling my nose, something light and clean.

Light and clean.

I wanted her. I wanted her so badly I was shaking with it.

What is this? I was almost tempted to pick her up and carry her to one of the deserted tables, to lean her over it and relieve the terrible ache between my legs. Somewhere in my bleary, muddled mind, it even seemed possible that this girl could soothe the deep, dark, pained places inside myself that I had no idea how to access.

Just for tonight—*just one damn night*—I wanted to lose myself in the sweetness so clear in this girl's eyes, the pure innocence I could feel emanating from her.

There was no place for sweetness in my life. And definitely no place for innocence.

But, ah, I wanted it so badly. And on that starlit deck on a cool Paris night, I admitted how much, even if only to myself. It beckoned like a sleepy lover. Like a muse that promised to stay longer than a brief moment or maybe two. And I didn't deserve it, but I didn't care.

I broke the kiss, trailing my mouth across her cheeks, feathering my lips over those angel kisses scattered so delicately on her skin. "Come home with me," I whispered, unable to disguise the neediness in my voice.

"You're drunk," she whispered back. "I've been watching you drink all night."

"Yes." I didn't deny it. "It won't affect my performance. It never does."

She stilled in my arms, and I realized how crass my words must have sounded, how common I must have just made her feel. And yet wasn't she? When it came down to it, wasn't that exactly what I wanted to make her? Common? Could I really pretend she'd be any different from the rest? Different from the myriad women I was with for a night and never again? I had nothing to offer a girl like this, so why did it feel like something that had been blooming a moment before had just withered inside me? I didn't know what it might be, but it felt like *something*. I'd *felt* something…

"You're different," she said, and sadness laced her voice. It had been a long time since anyone had wasted sadness on me. And what did she mean by *different*? Ah, she knew who I was. She'd recognized me. Maybe she had some fantasy that Callen Hayes was someone different from who they reported me to be. Maybe she thought I was just misunderstood. For a crazy second, looking down into her soulful eyes, I wanted to believe it was true. But I knew it wasn't. I opened my mouth to say something, to try to correct my mistake maybe, or perhaps just to apologize, when suddenly the door swung open behind us. I let go of the girl, and we both stumbled, turning at the same time.

Charlène stood in the doorway, her arms crossed under her small, round breasts, one eyebrow raised and a sardonic tilt to her shiny red lips. "If you're done feeling up the help, can we leave now? You did ask me to come home with you, *oui*?"

I cringed internally as the girl's shoulders drooped. *Jesus Christ*. I'd said those exact words to her. She glanced at me—her pretty mouth swollen, her hair hanging loosely around her shoulders—and I saw deep disappointment in her expression. For the first time in a long while, I saw myself through someone else's eyes, and I hated what I saw. She pulled her shoulders back and stepped away from me, past Charlène and through the door. Just like that, she was gone.

CHAPTER TWO

JESSICA

"How'd it go?" my roommate, Francesca, asked as I came in the door.

I threw my purse down and went straight to the refrigerator directly off the living room, removing a bottle of water and taking a long sip. "Fine if being officially unemployed is a good thing." I offered Frankie a rueful smile, taking another sip of the cool water. The apartment was stifling, and I felt a bead of sweat roll down my back.

"I'm going to change and then I'll be right back." I went to my tiny room and began peeling off my skirt and blouse, hanging them both carefully in my closet. I didn't have many professional work clothes, and I needed to treat the ones I had gently, given I now needed to apply for a new job.

Throwing on a pair of cotton shorts and a loose tank top and gathering my hair into a high ponytail helped cool me off before I headed back to the living room.

A *pop* startled me, and I laughed when I saw that Frankie had just opened a bottle of champagne and was pouring it into two champagne flutes.

"*Santé, mon amie*," she sang as she handed me one of the flutes and raised her own glass. I grinned and took a sip of the cheap bubbly. "This is the first step on the road to a wonderful career."

"*Merci.*" I plopped down on the couch, putting my flute on the coffee table and bringing my legs under me. Frankie sat down on the other end of the couch, taking another sip of champagne and screwing up her face.

"The best I could afford," she said.

"As soon as I find a job, the champagne is on me. Let's hope I'll finally be able to afford something decent."

She smiled. "You will. I'm proud of you for taking this leap."

"Yeah, yeah. But if I end up in the poorhouse, I'm blaming you."

"Fair enough. Although I don't think there are poorhouses anymore. It's the cold, lonely street you'll end up on, my little cabbage."

"Great." I smiled at the term of endearment, our familiar joke. She'd heard the term *ma choupette* somewhere and asked me what it meant, and I'd translated it literally. It was now Frankie's favorite nickname. Despite her Italian first name, Frankie wasn't fluent in *any* of the romance languages, and when we'd met she'd spoken only a few words of French. I'd met her at an Internet café when I'd first arrived in Paris, heard her fumbling her way through an order for coffee and a croissant and helped her out. We'd struck up a conversation after that and hit it off. We'd both been looking for a roommate, and it felt like it was meant to be. Thankfully, simply living and working in France had improved her French. Frankie worked at the fashion house of a hip new designer named Clémence Maillard. She loved her job, but her salary wasn't much better than mine.

Actually, I reminded myself, everyone's salary was now officially better than mine. I no longer *had* a salary.

"How'd Vincenzo take you quitting?"

I sighed. "Fine. He'll have no trouble replacing me." I picked up my glass and took a sip. Vincenzo had probably already filled the spot. Lounge La Vue was one of the most popular, swankiest hotel bars in Paris, and the tips were usually great. But I'd spent enough time as a part-time cocktail waitress.

A year ago, I'd graduated from Cornell University with a major in French and a minor in French medieval history, moved to Paris, and started applying for jobs. When the only offer I received was from a small newspaper that didn't pay enough for me to eat three meals a day, I'd taken the serving job at Lounge La Vue and fed my brain with short (unpaid) internships in museums. My most recent internship had just ended, and quitting Lounge La Vue was going to force me to get out there and find something in my field that paid real money. Frankie was right— it was time to take a leap of faith.

Through my studies I'd found that I had a particular talent— and affinity—for translating old French. If I managed to find a job where I could put that skill to use, it would be a dream come true.

I could have asked my father for help, which would have allowed me to get started on my career faster, but I was bound and determined not to ask him for anything. He had decided the French school in my hometown offered the best education, and it's where I had first discovered my love for the study of language and all things French. For that I was grateful to him, though there was little else. My mother had passed away from cancer when I was twenty, and given that the diagnosis had come when she was already stage four, it seemed she was there one day and gone the next. Four years later, I still mourned the loss of her, but I was also sad about the life *she* had accepted for herself. She'd lived for only forty-eight years and had spent more than half that life living with a man who treated her like she was no one special. I wanted more for myself. I would never accept a life like that. My father had promptly remarried, to a girl only a year older than me. I was sure he was already cheating on her, too. It's not as if I would ask. *Or care.* We'd never been close to begin with, and now we barely talked.

Thank goodness for Frankie. I had a small circle of friends in Paris—girls I'd met at Lounge La Vue mostly—but Frankie was more like the sister I'd never had. I'd created a family of my choosing here in France.

I leaned my head back on the couch. I hadn't eaten anything since breakfast, and the champagne was already causing me to feel sleepy and languorous.

"He never came in to the lounge again, did he?" Frankie asked, eyeing me. I almost pretended I didn't comprehend who "he" was, but she'd know very well I was just being bitter and purposefully dismissive.

"No." I'd returned to the tiny apartment I shared with Frankie after the night two months ago when Callen Hayes had come into Lounge La Vue, kissed me senseless, and then left with another woman. Not that he shouldn't have...He had clearly arrived with her. I'd seen her sitting close to him at the crowded table, but he'd been staring at *me*, and I'd hoped...

Well, I had hoped he would recognize me at the very least. But he hadn't. He had no idea who I was, other than a barmaid who he probably thought had been making googly eyes at him all night. Which I had been, sort of, but it was more a case of disbelief. After all those years, my Callen had walked back into my life. Although, he had never really been *my* Callen. And, well...he never would be.

But at the time I hadn't been able to help the low-simmering thrill that had sparked inside me at the possibility he would remember me as the little girl he'd sat with in a boxcar on a deserted stretch of train track long, long ago. The little girl he used to go on adventures with, play games with, and indulge her overactive imagination.

He'd kissed me on the patio, and he hadn't tasted like warmth and hope, not like I'd remembered. He'd tasted like alcohol and sin. He wasn't the boy I'd known—not even close—and it had broken my heart just a little bit. I'd come home and cried on Frankie's shoulder, telling her the whole story from the beginning. It was the second time in my life he'd kissed me and left. *And never returned.*

She knew who Callen Hayes was, of course. I figured any female between the ages of fifteen and fifty must. The first time I'd seen him on *Entertainment Tonight*, I'd almost fallen over. I'd first been mesmerized by the gorgeous man on the television, and although he looked familiar in a way I couldn't quite place, when they said his name, I'd known immediately who he was. I'd put my hand over my mouth to contain the loud gasp of surprise and sank down on the couch, watching in a daze as he effortlessly charmed the simpering female host.

That smile. He'd been a handsome boy, and now...he was devastating.

I'd taken the old, torn piece of paper out of my copy of *King Arthur and His Knights of the Round Table* and run my finger over the faded notes, wonder flowing through me that the famous man on TV was the boy who'd once drawn them. I'd downloaded all his compositions and recognized a piece of one from that boxcar so many years before—the melody he'd finally figured out how to finish. I listened to it over and over on my iPod, my headphones in my ears, as I closed my eyes and traveled back in time. I swore I could feel his boyish, calloused hand in mine. Silly. Stupid. Yet oh so true.

I'd followed his career since then, watched his star rise, his fame grow, and I was…proud. I had so many questions about why he'd disappeared without a goodbye, but I couldn't deny the pride that filled my chest whenever I saw a glowing article about him. Not that he wasn't also featured in the tabloids for his so-called bad-boy antics. He had a reputation, one the media seemed to find fascinating and women found alluring. I'd wondered how much was reality and how much was manufactured, but seeing him at Lounge La Vue had answered that question. He was exactly who they reported him to be, or at least pretty damn close. He drank, he partied, and he…kissed stupid girls on patios just because he could. Because I—*they*—were putty in his hands.

And why should I be heartbroken? He owed me nothing. I had known him for only a brief span of time so long ago, when we were both children. So he'd grown up to be a conceited, womanizing manwhore—a wildly successful, crazy talented, conceited, womanizing manwhore. Well, good for him. *And lucky for me he'd left that night with the French blonde.* His ability to step away from his date and kiss a stranger within three minutes told me more than I needed to know about Callen Hayes of the present.

Whatever was on my face made Frankie offer me a look of sympathy. I downed the final sip of the champagne and held the glass up, requesting more. Frankie grabbed the bottle and re-filled my flute. "Have you considered trying to contact him?"

"God, no. Why would I?"

She shrugged. "You didn't even tell him who you were. Don't you think he might have—"

"Might have what? Gifted me with one of those one-night stands he seems so famous for?"

She grinned. "Would it have been so bad?"

I rolled my eyes, giving her my best look of disgust. Unlike me, Frankie was never without a boyfriend or at least a crush. She flitted from one man to another, constantly falling in and out of love. But love would have had nothing to do with what Callen Hayes offered me that night, if he'd have offered me any-thing at all. "To be one in a sea of many? No thanks. Plus, I...I didn't want to tell him who I was. I wanted him to remember." I wanted to believe he'd know me anywhere...that he treasured the memories of that time, brief though it was. That he had a great reason for never coming back, for never even saying good-bye, and that he'd lived with regret all these years. I groaned. What a bunch of childlike, stupid, romantic drivel.

Frankie raised a brow. "I've seen pictures of you at thirteen, Jess, and no offense, but thank goodness he didn't recognize you."

I laughed, spitting out a tiny bit of the champagne I'd just taken a sip of. I wiped at my lip with my thumb. "Gee, thanks."

She laughed along with me, winking. "I'm kidding. Mostly."

I stuck my tongue out at her and laughed. It ended on a sigh. "No, we're nothing to each other now, and maybe we never were. Or maybe he meant something to me, but he didn't feel the same way. In any case, I could have told him who I was, but why? We're different people, strangers now, and we'll never cross paths again."

She leaned forward and patted my knee. "All right. Speaking of strangers, what do you say we go out dancing tonight and find a few cute ones?"

I was feeling drowsy and slightly drunk from the two glasses of champagne, and so I groaned and shook my head. "No way. I'm making dinner, and then I'm crawling into bed. I need to start sending out résumés or I won't be able to pay the rent."

"Fine. You're no fun. I'll call Amelie." She stood, and I grabbed the remote, turning on the television and taking a last sip of champagne. It'd already gone flat, and a headache was setting in.

A talk show of some sort was on, and when Callen's face suddenly came on the screen, his broody expression both sexy and annoying, I made a disgruntled sound and fumbled for the remote, punching at the off button. "God, *really?*" I stood and brushed my hands together, determined to say goodbye to Callen Hayes for the second time in my life. Too bad I hadn't said either one to his face.

CHAPTER THREE

CALLEN

I woke slowly and groaned, my head aching and my muscles so sore I wasn't sure I could move. I stretched and felt something warm at my back. *Oh no. Fuck.* This was the part that was beginning to get tiresome and uncomfortable—confronting my mistakes from the night before. "Good morning," a familiar voice purred. I froze. *Oh God, even worse.* Rolling over, I opened one eye cautiously. "I thought I told you this wasn't happening again."

Annette plumped the pillow behind her head and lay back on it, scowling and crossing her arms over her naked breasts. "I knew you didn't mean it."

I sat up and then fell back onto the pillow when a sharp knife sliced through my skull. "Fuck, how much did I drink last night?"

"From the number of empty bottles in your living room, I'd say a lot."

"Well, that explains why you're here. I was too drunk to realize who you were."

She let out an angry snarl and slapped at my shoulder. The jostling caused more pain in my head, but the insult worked to get her out of my bed. She swung her legs over the side and stood, turning slowly and placing her hands on her hips. My eyes ran lazily down her nude body, and for a flash I considered going for another round—despite no memory of the *first* round—but I knew from experience that Annette liked it rough and rowdy and my head hurt too much for a naked wrestling match. A quick glance at my chest showed that she'd used her fingernails and teeth last night. Disgust, and something that felt like depression, settled in my chest. "Where does Larry think you are?"

"Maybe I told him I was coming to you."

"Doubtful. I can find another agent, but you'd be hard-pressed to find another husband as rich as him and as willing to believe your lies."

She thinned her lips. "If he's so stupid, why do you keep him around?"

"He's only stupid when it comes to you." I yawned.

"Do you think he doesn't have his own…interests on the side?"

I ignored her. I didn't give a rat's ass about the details of Larry and Annette's marriage and less about what Larry's side interests might be. I knew very well Larry would be less than thrilled to know I had fucked his wife. More than once. Not that I meant it to be an ongoing thing—Annette was just more persistent than most and had a way of catching me at my least resistant.

She turned toward me and ran her hands over her large,

perky breasts, playing with her nipples as she eyed me through half-closed lids. "Mmm," she purred.

Her show wasn't even mildly arousing. I could see a stack of music ledgers on the desk near the window, and they were the only thing that interested me right now. *Please, please, please let something good be on that paper.* "Go home, Annette. I'm done with you, and I have work to do."

She dropped her hands from her breasts and huffed indignantly, picking up a pillow and throwing it at me. I dodged it, and when I looked up she was storming around the room, gathering her clothes. "You weren't done with me last night!" She began pulling on her clothes violently, and I was surprised she didn't tear them to pieces in her anger. "You're a fucking prick and a miserable drunk."

"Flattery won't work this time," I said easily. She glared at me as I smirked in amusement, and then she turned with a flourish and fast-walked out the bedroom door.

I got up and stood in the doorway, watching as she grabbed her purse off the couch and headed to the door. "Thanks for the memories," I called sarcastically.

She turned around stiffly, anger radiating off her, picked up an empty bottle of whiskey sitting on a table near the entry, and hurled it at me. I ducked, and the bottle barely missed me, sailing over my head and exploding on the wall behind the bed as the outer door slammed. I laughed. Drama, much?

But my laughter was quick to fade as I returned to my bedroom, picking up the stack of papers on my desk and riffling through them, my heart sinking like a stone when I saw what was on them. *Nothing.* I hadn't written a goddamn thing, not one fucking note. I tossed the papers across the room, and they rained down on me. "Fuck!" I yelled as I sank into the chair, putting my elbows on the desk and gripping my head. "Fuck," I said more softly, despair filling my chest. "Fuck, fuck, fuck."

You're a worthless idiot. I'm ashamed to call you mine.

He was right.

Worthless idiot. Ashamed to call you mine.

God, who wouldn't be?

I sat there for a while, allowing myself to wallow in my own misery, my own self-contempt, before getting up and going to the bathroom. I tossed a couple of Tylenol in my mouth, chewing them as I stepped into the shower, cringing at the bitter, grittiness of the pills as I washed the smell of sex and alcohol from my body. Sadly, nothing could be done to cleanse my soul.

* * *

The Gift of Music Charity Ball was already in full swing when I arrived, the smooth sounds of a jazz band drifting across the room from the stage up front. Couples danced, the women's evening gowns moving at their feet, a swirling river of reds and blues and purples. Chandeliers glittered overhead, and the smell of exotic flowers drifted in the air.

I stood in the doorway for a moment, looking around idly, catching sight of a sleek brunette ponytail. My heart stuttered for a moment, and then the woman turned, and I released a small huff of air. Why did thoughts of that girl I kissed in Paris still come to mind at the strangest times? It was bizarre. I rarely ever thought of the women I'd slept with, and I'd only *kissed* that girl. I could barely picture what she'd looked like. Maybe that was it. Maybe it was simply that I'd wanted more and hadn't gotten it, and the regret of not experiencing her lingered. I sighed. It was as good an explanation as any.

Or maybe it was about Paris. Some romantic mystique that shrouded the City of Light. Even I wasn't immune to it apparently.

A girl carrying a tray of champagne flutes passed by and I grabbed two, downing one quickly and then the other. *Fuck, I don't want to be here.* But it was a benefit for childhood cancer research, so I'd forced myself to come—a good reminder that life wasn't all about me and my stupid problems. I set the empty glasses down on a table behind me and surveyed the room again. I spotted Larry and Annette through the crowd, standing with two men, one of whom was wearing a garish, god-awful suit, and I made my way over to them.

"Callen," Larry greeted me, stepping aside and making room for me in the circle. "So glad you're here."

"You know how much I love fancy parties, Larry," I said sarcastically, taking another glass of champagne offered by a passing server.

Larry chuckled. "It's a rough life. You know Anders Hanson, don't you?" he asked, gesturing to the man standing next to him. Anders was wearing a skinny-fit, off-white suit, sleeves rolled up to his forearms, paired with a bright blue shirt and a multicolored, flowered bow tie. "And this is his assistant, Ralph." I glanced at Ralph, giving him a nod, and then looked back to Anders. I recognized his name. He was the music critic for one of the most popular classical music magazines. I hadn't met him in person, but I knew of him by reputation. He was known for his brutal honesty and "edgy" fashion sense.

Anders gave me a chin tilt that managed to be both arrogant and bored, and looked off over my shoulder as if he were searching for someone more interesting. *Pretentious dick.*

I looked at Annette, who raised one eyebrow and gave me a

fake smile. Clearly she was still disgruntled over my treatment that morning. Not that it would keep her away from me. I needed to stop getting drunk and answering my damn door.

I gave her a blank stare as I raised my glass, and her smile slipped into a momentary scowl before she pasted another phony smile on her face. It was all a game. All of it. "I'm surprised to see you here without a date tonight, Callen."

"Oh, you know me, Annette; I'm sure I'll remedy that before the night is through."

Her eyes narrowed, but then she looked away, feigning sudden disinterest.

"So *anyway*, like I was saying"—Anders chortled—"Brenton Conrad's composition was so bad, the paper it was written on wasn't worthy of being used to wipe my ass." He laughed heartily at his own *joke*. "It was his first album, and I told him for the good of all humanity, it needed to be his last. I titled my review"—he held his hands up as if his own words were worthy of a marquee—"'From Hell: Atrocious, Nauseating, and Flagrantly Desperate.'"

Brenton Conrad was a new composer I personally thought had some promise. His first composition had been mediocre, it was true, but nevertheless, a cold wave of anger slithered slowly down my spine—a feeling of disgust at the fact that this man thought obliterating someone with his words was even remotely entertaining. I leaned forward, feigning a look of confusion. "Flagrantly desperate? I'm sorry, was that a music review or the description of your outfit?" I looked him up and down, my gaze moving past the tapered bottoms of his pants and settling on his bare ankles. He wasn't wearing socks.

Enraged disbelief simmered in his eyes before he managed to

replace the expression with an overly large grin. "You didn't tell me he was so amusing, too, Larry."

Larry opened his mouth to speak, but I cut him off. "Oh, I wasn't being funny, Anders. Your outfit is seriously nauseating."

"Jesus, Callen," Larry muttered.

"So, Callen," Anders's assistant interjected quickly, his tone apprehensive, clearly trying to change the subject and head off whatever he imagined was about to happen between me and his dipshit boss, "I heard you're writing the music score for *Discovering Hart*."

My stomach tightened, but I moved my eyes from Anders's angry face to his assistant's nervous one and smiled. "That's right."

He raised his shoulders and made a sound of excitement. "I'm in *love* with Marlon McDermott." The star of the movie. "How's the music coming?"

I took a drink. "Great. I have about half written already." The lie rolled off my tongue easily. I wanted it to be true. Maybe lying about it would apply the extra pressure I needed to get something started. As if I didn't have enough pressure already.

"That's great, Callen. Why didn't you tell me?" Larry asked.

I gave him a tight smile, downing my champagne and looking around for more. Last time we'd talked, I'd had Larry ask the studio for an extension and told him in confidence that I was experiencing a little writer's block. Understatement of the fucking year. "I didn't want to jinx it." I grabbed another glass off a passing tray.

Anders laughed. "You artists and your ridiculous superstitions."

Ridiculous.

Ridiculous.

You can't do anything right. You're ridiculous.

My skin was hot. The room was suddenly stifling. I pulled at my bow tie, needing air, needing to get away from these people. "Not quite as ridiculous as you thinking anyone cares about your worthless opinion." Before he could even react, I turned and walked away, headed for the bar.

Twenty minutes and two drinks later, as I was beginning to feel nice and numb, Larry approached me, leaning against the bar. "The moody artist persona is only appealing to a point. You've gotta lay off the alcohol. It's turning you into an asshole."

"I was already an asshole before I started drinking, Larry. And I fucking hate critics," I mumbled. "Especially ones like him."

"Everyone hates critics, Callen. But they're a necessary evil. And you might have been an asshole before, but you knew enough not to insult people who will go out of their way to post scathing reviews of every piece you write from now until kingdom come. You might not like that guy, but people listen to him. You're going to end up losing us both a lot of money. What's going on?"

I shut my eyes, sighing. He was right. The guy was a dick, but I hadn't done anyone any favors by insulting him. I'd just made an enemy. An enemy in a flowered bow tie and no socks, but an enemy nonetheless. I placed my drink on the bar and turned toward Larry. "The truth is, I haven't written as much of the *Discovering Hart* score as I said."

Larry frowned. "How much have you written?"

"Not much. Not as much as I hoped I would by this point." *None.*

Larry pressed his lips together and then sighed before taking a long sip of his drink. "Listen, Callen, why don't you take a vacation? Go somewhere tropical and sit on a beach and get your head on straight. When you're feeling relaxed and destressed, that's when the writer's block will disappear."

I wanted to believe him. I really did. But I was afraid to hope. Still… "Somewhere tropical?" I murmured.

"Sure. Or better yet, go back to France. We were only there for three days for the Poirier Award ceremony, and you complained you didn't get to see anything. Take a trip to the Riviera. It's beautiful and very luxurious. It's where all the jet-setters vacation. We could join you for a weekend after you've taken a couple of weeks to yourself. Annette and I have been there before, but we never get tired of it."

"I've never been on vacation alone."

Larry sighed. "Then take a friend with you, as long as it's not a woman and as long as it's not someone who'll distract you."

A friend. The only person I considered a real friend was Nick, and I hadn't touched base with him in two months. But maybe he'd forgive me if I invited him on an all-expenses-paid trip to France.

How long had it been since I'd taken a vacation? I figured most people thought of my *life* as a constant celebration, a never-ending slew of late-night parties, late sleep-ins, do-whatever-caught-my-fancy days. Problem was, it had lost its allure. What had once felt like fun now brought nothing but emptiness and depression. I fucking hated pretending. Was sick of all of it. And, Jesus. I sure as hell didn't want Larry and his been-there-won't-be-going-there-again wife joining me.

France.

A starlit deck.

Innocent eyes and angel kisses.

Maybe a quick stop in Paris, too.

It wasn't a bad idea. I nodded. "I think I'll take your advice, Larry."

"It's about damn time."

CHAPTER FOUR

JESSICA

The office was windowless, small, and stuffy, with floor-to-ceiling bookshelves crammed with books lining three of the walls. Dusty-looking hardbacks littered every available flat surface, including several piles on the floor. I sat in the rickety chair in front of the desk, my knees pressed together and my hands laced in my lap, trying to take up as little room as possible lest I topple one of the many piles.

The door squeaked open, and I glanced behind me, smiling as I stood. The older gentleman gestured for me to sit back down, stepping over several stacks on the floor and making his way around the large wood-carved desk. "Madame Creswell"—he reached out his hand and we shook—"it's very nice to meet you. I'm Dr. Moreau. I appreciate that you could come on such short notice."

"Of course, Dr. Moreau. I appreciate the opportunity. I can't thank you enough." My heart thumped in my chest and I willed it to slow down, not to get too excited. Getting this job was a long shot. The listing had advertised for an assistant to Dr. Christophe Moreau, the director of romance languages at the Louvre, for a project translating recently found documents thought to be from the Middle Ages. From what I'd heard, the list of applicants was a mile long.

Dr. Moreau moved a few stacks of papers aside and riffled through a folder, taking out what I assumed to be my résumé. He lowered his glasses, glancing at it with raised brows. "Your list of workplaces is very impressive, although I see you've only held unpaid internships to this point. Why is that?"

"Well, Dr. Moreau, the truth is, I found that the internships provided more for me than the paid positions I was offered when I first graduated college."

"Except in a salary."

I laughed softly. "Yes, except for that." I paused. "There are always ways to earn enough money to live. I want to do work that challenges me and uses my strengths to make a difference."

Dr. Moreau sat back in his chair, finally giving me his full attention. "Lofty ambitions, especially for a language scholar." He eyed me. "Tell me what you know about Jeanne d'Arc."

Joan of Arc? "I . . . Well, I know a great deal, actually. In addition to French language studies in college, I focused on medieval French history." When he kept watching me, I sat straighter and went on. "Jeanne d'Arc was a martyr and a saint, a military leader acting under divine guidance who led the French army to defeat the English during the Hundred Years' War."

"And do you believe?"

"Believe she acted under divine guidance?"

"*Oui.* Do you believe God spoke to her and gave her a mission?"

I bit at my lip for a moment. "I don't know. I believe *she* believed so."

His lip quirked. "Ah, a good answer. Intellectuals who pretend everything can be known are the very worst sort of scholars. Those are the people who have stopped learning." He opened a bottom drawer and took out something enclosed in a clear plastic sleeve. "Six weeks ago, some writings—they seem to be a diary of sorts—were found in a cave in the Loire Valley. We believe they were written by someone close to Jeanne d'Arc, and though it is largely this individual's personal account of their own journey, they detail the military battles, speak of the saint's expressed thoughts, and recount conversations between the two. Unfortunately, not all the entries were preserved, but many were." He handed the clear sleeve to me, and I saw that there was a very old piece of parchment inside. "That is one of the writings, Madame Creswell."

I held it up to the light, studying it and reading the old French. My brow furrowed as I read, and after a moment I set it down on my lap and looked at Dr. Moreau. "Dr. Moreau, I'm sorry, but this can't possibly be from the fifteenth century."

He raised a brow. *"Non? Pourquoi?"*

"Well..." I pointed at one of the words on the document. "This description—*baroque*—wouldn't have been used in France until a hundred years after Jeanne d'Arc's death. It was an artistic style that didn't begin until the sixteen hundreds. These were written well after anyone who would have known Jeanne d'Arc personally was already dead as well."

Dr. Moreau smiled. "Indeed." He reached in his drawer again and brought out another clear plastic sleeve and handed it to me. "That is a copy of one of the real documents."

I blinked at Dr. Moreau and then examined the document he'd handed me, reading the text slowly.

"What can you tell me about the person who wrote that, Madame Creswell?"

I took another moment to study it before answering. "The author is a woman. The language is feminine."

"*Oui*. I agree."

"And she's of the upper class. It would have been rare, though not unheard of, for a commoner to read and write. Especially this well. It's lovely." I took a moment to read a paragraph, and as I read I envisioned the feather at the end of a quill wafting gently with the motion of the girl's moving hand. "Yes, definitely of the upper class. She makes a joke here comparing one of the generals to a swan and says the last time she saw such a bird was on her dinner table and she'd like to see him carved up similarly." I looked up at Dr. Moreau, whose lips tilted upward along with one brow. I let out a short breath. "Only the very rich ate a delicacy like swan in the Middle Ages." I paused, reading a few more lines. "And this headpiece she speaks of here, a *fronteau*, which is a tiara of beads, would only have been worn by a young girl of high birth."

I glanced up at the doctor, and he was watching me with a smile on his face. "I believe, Madame Creswell, I have found my newest assistant. If you're willing, that is."

My heart leapt, and I suppressed the grin that wanted to break over my face, giving him what I hoped was a controlled, professional smile instead. "I accept, Dr. Moreau."

* * *

I bounded up the stairs to my apartment as quickly as I could in a pencil skirt, resisting the urge to squeal. I threw the door open, and Frankie, who was on the couch eating a bowl of cereal, started, milk sloshing down her tank top. "Good Lord, what's wrong with you?"

I closed the door, grinning at her. "I got a job."

She set the bowl of cereal down on the coffee table and jumped up. "Oh my God! What is it?"

After tossing my portfolio onto the table by the door, I gave her a quick, excited hug and sat down in the chair across from the couch. She sat back down as well, looking at me expectantly. "Well, recently, some writings were found in a cave in the Loire Valley and they're thought to be connected to Joan of Arc."

"Holy cow! They need a translator?"

"Yes. They've already read through a few of the writings, but they're very old, most likely from the fifteenth century, and some of the words and phrases are difficult to understand. It's my specialty. They need to have every word carefully translated to ensure we keep the authenticity of the writing, but in a readable prose, and saved to a secure computer server. They've formed a team to confirm the dates and determine whether they're actually connected to Joan of Arc."

"Oh my God. That sounds really important."

"It sounds…amazing. They've put a whole group together to study these writings—paper experts and archaeologists who are still digging in the caves to see if they can find anything more that might carbon-date the pieces. I'm going to be working with another translator with a different specialty and under one of the leading language historians in France."

"Holy shit. This is huge. Why didn't you call me at work?"

"It's been a whirlwind. I haven't had a second. It's a temporary job, though, and it doesn't pay a lot, but Dr. Moreau told me if I impress the team, there might be further opportunities."

Frankie let out a shriek and covered her mouth. "This is so exciting. But when you say temporary, how temporary?"

"They've assigned a month." I sat back in the chair, stretching my legs out in front of me. "This is my dream job, Frankie. Just to get a chance to read those writings up close and personal. I'm so excited and nervous I could scream."

"Well, scream your way into your room and put on something fancy. I'm taking you out tonight to celebrate."

I grinned at her. "We'll go dutch. I can afford it now. Sort of." My smile slipped. "There's only one other thing."

"Uh-oh. What?"

"The job is in the Loire Valley."

Frankie's eyes widened. "The Loire Valley? *Quoi? Tu plaisantes?*"

What the hell was right. I sat up, leaning forward. "I know. But that's where the writings were found, and they want the team to come to them, see the spot where they were uncovered, et cetera. The writings are being kept in a museum in the Loire Valley for now, and they're putting our team up in this beautiful château nearby that's provided a work space as well."

"A château? Well, damn, girl. You've hit the jackpot."

"Project-wise, yes. Monetarily, no. Still, Frankie, if I do a good job on this, make some connections, this could be a career starter." A quiver of excitement moved through me, quickly followed by a flash of insecurity. Paris, this apartment, Frankie, they were my comfort zone, my safe haven, and I was going to have to separate myself from them, even if only for a short time.

"We're ordering the good champagne tonight, and you're wearing the backless Clémence Maillard."

"Oh, I couldn't, Frankie." The backless dress was a swath of drapey, silken material with cape sleeves and a sheath skirt that, when on a hanger, barely looked like a dress. But something magical happened when it was put on a woman's body that transformed it into one of the most gorgeous items of clothing I'd ever seen. It was ridiculously expensive, but Frankie was lucky enough to get samples of fabulous clothing from her employer, and that was one of them.

"Why not? You look fantastic in it, and this is a special occasion."

"That's your favorite dress."

"And you're my favorite newly employed friend."

I smiled at her, my heart overflowing with gratitude for her friendship. "I'm so lucky to have you."

She grinned. "I know. Now get your butt in there and start getting ready. We have some major celebrating to do."

I laughed. "Okay, fine. But I need an hour. Dr. Moreau gave me a copy of one of the writings so I could familiarize myself with the style and the voice of the writer. I can't wait to look it over and get to know her a little bit." I shot Frankie a grin.

"All right, all right. Go meet your new friend and then—"

"I know. And *then* the backless Clémence!"

In the year of our Lord 1429, on the tenth day of April

I am no longer myself. Now I am Philippe, dressed as a common boy of seventeen who will assist the Maid of Orléans as she prepares for battle and report back that of which I see and hear. She wears white armor, I am told, and rides a white steed as she forces the Anglo-Burgundians to retreat across the Loire Valley. I travel there now, sent off with great fanfare as though I myself am heading to war. And perhaps that is exactly what I should consider it, as the choice was not mine, and I sense a battle in my own future, though I know not why I should feel this way. After all, my place will only be at camp as I serve the girl they call a saint and wait in safety for her return. And yet, despite the assurances given by my father and by Charles VII of my well-being, both excitement and unease reside in my heart. The feather on my quill flutters in the breeze coming through the window of my carriage as I begin my journey. And likewise, I feel destiny swirling around me, a churning gale, and I know not if the winds of fate are benevolent or merciless.

PART TWO

All battles are first won or lost, in the mind.

—*Joan of Arc*

CHAPTER FIVE

CALLEN

The French countryside zipped by, and I stared out at it morosely. "You look like you're marching to the gallows," Nick said from the limo seat across from me. "Vacation isn't supposed to be a death sentence, you know. Almonds?" He held up a tray of snacks.

I pushed my sunglasses to the top of my head and squinted at him. "No." I resisted the urge to open the minibar and see what they had to offer drink-wise. I was laying off alcohol on this trip. Or at least, I was cutting down. Before five anyway. Or at least noon. I checked my watch. Ten forty-five. *Damn.*

Nick must have somehow been following the subject of my thoughts because he said, "You had enough last night." He ripped open a package of almonds and threw back a handful. "You've gotta get some work done, Cal, or you'll be in breach of contract. You told me to remind you of that."

"I didn't realize you'd start lecturing me five minutes into our trip," I snapped, more hostility in my tone than I'd intended. Maybe I *had* brought him along to lecture me. Maybe I knew in some part of my brain that was still reasonable that I needed all the help I could get.

Nick shrugged, obviously unaffected by my sour mood. "I take my job as the only responsible person in your life seriously." He winked, and I looked away. I knew I'd been avoiding him for just this reason. I'd known what he would say to me, and I hadn't wanted to hear it. *Still don't.* Who *ever* wanted to truly have their faults dissected, especially when they didn't know what the fuck to do to change them?

After a minute I sighed. It wasn't just that I had the weight of the world on my shoulders because of the compositions I owed the studio, but I was hungover and frustrated. We'd flown into Paris the day before and had gone to the bar where I'd met the cocktail waitress I couldn't stop thinking about. Hell, I hadn't really *met* her; I didn't even know her name. But I'd kissed her. And for some crazy reason that made no sense at all, she kept popping into my mind. So I'd gone back to the bar to find her, and when I'd described her to the manager, he'd informed me the girl no longer worked there. I'd asked for her name, but the manager had said he wasn't allowed to give out personal information—even of ex-employees—but that he'd take mine and pass it along. I'd declined. I was only in Paris for a day, I had no idea when I'd be back, and it was very possible the effect the girl had on me that night was a result of far too much alcohol.

At least that's what I'd told myself to stave off the disappointment. I sighed again, running my hand through my hair. "The thing is, Nick, my last album wasn't great, and I need to get my mojo back on this one." *I have to.*

Nick paused, looking as if he was considering what I'd said. "Your last album wasn't bad, Cal. I heard where you were going. You just...didn't quite make it there. It felt almost like you were holding back."

I shook my head. "I wasn't, at least not on purpose." I pressed my lips together. "I don't know. I don't know what the problem is."

"Maybe you need to stop dwelling on what the problem was with that album and let yourself focus on your current project. You're looking in the wrong direction, Cal."

I nodded, staring unseeing out the tinted window. "Yeah. Maybe." I looked at Nick, feeling marginally better for having talked about it with someone I could trust. "Thanks for coming along, Nick."

"I'm happy to. I needed a change of scenery. But I have work, too, so you'll be on your own most of the time."

I nodded, looking away again. Hopefully he was right. His faith in me felt like both a certain pressure and a blessing.

I'd met Nick when we were both seventeen-year-old punks who'd been sent to juvenile hall. I'd been fighting in an effort to get kicked out of school yet again, and Nick had stolen something so he'd get sent there to avoid his foster parents, if only for a night or two. He was a skinny, nerdy kid with glasses, a weird haircut, and worst of all, an expression that let everyone know he was scared. Easy prey. When some tougher kids focused on him, I'd fought them off. I'd always despised bullies.

We'd found that despite outward appearances, Nick and I were more alike than different—both constantly choosing between the frying pan and the fire—and we forged a bond. When we were both eighteen and finally free to make choices that didn't include regular residency at juvenile hall, we took odd jobs, found couches to sleep on, and shared both food and a very meager supply of hope.

Music was my passion, and I practiced every spare second I had, carrying around backpacks of notebooks filled with compositions and CDs of my work, which I gave to anyone and everyone who might be able to give it to the right person. I'd met the wife of a bigwig in the music industry at a cocktail party I'd all but crashed, and—after some personal attention in her grand, velvet upholstered bed—she'd put my work on her husband's desk. So yes, my first break had been a result of my willingness to trade sex for favors, and I wasn't necessarily proud of that. But it'd gotten me where I was, so I tried not to think about it very much. When an afternoon of casual fucking was the difference between living your dream or delivering pizzas to make ends meet, you did what you had to do.

After that initial break, I'd sold a few jingles that were used in commercials and a ringtone that became extremely popular. I did a couple of video game scores and then the music for several two-minute film trailers. One (legitimately) lucky break turned into another, and I was able to strike out on my own. Nick, who had always been brilliant with computers, had a few lucky breaks as well and started his own website design company and was successfully self-employed. Hence his ability to come on vacation with me with not much notice. As long as he had his laptop, he could just as easily do business from Los Angeles as from the Loire Valley.

"So, tell me about this girl you went to see last night." He used his index finger to push his glasses up his nose.

"Temporary insanity," I murmured.

He raised a brow. "As opposed to all the *sanity* of your recent relationships?"

"I don't have relationships, Nick. I have one-night stands."

He sighed. "That's going to get old one of these years."

I made a scoffing sound, and Nick raised his eyes to the heavens and shook his head as if apologizing to the angels for my sins. I laughed quietly and looked back out the window again. "I kissed her last time I was here, nothing more. And...I don't know, maybe I just didn't get enough."

I could feel Nick studying me. "You not get enough? This is different. Have you thought about looking her up online?" He paused. "I could see what I could come up with if you want me to."

"I don't even know her name." I ran a hand through my hair as I looked back at him. "And it doesn't matter. She was just a pretty girl, and there is no shortage of pretty girls anywhere in this fucked-up world." *So why the hell can't I forget about this one?*

"Hmm," he said, not sounding convinced for some reason I didn't care to know about. But he didn't elaborate, and instead picked up a travel brochure the limo company had provided, obviously willing to move the conversation to a different topic. The brochure featured a picture of a large castle on the front cover, and I assumed it covered nearby attractions. "Is this where we're staying?" he asked.

"I have no idea. My assistant booked it." The only directive I'd given my assistant when I'd told her to book me a vacation spot in France was that it should be somewhere other than where the so-called jet-setters went but still somewhere with style. "All she said is that it's spectacular."

"Liza?"

"No. The new one's name is Myrtle."

"What happened to Liza?"

"What do you think happened to Liza?"

He made a disappointed sound in his throat and shook his head. "You slept with that one, too? Jesus, Cal. How do you expect to keep anyone employed at this rate?"

"Myrtle is seventy and has fourteen grandchildren."

"It depresses me that I'm still concerned."

I laughed. "Touché. I'm not that bad."

"Pretty damn close," he muttered.

"Myrtle does have this interesting blue hair. I'm sort of tempted to find out if the curtains match the carpet."

Nick groaned. "Ugh, you're the worst. I'm surprised you haven't put the moves on me yet."

I raised my brows. "Don't underestimate the romance of France, *mon ami*. You won't be able to resist me for long."

"Oh, I'll be able to resist you—don't worry about that."

I laughed. "Seriously, what about you? When's the last time you went on a date?"

"I was seeing a girl in L.A. for a couple of months. She said I work too much."

"She was right."

Nick bounced his knee. "I know. It's just…building financial security means more to me than a relationship right now."

I watched him for a second as he looked back down at the brochure. I knew what he meant. He didn't want to live the way we'd lived for so long—surviving day to day, no guarantees of a roof over our heads, no safety net, just each other and a fire that burned in our guts for *more*. Of course, I had enough money now that *I* was his safety net if he needed one, but I understood that he wanted to make his own way, too. "I know, Nick."

He looked at me and gave a small smile, a nod. "I know you do."

We lapsed into a comfortable silence, and I gazed out the window at a train speeding by, heading in the same direction. The blurred profile of a brunette caught my eye and my heart gave a strange jolt, but as quickly as I'd seen her, she was gone. I sighed, closing my eyes. I was obviously so tired, my mind was playing tricks on me.

* * *

I doodled a monster made of musical notes between the staffs, stared at it, and then threw my pen across the room, crumpling the paper—empty except for my bad art—and tossing that as well. "Goddamn it!"

I stood, running the fingers of both hands through my hair and holding my head forward for a minute. I grasped my skull and shook my head, hoping that the movement might make something click back into place. Specifically, the creativity that seemed to have fallen loose and was free-floating through my brain, lost and unobtainable. I shook my head harder, using my fist to box my own ear so hard that a gasp of pain escaped through my lips. *Fuck!*

The impressive balcony off my room overlooked a river, and for a minute I stood at the iron railing looking out into the night, watching as starlight danced on the water. The pain in my ear faded, along with the last vestiges of the hope I'd held as I'd sat down to write.

Now what do I do? Nick and I had checked in to the castle featured on the front of the brochure that afternoon, and I'd taken a short nap. When I'd woken, my headache had lessened and I'd been filled with cautious excitement. While I showered, a melody—just the echo of something that floated on some inner breeze—had drifted through my mind. I'd stumbled out and tried desperately to catch it, to get it down on paper, but it was gone. As wispy as the fragment of a forgotten dream.

Useless. You're nothing but a waste of time.

Useless.

Useless.

Useless.

I turned away from the river and went back inside, putting my shoes on and grabbing my wallet. I knocked quietly on the door to Nick's room, which was right down the hall, but he didn't answer and it looked like the lights were off inside.

There was an older couple in the elevator, and they gave me a polite smile. When I stepped inside, the woman pointed to the panel of buttons and said something in French that I assumed was, "What floor?"

"Uh, *le* bar."

"Ah, *oui*," she said, pressing the lowest button.

As soon as we stepped off, I could hear the familiar sounds of music, laughter, and clinking glasses. I followed the noise and ended up in a lavish room with an ornate mahogany bar taking up the entire far wall. A mirror ran the length of the wall behind the bar, reflecting the multicolored bottles on glass shelves and the sparkling chandeliers hanging from the ceiling. It was stunning, and for the first time since we'd arrived, I took a moment to look around. This is what it must have felt like to be lord of the manor—king of the castle?—back when châteaus like this one were built in...what year? I had no earthly idea. I knew nothing of history, of eras, of titles, and the reminder of my lack of education depressed me as it always did. I had money and I had fame, so why did I always feel like an imposter? Like any success I enjoyed would be taken away once people realized I had no real talent? I always felt like I was only one step ahead of a universe that was looking to expose me for the fraud I was. It made me feel sick and alone. The dread was a block of stone that sat heavily in my gut.

"Bourbon, neat. Make it a double."

"Oui, monsieur."

The drink was put in front of me, and I scrawled my signature on the tab, taking a sip of my drink, enjoying the smooth burn and turning toward the open room. There was a group of women standing by a seating area looking at me, whispering and giggling. When I raised my drink to them, I heard several squeals. "Five, four, three," I muttered, barely moving my lips. I took a sip of my drink. "Two, and..." One of the women began making her way over to me.

She had nicely rounded hips and smallish breasts, and she swayed seductively as she walked, pulling at the hem of her tight red dress as if she wanted to make sure it didn't slide up her thighs. Which was amusing considering it was so tight I could see every curve, bump, and crease of her body beneath the thin material. She came to stand in front of me, giving me a coy smile and twirling a lock of strawberry-blond hair around one finger. "My girlfriends and I have a bet. They don't believe you're Callen Hayes, but I think you are."

"What do you win if you're right?"

She giggled. "With them? Just bragging rights. But I'm hoping you'll sweeten the pot."

I chuckled. "Sweetening pots is my specialty. How do you feel about hot tubs?"

CHAPTER SIX

JESSICA

The Château de la Bellefeuille was a masterpiece of Renaissance architecture, majestic and elegant, surrounded by expansive, formal gardens and situated next to the Loire River. I stood in the center of my room and spun around slowly, taking in the ancient stone walls, the pale green silk draperies and matching bed linens, and the simple but lovely French furnishings that looked to be refurbished originals. I was in one of the smallest rooms on the bottom floor, and even so, it was utterly charming. I could only imagine the splendor of the top-floor suites.

I had arrived via train earlier that day, checked in to the château, and taken a long walk through the gardens. It was Saturday, and the other members of the team—some of whom were not living in France—were supposed to arrive Monday. I was delighted to have the opportunity to see parts of the village we were in before diving into work. I had always loved meandering through obscure places, without the rush of a tour guide. It allowed me to *feel* my way around. I'd eaten alone in the château restaurant and come back to my room, intending to turn in early, but I was too excited to sleep. All day I'd had this nervous energy running through my veins, a fluttery anticipation that had only increased as the train I'd taken had sped closer to the Loire Valley. As if the area itself was luring me, as if I was meant to be here. *Just like the girl dressed as Philippe had described her feelings.* I'd read only one of her writings, and yet I already felt somehow close to her—connected in some vague sense—and I was eager to know where her story led.

I picked up a brochure on the writing desk and opened it, glancing at the professional photos of the château and reading the short history of the castle. Apparently, the king who originally had it built left it to two of his mistresses upon his death, rather than his children. It caused a great scandal, and despite the children's many attempts to get it back, the mistresses— who were not friends and each occupied separate wings of the château—lived here until their deaths. A sound of irritation escaped my throat, and I tossed the brochure back on the desk. Men and their vast array of women! Did any man want to be faithful to just one?

I hefted my suitcase onto the luggage stand and zipped it open, pulling out the dresses and various clothing items Frankie had insisted I take with me. I should have remembered to hang them up right away, but I'd been too intent on exploring this massive castle to remember the garments wrinkling in my suitcase. The material must have been spun by magical fairies, though, because when I held them up, there was not a wrinkle in sight. I placed them in the closet and then set the shoes on the

floor below. Frankie had loaned those to me as well, and I eyed
them warily. I supposed I was very lucky we were the same size,
though I had doubts I'd be able to walk in the strappy, spiky-
heeled, pointy-toed contraptions in front of me. Hopefully there
wouldn't be an occasion to wear such things. Frankie had insisted I humor her and be prepared for anything. Fashion-wise
at least.

I unpacked my pj's and underwear and took my toiletries
into the tiny bathroom, securing my hair into a messy bun. The
shower felt wonderful as I washed the travel dust from my body,
the bathroom filling with the steamy fragrance of my body wash.

Back out in my room, I eyed my pj's, that same buzz of anticipation causing me to hesitate. I just wasn't tired. Which was
surprising, considering I'd woken early and had had a long day
of travel and exploring. I stood there, holding the towel tightly
around me, trying to figure out what to do. Maybe a drink at
the lounge would appease the restlessness. Being that I'd spent
a lot of my working hours at a bar in Paris, it wasn't my normal distraction. *But hey, I'm twenty-four.* Wasn't that what other
twenty-four-year-olds did? I'd at least have one drink and enjoy
a little people-watching.

I perused the clothing I'd hung in the closet and pulled out
a silver dress with shimmery pale silver threads woven through
the fabric. It was somewhat demure-looking, with an asymmet-
rical V-neck and a short A-line skirt, but when I pulled it on,
it hugged my body in a way that made my waist look tiny and
showed off my cleavage to its full advantage. "Oh, Clémence,
you evil genius," I murmured, turning this way and that in the
full-length mirror and slipping on the silver shoes. They weren't
as uncomfortable as they looked, so I teetered into the bathroom,
where I put on a bit of makeup and brushed out my hair, pulling

it up into a twist and taking out a few pieces around my face. I studied myself in the mirror, feeling pleased with the effect, even though it was only for me.

* * *

The lilting strains of "La Vie en Rose" drifted from the lounge, luring me forward, the buzzing in my veins suddenly increasing and the surge of adrenaline causing me to stumble on the stone floor. Despite the instability of my borrowed shoes, I had the brief, intense urge to run, as if I were late for something and time was of the essence. "Get a grip, Jessica," I whispered to myself. I needed to settle down, and quiet my excitement at being in this grand place, or I'd never be able to focus on the work I was here to do.

I took a deep breath, the music and lyrics of the famous French ballad calming me as I entered the lounge, standing in the doorway for a moment. The room was magnificent, decorated in shades of royal blue, light blue, and gold, with a striking, ornate bar on the back wall. I felt suddenly uncertain as I watched groups of people laugh and chatter, the crystals from the chandeliers overhead causing the light to shift and shimmer. I bit my lip and moved farther into the room, that electric feeling settling into a warm hum that relaxed my muscles and made me want to sink into one of the comfortable-looking upholstered chairs in any one of the small groupings of furniture. *Stay*, it whispered.

I stepped up to the bar, and the bartender turned my way. *"Madame?"*

"Un verre de vin blanc s'il vous plaît." The bartender handed me a *carte des vins*, and I chose a sauvignon blanc that came

from a winery in the Loire Valley. I turned and glanced around the bar as the bartender was pouring my wine. There was a group of women gathered around a man with dark hair, and he was laughing and saying something that they evidently all found completely delightful, as they were laughing giddily and flipping their hair in unison. I felt an inexplicable jolt of annoyance and turned back around just as the bartender slid the glass of wine and my tab onto the bar. I signed the slip, taking my wine with a smile and a muttered, *"Merci,"* as I began walking away.

"Excusez-moi, Jessica Creswell. Eh, Madame Creswell?"

It took a moment for my name to register, and I turned back around in confusion to see the bartender holding my evening bag toward me. I'd left it on the bar. I let out a short breath, reaching for the bag and smiling in embarrassment. *"Que je suis bête." Silly me.*

I wandered away from the bar, toward the doors to what must be a balcony, glancing outside. The balcony looked out over the gardens I'd walked through earlier that day, and I considered taking my wine outside but decided against it when I noticed a couple standing at the railing, their heads bent together intimately. They were obviously enjoying the privacy. Feeling a strange sort of heat on the back of my neck, I tensed, a shiver running through me as I slowly turned around.

I sucked in a startled breath as my gaze clashed with that of Callen Hayes.

My hand trembled, and I brought my other hand up just in time to stop myself from dropping the wineglass I was holding. *Oh dear Lord.* It felt like all the blood in my body had drained to my feet.

How in the *world*? How in the wide, wide world was this happening to me *again*? It couldn't be. It *couldn't*. He was moving toward me, eyes wide, his expression stunned, as if he'd just seen a ghost, and all I could do was stare back. Frozen.

I felt caught in his gaze, paralyzed with this feeling of unreality, as he stepped between two women and moved closer…closer. Some part of me wanted to run away, and another, stronger part, wanted to move toward him so we'd come together sooner. This was…This was impossible. Only somehow it was not. *Somehow*, I felt this odd inevitability, as if a part of me had been waiting for this to happen. I couldn't explain it, not even to myself.

I sucked in a breath of air, watching him approach. He was gorgeous. I remembered the first time I'd seen him sitting in the back of that abandoned boxcar, bruised and alone. He'd been only a boy, but beautiful even then, and I'd been mesmerized. Just as I'd been in Lounge La Vue. Just as I was now. How was he *here*?

"Jessica Creswell? *Jessie?*" he asked, his voice slightly hoarse.

My heart was beating a mile a minute, and I let out a whoosh of breath, gripping my wineglass so tightly I was surprised it hadn't shattered. Callen Hayes was here…*somehow*, and he'd obviously heard the bartender say my name. I swallowed, my eyes darting around the lounge, looking for what? A distraction? An escape? "Hi, Callen."

He shook his head very slowly. "Jessie Creswell? You're…my God. You're…Paris…You're *Jessie* and you're here. How?"

"Yes…I…" *What did he ask? How am I here?* "Uh…well, I— I'm here for a job. I'm working here." I shook my head. "Not for the château, but *at* the château…and I'm staying here, temporarily."

His eyes moved over my face incredulously. He still looked

slightly shattered, as if he was having trouble putting the pieces together. I could relate. "What—what are *you* doing here?"

He ran a hand through his hair, blinking as if he couldn't quite remember. "Ah, I'm here on vacation for a couple of weeks. My God, this is...unbelievable. Jessie Creswell. And I've run into you twice now." He paused, looking me over once again. I felt the heat of his gaze as it moved down my body, and I took a sip of wine, willing my heart rate to slow. "That night at the bar in Paris, you knew who I was. You tried to tell me."

The warmth of the wine slid down my throat, and I felt better, my hands more steady on the glass. "Yes." I nodded. "It's okay, though. I wouldn't expect you to remember me." *I'd only hoped...*

"Of course I remember you. Just now...when I heard your name, I knew it immediately. I just..." His voice was so deep and smooth, and his eyes held something, some emotion I didn't know how to read. "I haven't thought about Santa Lucinda in so long, and...you've changed. You were always pretty, but you're beautiful now." A flush of happiness flowed through me at his words, and I looked down for a moment. When I met his eyes again, he was still staring at me. "You're...all grown up." He sounded almost shocked, as if he'd kept me in his mind as a little girl and he was having trouble connecting me with that child. I could understand. Perhaps I'd feel the same way if I hadn't had time to process and accept the grown-up version of Callen Hayes.

I offered a small smile. "I guess we both are. Grown-up I mean."

"Yeah, I guess so." Something moved between us, a charge in the air that made my stomach tighten. Like cresting the peak of a roller coaster and anticipating the drop. *Fear. And delight.*

He frowned. "I owe you an apology for that night. I'm sorry—"

"There's nothing to be sorry for. Really. It was fine. It was just...Paris." I shrugged one shoulder and gave him a smile.

"Paris," he murmured. "There is something about Paris..."

"*La Ville des Amoureux*," I said before I'd considered the words. *City of Lovers.* Only, we weren't lovers, and we never had been. He'd had a different lover that night, in fact. One of his *vast array* of women. My face felt warm, and I hoped he couldn't tell I was blushing.

We stared at each other, and the moment suddenly felt weighty...awkward—as if there was something we should be saying and neither knew what that was. I shifted on my feet. "I'm, ah, so happy for all the success you've had." I smiled. "I've followed your career...a little bit." *A lot.*

"Thanks. I...You know it was because of you I discovered music."

"Really?" I shook my head. "No. I'm sure you would have discovered music with or without me. It's obviously your passion. Your gift."

He sucked his full bottom lip into his mouth, and my stomach muscles clenched, along with places lower and deep inside. Places I didn't necessarily want to consider. "Maybe. I don't know. I still have that keyboard you gave me."

I laughed in surprise. "Do you really?"

He smiled, and for one moment he didn't look like Callen Hayes the famous composer, the playboy of classical music—he looked like Callen, the prince and hero of my girlish heart. I felt possessive of that smile, as if it belonged to me and no one else. *Stupid, Jessica. So stupid.* I looked away. I didn't want to be having these feelings for Callen. They were useless and slightly painful.

Still, this moment felt like a dream, and I couldn't quite convince myself to embrace what I knew was reality.

"What kind of work are you doing here? You were working at that lounge a couple of months ago."

I nodded, taking another sip of wine. "Just to pay the bills. I'm a translator. That's what I'm doing in the Loire Valley. I'm working with a team to translate some documents."

He nodded, tilting his head. "French. Yes, I remember." He paused. "You were always so smart, Jessie." There was something in his expression, sort of tender and sort of sad, and it confused me. But then he smiled and the shadows in his eyes melted away. "You did what you said you would do—you moved to Paris. Only, you must not be eating as much chocolate as you planned." He glanced down my body, his expression appreciative as he raised a brow.

I laughed, a thrill moving through me that he remembered at least some of what we'd talked about; he hadn't completely forgotten me or the pieces of my heart I'd once shared with him. "I can't afford to eat much chocolate just yet. That particular dream remains on hold for now."

He laughed. "We should all have a dream or two."

I smiled and opened my mouth to say something when a woman in an obscenely tight red dress approached us, draping herself on Callen and shooting me a cool smile. "You about ready for our Jacuzzi date?" she cooed. "I can't wait to slip out of this dress."

I tensed, the warm happiness that had filled my heart a moment before turning into cold disappointment. Callen Hayes was not the boy I'd known, and I shouldn't have forgotten that, even for a moment, even here in this gorgeous room in the Loire Valley, where fate seemed to have once again brought us together. I smiled, hoping it didn't look as stiff as it felt. "I have to get up to bed anyway. It was nice seeing you again."

I began to turn away, but Callen grabbed my arm, shaking himself loose of the red-dress girl. "Wait, Jessie. Don't go yet." He turned to the girl, who now had an angry scowl on her face. "I'm sorry. I'm going to have to cancel the hot tub. Maybe I'll see you later."

She huffed out a breath and crossed her arms over her chest. "You promised," she whined, "and you owe me."

Ew. Whatever that meant, I didn't want to know. I pulled my arm gently out of Callen's grip. "Really, there's no need to cancel your plans. I have to turn in. I'm going on a museum tour in the morning, and it starts early."

There was a tic in Callen's jaw, but he smiled and nodded. "Can we do dinner while you're here?"

Red dress was glaring at me and tapping her foot impatiently. A vision of her in the hot tub draped over Callen flashed through my mind. I didn't like the picture my brain created, but it was a good reminder of why I needed to stay far away from him. I'd already had my heart broken by one womanizing lecher—my father—and I refused to add another to the list. Callen and I had been friends before, and maybe we could be again. It didn't have to be anything more. But what would be the point? So I could end up with hurt feelings and the definitive knowledge that even if I had meant something to him once, I didn't now? I'd been reminded twice how Callen viewed women: temporary and disposable. To become even more acquainted with what he'd become was only *asking* to be hurt. "I don't think so, but thank you anyway. I hope you enjoy your vacation. Good night." And with that I turned and walked away, not daring to look back, not even once, taking some small satisfaction in the fact that it was *me* walking away this time.

CHAPTER SEVEN

CALLEN

Jessie Creswell. *My* Jessie Creswell. Holy shit. I was still trying to wrap my head around it. Jessie Creswell was the girl I'd kissed on the rooftop in Paris? The girl I hadn't been able to stop thinking about? Was *that* the reason for the strange draw I'd had to her? A familiarity that I hadn't known how to explain? Was it the reason my mind had kept returning to her? I'd always had a special place in my heart for Jessie, and perhaps it was that long-ago closed-off piece of me that had taken notice.

But it felt like…*more* than that. I just wasn't sure exactly why or how. Her hair was longer and darker, her freckles barely noticeable, and she obviously didn't wear braces anymore, but now that I knew who she was, I could see the remnants of the child she'd been. Although other than that echo of recognition, she definitely wasn't remotely childlike anymore.

Her body was slim yet rounded in all the right places, and I'd had to force myself not to stare at her full, luscious breasts. Jessie Creswell. Goddamn.

The two years I'd spent with her had been the only real childhood I'd had, the only time I'd allowed myself to *play*, and to lose myself in lands of fantasy, where anything was possible. She had been the only *good*. And yet that time was riddled with pain, too, and memories I didn't want to look at, memories I constantly tried to push away.

Fuck, she'd been all I could think about since running into her last night.

I heard the *ding* of the elevator and stood, my heart picking up speed as I watched to see who got out in the lobby where I...well, where I'd been sort of loitering in a corner for the past hour.

An older couple stepped out, and my heart sank but then lifted again when I spotted Jessie behind them, looking at a pamphlet of some sort held open in her hands. She was dressed in jeans, a loose white top, a pair of sandals, and she had a large purse over one shoulder. Her long brown hair was pulled into a ponytail like the night I'd kissed her in Paris, and she had a pair of sunglasses perched on her head.

"*Bonjour.*"

She looked up, and I laughed at the startled look on her face, surprise that morphed into something that resembled irritation. "Callen. I wouldn't have pegged you for an early riser."

I cleared my throat and fell in beside her as she began walking toward the front desk. "Yes, always. Best part of the day. I never miss, er..." I searched my mind for what happened before noon.

"The sunrise?" she offered, amusement lacing her tone.

"Yup."

She looked at me sideways, clearly skeptical, and I couldn't help smiling. She was so pretty. Those big hazel eyes, full lips that I knew tasted sweet, and a light scattering of freckles that I could only see when I was close. *Very close.* I leaned toward her and she leaned away. "What are you doing?"

"Ah...nothing."

She gave me a suspicious look and then stepped up to the front desk, speaking in rapid French to the man who greeted her. I didn't understand a word of it. She smiled and turned, and I nodded to the man, catching up to her.

"Where are you off to this morning?" she asked.

"Museum tour."

She stopped and turned toward me, raising a brow. "Which one?"

I waved my hand toward the front door. "The one down...thát way."

She crossed her arms over her breasts. "Mm-hmm. We're going on the same one, I'm assuming?"

I shrugged, enjoying this. Enjoying *her*. I felt...eager. *When was the last time I felt eager?* "How presumptuous of you. There must be hundreds of museum tours in the area."

Her lip quirked. "Crafts and exhibits relating to a former abbey from the Middle Ages?"

I pretended to be shocked. "What a coincidence. Fate really seems to keep throwing us together, doesn't it? I'm fascinated by alleys of the...ages."

"Abbeys."

"That's what I said."

"Right." She sighed, her expression becoming serious. She fidgeted as if she might be a little uncomfortable. "Listen, um, Callen...it's been great seeing you and knowing all you've accomplished. But we've both changed a lot and I don't think...well, I just don't think there's any reason for us to spend time together. It really wouldn't come to any good."

I frowned, drawing back slightly, the unfamiliar rejection hitting me like a smack. "Why not? We were friends once. We enjoyed each other's company. Why shouldn't we enjoy it again?"

Her lips thinned, and she looked off behind me for a moment, as if gathering her thoughts. When her eyes met mine again, her expression was grim. "It doesn't seem you're lacking for...*friends*. And I'm not interested in any of that. The friendship we shared as children is a sweet memory for me, and I'd like to keep it that way."

"But...we could create new memories. *Better* memories." I gave her my best seductive smile, but it only caused her eyes to narrow with disapproval. My smile slipped, and I felt strangely chastised.

She put a hand on my arm as if in comfort. "Thank you, no." Then she turned and walked away from me for the second time in twenty-four hours.

Thank you, no?

I followed her out the hotel door, fast-walking to catch up. Outside, the air was cool and fresh, the sky already a bright, cloudless blue. "Thank you, *no*?"

She turned abruptly, and I collided with her. Her body was both firm and soft, and I wanted to press in closer, but she stepped back, taking a deep breath. "Listen, half the women of the free world would love to spend time with you. You won't miss the company of one girl."

She turned again and walked to the curb, where she took her cell phone from her purse, glanced at it, and dropped it back inside.

I went to stand next to her. "Forty percent."

She glanced at me, furrowing her brow. "What?"

"Half the women of the free world is a bit of an exaggeration. Forty percent, forty-five max. I don't take a single one for granted." I brought out the big guns, smiling, sort of lopsided, the one I knew women went crazy for.

But once again, apparently not this one. She tilted her head as if she was trying to figure something out. "Funny," she muttered, drawing out the word, though she didn't sound amused at all. She took a few steps forward, tapping her foot and looking toward the bend of the long driveway, as if impatient for her ride to show up.

This wasn't working. I wasn't charming her. At all. Maybe it was little wonder after our first two encounters. "So…okay, you're mad about the women who interrupted us both times we've run into each other—"

Her head whipped toward me and she gave it a quick shake. "No." Her chest rose and fell on a deep intake of air. "No. I'm not mad. I have no reason to be mad. I just…don't want to be a part of it. I *can't* be a part of it."

A shuttle bus pulled up to the curb, and she headed to it. I paused for a moment, telling myself I should walk away. But my feet had a mind of their own, and they followed Jessie, stepping onto the bus. She was already sitting, and her eyes widened when she saw me. She pulled her sunglasses down and looked out the window. I took the seat across from her, putting my own sunglasses on.

An older woman took the seat next to Jessie, and they struck up a conversation in French. I stared out the window, wondering what I was doing. I'd never chased a woman in my *life*. Much less to a *museum*. This was either a new low or a new high; I couldn't tell which.

As I watched the scenery go by, I realized I hadn't been up this early in years. I'd forgotten what the morning sky even looked like. But I'd woken this morning with an excitement running through my veins that I hadn't felt in what seemed like forever, and I knew it had to do with Jessie. I wanted to see her, to spend time with her, to hear the things she thought about, to find out the details of her life and all I'd missed since the last time I'd seen her.

But she *didn't want to be a part of it*. Of me. I should have walked off and found any number of women who desired my company, but I couldn't because I only wanted to spend time with her. *Jesus.* Maybe it was the challenge. Lord knew I hadn't had one of those for a long damn time. Still, I knew she wasn't playing some sort of game to get me to chase her, so again, what the hell was I doing?

The shuttle drove through the quaint downtown area, turned and bounced down a short, dirt road, finally lurching to a stop in front of a square stone building. We all stood and filed off the vehicle, but I held back, following behind Jessie, who was still chatting animatedly with the older French woman. I picked up a brochure at the museum's front desk, purchased a ticket, and followed the group through a lobby area and into the dim, quiet interior of the gallery. The space was roomy and open with display cases lining the walls and placed in the middle of the room, creating wide rows that patrons could wander between. Large, framed paintings hung on all four walls, with small gold placards beneath each one.

A tour guide greeted our group and asked if anyone spoke a language other than French. I kept quiet. I didn't care to hear about any of the items, so what did it matter what language he spoke? He began his talk, and I tuned him out easily, leaning against one of the display cases and stifling a yawn. I saw Jessie's lip quirk up as if she'd seen me in her peripheral vision, but she schooled it quickly and laced her hands in front of her, tilting her head as she listened to the guide.

I moved along with the group, glancing at a few items, mostly watching Jessie as she walked in front of me, bending toward each display and reading the descriptions, her lips moving along with the words. Why I found that so sexy I had no idea. I took a moment to look at the pieces that seemed to draw her attention, wondering what I could figure out about her from the things that piqued her interest.

I put my hands in my pockets, then removed them, feeling out of place, but at the same time, not really wanting to be anywhere else.

At first I didn't think Jessie was paying much attention to me, but then I caught her glancing my way surreptitiously in the reflection of one of the display cases, and it made my heart thump faster in my chest. We wandered to the back of the room, and I saw her look at me again and look away, and I couldn't help the smile that made my lips twitch. Maybe she was only keeping me in her sights because she knew I was watching *her,* but I didn't care. It felt... good. But for the first time in a long time, I wished my life hadn't been as public. I wished she didn't have so many reasons to write me off so quickly, that she wanted to know me like I wanted to know her. *Like she had thirteen years ago, when she'd first looked past the bruised and battered face and had seen the lonely, sad boy within.*

The tour guide had finished his spiel and was standing near the back of the room, answering questions quietly, when someone came up to him. The near-silence of the room was suddenly broken when my cell phone began ringing shrilly from my pocket. "Oh, fuck." My words—meant to be muttered—echoed around the tall room, some strange acoustics causing them to bounce from wall to wall. Several older women looked at me with shocked disdain, *tsk*ing softly. I fumbled in my jeans, trying to remove the damn thing as quickly as possible. I smiled in embarrassment as I glanced around, catching Jessie's wide-eyed stare. The phone finally came free of my pocket, and I punched the first button I could get to, which unfortunately was the answer button. Myrtle's loud, crackly greeting rang through the gallery, and I turned and walked quickly to the front of the room, exiting into the lobby that, thank God, was empty.

"Myrtle, I have to call you back."

"What? This isn't a good connection." The phone crackled directly in my ear, and I winced. *Ouch.* I hit the speaker button, turning the volume down and glancing back at the closed door to make sure I couldn't be heard as Myrtle went on. "I called to give you the transcriptions of your text messages."

"Myrtle, I need to—" I whispered, walking to the other side of the open area.

"I see why you don't have time to read them. There were fifty-seven. Some were from women that sounded like brazen hussies, and I just deleted those. In my day and age, no self-respecting female would talk to a man *that* way." She made a disgusted sound in her throat, and I tried to break in one more time. "One of them sent you her address and suggested you come to her house and do things to her that were so lewd, I wrapped up a bar of Ivory and sent it to her with a note that said, 'Please use this to wash your whore mouth out with soap, regards, Myrtle.' The other ones—"

"Myrtle," I hissed loudly, thankful there was no one around. Still, the crackling faded, and I took it off speaker even though the ceasing of Myrtle's rambling let me know she'd finally heard me.

"Yes, dearie?"

Myrtle had finally figured out how to open the computer program I'd set up that allowed my assistant access to my text messages. There were only so many texts because they'd been building up for two months while Myrtle became acquainted with the twenty-first century. Damn my own tendency to give my number out freely when I was drunk. I usually came to regret it—like now.

I ran a hand through my hair, glancing back at the closed door to the room where Jessie was enjoying the rest of the tour. My gaze moved upward, and with a sinking in my stomach, I noticed that the high wall over the doorway was open and the vaulted ceiling of the hallway continued into the gallery. *Shit.*

"Myrtle, I don't have access to a pen right now. Can I call you back later to go through the messages?"

"Oh, of course, dearie. I just wanted to let you know I've got everything covered here. Nothing important at all. You just relax and enjoy yourself, and if you decide you want the messages before you return, you call me."

"Thanks, Myrtle."

I hung up my phone and turned it off, then headed back into the room. Jessie was standing in front of a huge portrait of an angel smiling down on a young girl, and she glanced at me quickly and then turned her attention back to the art.

She spent another several minutes looking at that painting, and I pretended to be interested in the statue next to me, resting my hand on its head and feeling one shell-shaped ear beneath my fingertips. The stone was rough and had broken away in a few spots. I wondered idly how one went about carving figures from rock, when the ear suddenly came loose and dropped with a small *ping* to the glass surface below. I froze.

Jessie, who had turned from the painting and was strolling to one next to it, looked my way just in time to see me grab for the piece of broken ear, bumping the statue and causing it to rock dangerously. I sucked in a breath, steadying it, and Jessie put one hand over her mouth, her eyes going wide with alarm. My breath wheezed out between my teeth as the statue stilled, and I stuck the ear in my pocket, looking over my shoulder to make sure no one had seen what I'd done.

The security guard standing near the front looked at me suspiciously, shifting back and forth on his heels as if considering whether to come over to me with some warning or another.

Before I knew what was happening, Jessie made a beeline for me, grabbing me by the arm and pulling me out the door. "Oh my God," she muttered. "You broke that statue of the Virgin Mary. Let me see."

I sheepishly reached into my pocket and pulled out the ear. She stared at it before looking back at me, a choking sound coming from the back of her throat. She pulled at my arm again, dragging me out of the museum's main entrance and into the bright sunshine. "Don't you follow directions? The signs all said 'Do not touch.' Good God."

"I'm sure it can be superglued."

She stared at me, her mouth slightly agape, and then her lip suddenly twitched and she started laughing, grabbing her stomach and bending forward. The whole thing suddenly seemed so ridiculous, and I started laughing, too. Really laughing, for maybe the first time since I was a kid. Maybe since the last time I'd been with Jessie. "We're going to get arrested or something."

"I did it. Not you."

"No, but I'm the reason you're here. I feel responsible for you." She dug around in her purse and pulled out an envelope, removing the contents and then holding her hand out. Understanding what she was silently requesting, I fished in my pocket, pulled out the tiny ear, and placed it in her palm. She put it in the envelope, sealed it, took out a pen, and wrote something on the front. Then I watched her walk the short distance to the mail slot, drop it inside, and hurry back to where I waited. "We have to go. Come on."

I held back a laugh. "Go? We're miles away from the château."

"At least it's a nice day for a stroll." She paused before glancing away. "I guess we're going to spend some time together after all."

CHAPTER EIGHT

JESSICA

The sun warmed my back, the birds chirped in the dense trees all around us, and I shot a look at Callen as we made our way along the dirt road that led back to our hotel, tempted to laugh again. He'd looked both bored and uncomfortable in that museum, and I'd been unable to hold back the wave of tenderness that accompanied my amusement. He'd followed me there despite the fact that he obviously had no interest whatsoever in the exhibit. I couldn't help feeling flattered and strangely charmed by the sight of Callen Hayes pretending to find enjoyment in church relics described entirely in French. And unwillingly, I'd caught a glimpse of that same boy who'd once followed me through overgrown fields, between trees, and around a train yard, playing the games I came up with and indulging my childhood fantasies. Yes, he was a man now, and

I knew his motives were different and probably not very honorable, but I still couldn't help the warm flush of affection for the boy that might still be part of the man after all. I'd thought he'd become nothing more than a suave womanizer. I'd seen him in action. But there was still sweetness in him and an endearing awkwardness that made my heart skip a beat. Stupid, maybe, but there it was.

"Sorry about that. I didn't mean to ruin your museum experience."

I sighed. "It's okay. I saw enough of the exhibit." I paused for a moment, glancing at him and remembering the phone call he'd taken out in the vestibule, the one that had been broadcast to the inside room at large. "I like Myrtle, by the way," I said, my lip twitching.

His eyes widened, and he let out a surprised laugh that ended in a groan. "Shit, you heard all that?"

"Most of it."

He ran a hand through his hair, the dark strands glinting a deep, rich chocolate in the sun. "She's my assistant."

"I got that, *dearie*." I gave him a wry smile, and Callen laughed, looking just slightly embarrassed. I hefted my purse on my shoulder, and Callen made a gesture that indicated he'd take it from me, but I shook my head.

We walked in silence for a few minutes, and I soaked in the peaceful quiet of the day, looking ahead to where I could see the tops of the town buildings. I was surprised there was no discomfort between us. Walking with him like this almost felt...normal, common, as if we were easily falling back into the camaraderie we'd once had, despite all my reservations about spending any time with him at all. With no one else around, it felt simple and...good.

"Remember that time we pretended that old train car was a pirate ship, and we sailed the seven seas?"

His words surprised me, but only a little because I'd been thinking of the past, too. Something inside me delighted to know his thoughts had followed a similar path, and a grin spread over my face at the memory. "You called yourself Captain Carver 'One Eye' Swales."

Callen laughed, the sound deep and rich. "Captain One Eye, that swashbuckling swain. Damn, I can't believe you remember that."

I smiled softly, looking away. "I remember everything about those years." *I remember everything about you, Callen. You were my prince and my pirate, my savior and my friend.*

I stopped suddenly, turning to face him. "Why did you disappear? Where did you go?" I shook my head, resisting the urge to cringe. I'd told myself I wouldn't ask, and yet it was as if the words had fallen from my lips of their own accord. Callen the man was clearly interested in me, but it was the *boy* I'd loved, and he'd left me. I needed to know *why.* Yet...fear raced through me, too. A part of me didn't want answers because the knowing might wound me even more than the wondering. "No, don't tell me. It doesn't matter." I began walking again, but Callen took my arm gently, stopping my retreat and turning me toward him. I stared at him, into those thickly lashed gray eyes I'd once known so well. Eyes that brought to mind storms and shadows and the early hours of dawn. The eyes that were the same, though almost everything else about him seemed different.

"Doesn't it matter though, Jessie?" he asked softly, pushing a piece of hair that had come loose from my ponytail behind my ear.

I shivered at the intimate touch, shutting my eyes briefly. A small sigh escaped my lips. "I made up all these fantasies about what happened to you. That you had been abducted by a caravan of gypsies...or were being held for ransom by a band of robbers...only I was too old for those games by then, and I finally had to face facts that you were done with me and had decided I wasn't even worth saying goodbye to." *That our kiss hadn't meant anything to you, when it had meant everything to me.*

"No, Jessie, that's not what happened," he said, his voice thick with some emotion. Regret? He ran his hand through his hair again and looked off into the distance. "The truth is, I told myself I wouldn't go back. After...after that day, I realized how..." He shook his head, obviously struggling with his own words, with the explanation I'd wanted so desperately then but was now so afraid to hear. "I realized how selfish it was of me to keep spending time with you. You were pretty and smart and full of so many dreams, and I was just a stupid nobody, Jessie. Less than that."

"No," I said, my fists clenching at my sides, a sudden fierce protectiveness racing through me. *I'd been there to save you.* "You weren't nobody to me. To me you were everything."

He shook his head. He looked pained, as if my words had hurt him. "I stayed away for a week and then I couldn't anymore. I planned to go back the next Saturday, but I came home Friday afternoon and my dad was packing up our house. He'd been laid off from his job, and I knew enough to stay out of his way and not to question his decision. I snuck back to the boxcar and left you a piece of music. I hoped..." He looked off in the distance, the corners of his eyes tightening minutely. "I hoped you'd know it was a goodbye...a thank-you." He shook his head. "The truth was, Jessie, other than you, there was nothing in that town for me. I'd burned every bridge there was to burn. My dad and I got in the car with all our stuff and drove to Los Angeles the next morning."

"Oh." It felt so strange to have the pieces of that long-ago mystery come together. And I had been scared that it would hurt, but mostly it just made me sad. I pictured myself returning to those train tracks day after day, month after month, continuing to hold on to the hope that Callen would return, and he was long gone, in a city four hundred miles away, beginning a brand-new life. But he'd *wanted* to return. That piece of knowledge made something inside me feel lighter. If only I had known it back then. "I found the music, but I didn't realize it was for me. I thought it was something you'd accidentally left behind. Couldn't you have left me a note? Or written to me later? Something?" *Anything*.

"No. I…" An expression, part pain, part embarrassment, moved across his face, and he opened his mouth to say something but then apparently changed his mind. "I thought it would be better if we just cut ties, if you didn't think about me again."

I blew out a breath. He'd been wrong about it being better that we just cut ties, and I wished he'd made a different choice. But he'd been a fourteen-year-old kid with an abusive father and who knew what other hardships that he might be keeping to himself. I found it difficult to be angry with him now. "I felt guilty for a long time," I admitted. *Sad, heartbroken, and guilty*.

"You? Guilty? For what? You didn't do anything wrong."

I shook my head, remembering the disbelief I'd felt when I'd seen him on television, but also the relief. "I knew you didn't have a good home life, and I worried that something bad had happened to you, that I should have tried to find you back then when I still might have been able to do something…I should have gone to a couple of schools to look for you, or asked my parents for help, or—"

"Jessie," he said, shaking his head. "No. You were a kid. We both were. God, I'm sorry that I made you worry. Forgive me for that?"

"I already forgave you for that, Callen," I said softly. And"—I let out a breath—"now that I know what happened, I'm glad the move was fortuitous for you as far as your music. It all started for you in L.A., right? It worked out the way it was supposed to, I guess."

His eyes moved over my face for a moment. "I guess," he finally murmured. He put his hands into his pockets and glanced up the hill toward the town. "Think there's any chance of us finding a place to eat up there?"

I smiled, aware that he was changing the subject but not minding. We'd said what needed saying. "I'm sure there is. Come on."

We walked the short distance to the downtown area in silence, stepping onto the cobblestones that lined the narrow streets. Flowers trailed out of window boxes, colorful awnings shaded shop windows, and girls rode by on bicycles, their front baskets filled with fruit and bread and morning purchases. The day had warmed even more, and there was something sleepy and old-fashioned about the town that filled me with a sense of dreamy happiness. I could have strolled the cobbled streets all day, window-shopping and exploring small, dusty stores, but I didn't figure Callen would find such things interesting. I was here for a month, though, and I'd have plenty of time on my own.

"We could get some things to go and have a picnic lunch somewhere nearby," Callen offered.

I raised a brow. "Why, Callen Hayes, that sounds perfectly...sweet. What will it do to your reputation if the paparazzi gets a picture of that?"

He laughed. "I'll be ruined. My bad-boy image will be shot to shit." He stopped in front of a storefront featuring a stand of hats and grabbed a ball cap with the French flag on it, perching it on his head. "I'll wear a disguise."

I laughed, though my stomach did a slow roll of appreciation at how cute he looked. What was it about boys in ball caps?

He paid for the cap, letting the shopkeeper keep the very generous change, and then we walked a few stores down to a market, where we bought a basket of ripe strawberries, a wedge of Brie, some sliced ham, and a bottle of sparkling water. A bakery across the street had just taken a tray of warm baguettes from the oven, and we bought a loaf and took cutlery and napkins from the counter.

I asked the woman who rang us up at the bakery if there was anywhere interesting to sit and eat lunch nearby, and she told me about some church ruins that overlooked the Loire River a quarter mile outside town. When I told Callen what she'd said, he smiled and said he was up for anything. *Why does he have to be so charming?*

As we turned out of town, something caught Callen's eye at a novelty store on the corner, and he stopped, pulling an object out of a tall box. *A kite?* I stepped closer and saw that the kite he'd chosen was in the shape of a red-and-black pirate ship, a white skull and crossbones on its topsail. I laughed. "Why, One Eye, look at that; it's your ship. I was sure it was in a thousand pieces on the ocean floor by now."

He laughed, too, taking the kite inside and returning a moment later with his purchase. I shook my head, turning my face up to the sky. "I don't know if there's enough breeze for a kite today."

"We'll have to see." He winked, and my heart flip-flopped

over itself, causing me to look away on a frown. I knew it wasn't a good idea to be swooning over Callen Hayes. I'd vowed not to do it, and yet here I was, strolling through a quaint French village on my way to a picnic lunch with him. I groaned internally. A couple of hours. I had to get to bed early tonight since I started my new job in the morning. And then it would be easy to focus on what I needed to focus on... which wasn't him.

I had no doubt he'd find ways to occupy himself very easily as well. I had a perfectly good idea about what *ways* those would be, and I hated that the thought depressed me. Still, it was wise I kept it in mind, wise I remembered who Callen was *despite* the temporary boyish happiness in his eyes today. Despite the romance of the Loire Valley and despite the erratic beating of my heart each time he turned his beautiful smile my way and looked at me with affection in his eyes.

I wasn't unique. This was part of his allure. *He used to make me feel special all those years ago, too.* But now? I refused to become one of many who fell for those same charms.

"What's the sourpuss expression about?" he asked, breaking my moody silence.

"Huh? Oh, I'm just hungry. Come on, the woman at the bakery said the ruins are this way."

CHAPTER NINE

CALLEN

I didn't like the suddenly somber look on Jessie's face, so I took her hand in mine and clasped it firmly. "Lead the way." She looked startled as she glanced between our latched hands and my face, but she didn't try to pull away. I grinned, finally eliciting a laugh from her as the mood lightened.

We were going to eat a picnic lunch and maybe fly a kite. I didn't think I'd been this damn excited when I'd taken the stage to accept that French award months ago—the biggest award I'd ever received. Weird. Inexplicable. But true.

We walked a short way, and then Jessie turned down a dirt road that led to the edge of a flower field. She let go of my hand, and I immediately missed her fingers threaded through mine and the warm clasp of her palm against my own. "Look, it's over there," she said, pointing.

All I could see was a strange pile of rocks at the edge of a cliff overlooking the river. "When you said remains, I thought there'd be more to look at."

She shrugged and started walking, and I followed. *As I always did when Jessie took me on an adventure.* When we got to the site, there looked to be an old tile floor peeking out through the rubble, but other than that, it really was just piles of collapsed rock. "There's nothing left."

Jessie was looking around with interest, though I had no idea why. "Not much. But I can tell it was beautiful once."

Whatever evidence had led her to that conclusion was obviously lost on me. "Well, it definitely had a nice view." I looked out to the river, where the blue-green water moved peacefully by, the trees that grew along the shore casting light green and yellow reflections. Sunlight sparkled on the surface as if a handful of diamond shards had been casually tossed into the water. For a moment I was lost in it, lost in the beauty. When I tore my eyes away and glanced at Jessie, she was smiling softly at me. "What?"

She shook her head, the smile remaining. "Nothing." She turned, setting the bag of food she was carrying near some rocks, and I followed suit. Apparently her hunger was momentarily forgotten as she explored the area, picking up tiny pieces of rock and rubble and examining them for a moment before carefully replacing them on the ground. She squatted and ran her finger along a piece of broken tile, leaning in to look more closely.

"So, tell me about the work you're here to do."

She looked my way and stood, walking toward a pile of rocks that might have once been a piece of wall. "There were some documents found in a cave in the area that are thought to have been written by someone close to Joan of Arc."

"Joan of Arc?"

"Hmm," she hummed, running her finger along a rock sitting at the top of a pile. "Do you know anything about her?"

"Not off the top of my head."

She looked out to the river, her finger continuing its movement. She had always been tactile like that, always exploring things with her hands, her fingertips. I wondered now if she'd express herself in bed like that, too, and just the *thought* was so exciting I almost groaned. I suddenly remembered her as a young teen and the way she would find my hand as she read and trace a fingernail with the pad of her thumb. She hadn't even known she was doing it, and I'd found it so arousing, I'd all but come in my pants. I took a deep breath, willing myself not to get hard, not to let her know how sexy I found her as she picked up a pebble and rubbed it slowly between her thumb and index finger. I instinctively knew letting her know how turned on I was would scare her off and she wouldn't respond well. At least not in this moment. Maybe never.

"Joan of Arc was a French peasant girl who believed she was acting under divine guidance when she led the French army in a victory over the English during the Hundred Years' War."

"Divine guidance?"

"She reported hearing voices sent from God."

"Ah. Lucky girl."

She looked at me, raising a brow, obviously hearing the sarcasm in my voice. "You think?"

"Don't you?"

She appeared to really consider the question for a moment. "I think it sounds like an incredibly heavy burden to bear."

"Why?"

"Because if God calls you to do something, you better do it.

And do it well. No matter what it is. Joan claimed God's mission for her was to save France from its enemies and ensure Charles the Seventh was crowned as rightful king."

"No pressure though."

Jessie laughed, and my heart gave a small jump. "I don't think God messes around when he's doling out missions. Joan, a seventeen-year-old girl, set out from her village with not much more than the clothes on her back to follow his instructions. And in this circumstance, the thing God called her to do ended up getting her burned alive at the stake."

I made a show of shivering. "No thanks. God can keep his divine missions."

She wrinkled her nose. "Exactly my point."

"Did others believe she, uh…?"

"Heard heavenly voices?" She smiled. "Many did. According to popular prophecy of the time, a virgin was destined to save France. It's said that when she first gained an audience with Charles and asked him to give her an army, she revealed things to him that only God could have known."

"A seventeen-year-old peasant with no military training walked into court and got an audience with the king, who then gave her an entire army? Just like that?"

"He wasn't the king at that time. He'd actually been disinherited by his father, who was known as the Mad King, and needed a different way to inherit the throne he felt was rightfully his. But yes. Whatever Joan said to him to get him to give her an army, it was obviously very convincing. At her trial, she asked not to be pressed about it because she wouldn't tell. She only said that he received a sign that what she said was true. It's one of history's great mysteries. In any case, she led the army that had, up until then, only known defeat and humiliation to immediate and repeated victory."

"Huh. That's pretty unbelievable. The Mad King? I can see why history fascinates you. It's like a real-life fairy tale."

"Yes, I suppose it is." She blushed and looked down. "And to be here, where it all happened, is just..." She turned her face to the sky suddenly and smiled before looking back to me. "Do you want to eat or fly that kite?"

I was taken off guard by her change of topic and tilted my head, my brow furrowing. "I thought you were really hungry."

"I can wait. I feel a breeze we should take advantage of."

I paused, tilting my head upward as well, and felt the wind ruffling my hair and flowing across my skin. "You're right. Let's do this."

I unwrapped the kite quickly and unraveled the string. It seemed pretty straightforward, but I'd never flown a kite before. "Come on, we need room," Jessie called, jogging toward the wide-open field. I followed her, letting the kite drift into the sky, caught by the breeze now coming off the water. I let out a half laugh, half holler when the kite suddenly whipped higher into the sky, dragging me along with it and causing me to have to jog to keep up.

I passed Jessie as the wind blew harder, and I began to run, my baseball cap whipping off and flying away, the kite leading me as I ran along behind it. I could hear Jessie's breathless laughter behind me, and a sudden, sweeping joy filled my body. I let out a loud *whoop* of delight, the wind in my face, the high grass swishing against my shins, the kite above my head making me feel like I was flying along with it.

I looked ahead and saw the edge of the field was coming up quickly and attempted to turn, but the wind was in charge and it wasn't changing course. "Oh, shittttt," I yelled, having no choice but to let go of the kite as it whipped higher and moved out over the river. I collapsed on the ground, laughing and trying to catch my breath.

Jessie's shadow came over me, blocking out the sun, and I grinned at her, my breath still coming out in sharp pants. She was laughing, too, and shaking her head. "You lost our ship, Captain."

I squinted my left eye, peering up at her with only my right. "Aye, matey. But it was worth it."

She reached out her hand and I took it, rising. I came to my feet directly in front of her, so close that I could feel the soft exhale of her breath. Our laughter dwindled, and for a moment we stood staring at each other before she stepped back, glancing behind me toward the water. I turned so I was standing next to her, and we both looked out over the river, our ship only a bare speck on the horizon now, off to sail to warmer seas.

After a few minutes we looked at each other, smiling as we made our way back to the ruins where we'd left our picnic, Jessie ribbing me about letting the kite take charge. I didn't regret it, though. It'd been exhilarating. I felt happy and alive and...so hungry I could eat a horse. "Over there?" I asked, and Jessie nodded as we collected the food. I walked to the edge of what had once been the church floor, sitting down on a low wall of stacked stones that still looked sturdy. I let my legs dangle over the edge, placing the bags next to me.

I could smell the river, sort of like minerals and mud, but it wasn't unpleasant as I breathed it in. Jessie sat down beside me and pulled a light sweatshirt out of her purse, opening the food and laying it out on top of the makeshift tablecloth on the portion of flat rock between us.

For a few minutes we ate in silence, and I enjoyed the sun on my face, the gentle sounds of the river lapping the shore below, and the occasional bird cry. A distant melody seemed to swirl softly in the air, dancing off the sparkling water, moving quickly from leaf to leaf, but it soothed me rather than making me desperate to catch it, and when I went to put a strawberry in my mouth, I realized my lips were pressed together and the snippet of music hummed in my throat.

I bit down on the bright red fruit, the sweet taste bursting across my tongue, relishing the fresh, delicious food. The strawberries were perfectly ripe, the ham rich and salty, and the cheese creamy as I spread it on the bread. I'd eaten in the finest restaurants all over the world, yet I'd never experienced a better meal than this. Jessie moaned softly as she bit into the soft bread, and my blood heated in my veins. I glanced at her, and her eyes widened as if she hadn't realized she'd made a sound that I could hear, but then she laughed softly, sort of bashfully. "This is so amazing."

Everything's amazing. The food, the day, this moment. You.

I smiled, reaching over and using my pinky finger to wipe a bit of cheese from the corner of her lip. She stilled, our eyes meeting and a flare of electricity moving between us before she lowered her eyes and brought the tip of her tongue to the place I'd just touched. My cock hardened, pressing against the zipper of my jeans, and it was a welcome ache, slightly painful but laced with a steady throb of pleasure. I wanted her. Jessie. What surprised me the most was that I didn't just want sex, didn't just crave the mindless oblivion of my own release. I wanted *her.* I wanted to smell her skin, to know the particular scent between her legs. I wanted to taste her everywhere and hear the sounds she made when she came. I wanted to feel her shiver and throb around me, and I wanted to hear my name on her lips when that happened. I *wanted*, and the feeling swelled inside me like an entire orchestra as it neared the crescendo, just beginning that heart-soaring rise. "Jessie…"

"Yes?" she whispered, a note of something in her voice that almost sounded like fear.

"I…You were my first kiss. Did you know that?"

She blinked, her lips parting. "No. I didn't know." Her delicate brows drew together, and she tilted her head. "I was?"

I smiled at her obvious surprise. "Yeah. I wasn't always…" I grimaced, not knowing how to end that sentence without reminding Jessie exactly who I'd become.

"Callen Hayes, international gigolo?" she asked, a glint of teasing in her tone.

I let out a laugh mingled with an exhale, squinting at her as my smile faded. "I thought about kissing you for a year before I worked up the nerve. All those days we'd sit in that boxcar as you read. I'd stare at your lips moving and…" I groaned, shooting her a small smile.

She offered a shy smile in return. "I thought one of the reasons you didn't come back was because you hadn't enjoyed kissing me." She glanced away, out to the horizon.

"No, Jessie. I did enjoy it." I shook my head. "I enjoyed it too much."

The sun shifted above, and when Jessie's eyes met mine again, they appeared gold, ringed in deep, twilight blue. Eyes like sunset. *Beautiful.* "I enjoyed kissing you too much, and I wanted to do it again and again. I want to do it now." My voice was a hoarse whisper, laced with the desire pulsing through my veins. Jessie must have heard it because she looked down, her lashes casting shadows on her cheeks. A faint pink color rose in her face. *A blush.* God, she was innocent and sweet, possibly even inexperienced—a saint, whereas I was a sinner. And I wanted her anyway. I wanted her more than I'd wanted anyone in a very, very long time.

She didn't say no. Her eyes fluttered closed as my lips touched hers. I moved in closer, weaving my fingertips into her hair, my thumbs brushing the smoothness of her cheekbones as I swept my tongue over her lips and entered her mouth. She let out a sigh, and I moaned as her tongue touched mine, dancing, exploring. Our kiss deepened, and my lust grew, but I wanted to draw this moment out as long as she'd let me.

Jessie broke from my lips, turning her face downward, and my hands dropped with her movement. She used her thumb to wipe at her lip and shook her head, just a small movement, before she glanced back at me, looking beautiful and uncertain. "I'm sorry, I—"

"Don't be sorry. I heard what you said earlier. I just couldn't resist." The truth was, I hadn't kissed anyone else's lips since our kiss in Paris. I hadn't considered why...didn't even think it'd been a conscious choice. I'd done...other things, but my lips hadn't touched anyone's since hers.

I felt her eyes on me as I looked out at the river. "Callen, do you remember anything about my family?"

I turned my gaze to her, surprised, trying to remember the things she'd told me so long ago. "Your parents had a bad marriage."

Her lips, still swollen and pink from my kiss, tipped up in a sad sort of smile. "To say the least. My dad was a chronic cheater. He couldn't stop, or he didn't want to. Maybe both—I don't know. My mom used to drag my brother and me with her to catch him in the act—sometimes very literally." She cringed at some memory, and I felt a pinching sensation in my chest at the

sorrowful look on her face. "In the end, I resented them both."
She shook her head and looked out at the water. "I promised
myself I'd never be like her. Not ever. One of many, competing
constantly for the attention of someone who was never going to
love her the way she deserved."

My eyes moved over the pretty lines of her profile—the feminine sweep of her jaw, her slightly upturned nose, her delicate
cheekbones, and I felt a thickness in my throat.

She saw her father in me, a womanizer, a man who didn't
have the capability or desire to be faithful to one woman. I
wanted to deny it. I wanted to tell her she had the wrong
idea about me. Hell, I even considered lying to her. But that
wasn't fair, not to either one of us. There were things about
me I didn't ever want anyone to know, secrets I'd gone to great
lengths to protect, so getting that close to anyone was impossible. And there were a hundred more reasons anything other
than friendship, or maybe a casual affair, wasn't in the cards.
Couldn't be.

I let out a gust of breath. "I realize I'm not relationship material, Jessie. I know that better than anyone." I ran a hand through
my hair, feeling surprisingly sad to say the words out loud. But
they were true, and I couldn't deny them, not to myself and not
to Jessie. "I just... We're only in the Loire Valley for a short time.
Do you think we could enjoy each other while we're here? Just
for the next couple of weeks. No promises, so no regrets. And
then we'll go back to our lives."

She pressed her lips together, shaking her head as she looked
away. "You want me to be a temporary plaything?"

I leaned back, remorse causing a burning sensation in my
throat. "No, Jessie...that's not what I'm asking for. I'd never
think of you like that. I'm attracted to you. I can't help that.

But…whatever you're comfortable with, that's all I want. Just to spend *time* with you while we're here."

She bit at her lip, staring at me, her expression seeming to reflect the mixture of sadness and possibility I felt inside myself. Finally, she let out a sad-sounding sigh. "I don't know, Callen. I'm here to work. I need to focus on that. And…I don't think getting involved in any way is going to be good for either of us. It seems you have plenty of company to keep you occupied without me. How was the hot tub last night, by the way?" As soon as the words left her mouth, she grimaced. "No, don't answer that. See? This is what would come of us spending time together—"

"I didn't use the hot tub last night. I went to bed, alone, so I could wake up early and follow you to a museum where I managed to make an ass of myself and break priceless relics."

She looked surprised for a brief second and then laughed, shaking her head. After a moment, she sighed. "I don't know."

"Just you and me, Jessie. Like old times."

"We're not kids anymore, though, Callen. Things aren't as…simple."

"We can make them simple. Because this has to be temporary. We live on different sides of the world."

"As friends, then? Is that what you're proposing?"

I shrugged, wanting to say no, but knowing I'd been honest when I told her I'd take what I could get. *Anything.* I wanted more moments—*more days*—like this one. When I didn't feel empty. Detached. I felt desperate for anything Jessie would willingly give me. If she insisted I keep my hands and lips to myself, I'd do it. I hoped she wouldn't, but I'd respect it if she did. "Like I said, whatever we're both comfortable with. We can take things as they come. You lead the way. If it stops being enjoyable for one or both of us, we end it, whether two weeks is up or not."

She looked so torn, and I held my breath. "And will you have other...friends while you're here?"

I shook my head. "No. Just you."

She studied me for a long moment, and I forced myself not to twitch, not to say anything as she considered her decision. "Okay. When and if I have free time from work. And only while we're here."

My face broke into a smile. "Only while we're here."

CHAPTER TEN

JESSICA

The shower water rained down on me and I turned, letting the water pressure massage my shoulders. My body was still sore from all the walking Callen and I had done earlier that day. *Callen.* Oh God, had I made a huge mistake by agreeing to spend time with him while he was here in France? *Two weeks.* Just two weeks, but why did I have the feeling they were going to alter my life in some way I couldn't even imagine right now?

He'd told me he was willing to take whatever I was comfortable with. But was I strong enough to spend even a couple of weeks with Callen—under *any* circumstances—without falling for him? And if I wasn't, would I regret it? If I decided not to give him the two weeks, would I come to regret that?

I was pitifully inexperienced when it came to men. I'd dated a bit, but no one seriously and no one long-term. I'd been a focused student, and the knowledge that I'd be moving to France after graduation kept me from getting too involved with anyone. At least that's what I'd told myself. And then I'd been busy trying to get my life in order when I'd moved to Paris. But I also had to admit that I was probably more hesitant than most when it came to relationships. From my experience, *love* resulted in tears and loneliness, heartbreak and despair. So yes, I was a twenty-four-year-old virgin who'd never shared my entire body or my entire heart.

Initially, I'd been insulted by Callen's proposal, but maybe the arrangement he had described was actually perfect for both of us. *No promises, so no regrets.* Just because we weren't going to have a relationship didn't have to mean I couldn't enjoy the pleasure of kissing him. Did it?

And kissing him *was* pleasurable. At the recent memory of his lips on mine, his taste, a shiver ran down my spine.

The pipes squeaked as I turned the water off, stepping out of the tile shower and grabbing a fluffy towel. I wrapped my hair and then stood in front of the sink, brushing my teeth. I needed to get to bed so I could be fresh for the morning. Callen consumed my mind, but my main focus needed to be my job. Which wasn't difficult because I was filled with excitement to get started, to get my hands on more of those writings and immerse myself in the words and descriptions of a time long ago, to step into the mind of a girl on her way to serve a saint in the midst of war.

I heard my phone *ding* with a text and stepped out of the bathroom to grab it.

Frankie: How's the château, cabbage?
Me: The château is gorgeous. So is Callen Hayes, who's here as well.

The phone remained silent for a good couple of minutes. I dropped my towel, pulling on underwear and my nightgown. My phone rang, and I chuckled softly, knowing it was Frankie without even looking at it.

"Hello?"

"Um...what the fudge?"

I laughed. "I know. It's crazy. Unbelievable. But yeah, he's here on vacation. I ran into him last night in the bar."

"Are you *kidding* me? Why didn't you call me? This is...I don't know. Wait, are you sure he's not stalking you or something?"

"No. God, I'm surprised he didn't think *I'm* the one stalking him. No, it's just a crazy coincidence."

"It's *fate*, Jess."

I smiled as I sat down on the edge of the bed. *Coincidence. Fate.* Were they one and the same? "I don't know, but...Frankie, he wants me to spend the next two weeks with him."

"What do you mean spend the next two weeks with him?"

"I mean, I'm working obviously, but when I'm not, he wants to...hang out, I guess. And we kissed."

There was a beat of silence. "And after the two weeks?"

"Say goodbye, I suppose. No promises. I agreed, sort of, but...maybe you should talk me out of this, Frankie."

There was another pause before she said, "I'm not going to, Jess. It might hurt to spend time with him and then go your separate ways, but, I don't know...I have this feeling..." She paused again, and when she continued, there was an excited tone to her voice. "Fate seems to have her own plans with the two of you, and who am I to mess with fate?"

I let out a huff of breath that was half laugh, half sigh. "The friend who's going to have to stock a lot of wine at our apartment when I come home?"

Frankie laughed. "You can count on me, cabbage."

"I know I can, Frankie. I miss you."

"I miss you, too."

We chatted for a few minutes longer and then said our goodbyes, me promising to keep her updated on everything unfolding in the Loire Valley.

Even though I wasn't entirely surprised Frankie had encouraged me to take a chance with Callen, somehow I felt better with her support. I would just do what felt comfortable. If agreeing to spend time with Callen meant another day like today, I would gladly take a bit of sadness when he left. It had been one of the best days I'd had in a long time. The picture of his joyful face below me as he'd lain in that field flashed in my mind's eye, and I felt my lips curve into a smile. He wasn't asking for anything permanent. He wasn't asking for anything I hadn't given before—*casual. No promises, no regrets.* Perhaps he'd go back to his playboy lifestyle, but that wouldn't be any of my business. I *wasn't* like my mother, and I never would be. *Whatever you're comfortable with.* This was on my terms. I was in charge here. *Two weeks.* Two weeks and that would be it. Callen Hayes and I would part ways once again, and I'd survive just as I had the first time, because this time I'd have the peace of a goodbye.

* * *

I stepped off the elevator and followed the directions I'd been given to a set of back stairs that led to the bottom floor of the château. Excitement drummed through my veins, and I took the stairs quickly, stepping into a dimly lit hallway and noticing immediately the one room that had light pouring from under the door. The low hum of voices met my ears, and I knocked softly before entering.

Dr. Moreau turned from the large conference room table where he was standing and smiled in welcome. "Ah, Jessica, come in. Good morning. How was your trip?"

"Très bien." I smiled and took his outstretched hand, squeezing lightly. There were two other men standing on the other side of the table, one older and one who looked to be in his late twenties.

"Jessica Creswell is the translator I was telling you about. Jessica, this is Dr. Irwin Roskow. He's leading the team of scientists testing the documents in order to date them and verify authenticity. He'll mainly be at the lab they've set up near the dig site." The older gentleman smiled politely and reached across the table to shake my hand.

"And this is my second assistant, Ben Roche, the other translator I told you about, who specializes in French military science. In order to finish the project on time, we'll need to split up the writings. I've given Ben the pieces that mention the name of a battle, and, Jessica, I've given you the entries that look to be more of a personal nature. Ben will be able to help with the military terms that may not be familiar, and Ben, Jessica will be able to help with references relating to French life during the Middle Ages. I'm hoping it will be helpful for both of you to bounce questions or ideas off one another." I nodded, smiling at the young man in glasses with messy dark hair. He nodded bashfully and shook my hand.

"Excellent," Dr. Moreau said. "Now, then, who would like to see the site where these documents were found? We can take a quick trip and then return to get started. *Cela vous convient?*"

"*Oui*," Ben and I both said in unison, and then laughed.

"There's coffee and to-go cups over there," Dr. Moreau said, pointing to a counter against the far wall that held a large silver dispenser and various coffee-making accoutrements. "Grab a cup if you'd like, and we'll get going."

Coffee. Oh, thank goodness. I headed for the counter and poured myself a tall paper cup, adding cream and then a lid. The men followed suit, and we all left the room, following Dr. Moreau up the stairs and out the front door, where he had a car and driver waiting.

I knew the cave where the writings had been found was about fifteen miles away, and I sat back, sipping the hot, rich coffee appreciatively and watching the French countryside go by. I wondered if Callen was up yet or if he'd slept in, and decided he was still in bed. The sunrise bit he'd tried to sell was *not* true. I'd wager that if Callen did ever see the sunrise, it was because he'd never gone to bed the night before. We'd parted after lunch and kite-flying the day before without making any particular plans. I'd needed to study up on a few things for today and ordered room service for dinner, but I'd given Callen my cell number, and he'd said he'd call me.

Jess, stop. You're on work time. I was bound and determined not to be distracted by him, especially not today.

We turned off the main road and drove through a little village before turning onto a dirt road that wound up a mountain in front of us. Our SUV bumped along for a short way, traveling uphill, before coming to a stop near a grove of trees where several other vehicles were parked.

"The caves are a short walk, but the path has been cleared," Dr. Moreau said as we all stepped out of the vehicle. I glanced down, thankful I'd worn flats, even though I hadn't known we were traveling to the dig site on the first day. I'd hemmed and hawed over what to wear that morning, finally deciding it wasn't the kind of job where I needed to look overly professional, as I'd be in a basement conference room all day, sitting and translating text. Comfort was paramount, so I'd chosen a nice pair of capri khakis, a white blouse, and a navy blazer. I patted myself on the back for the addition of the sensible floral-patterned flats I'd paired with the outfit. Hiking up a dirt trail in heels would have sucked.

The morning was warm and clear, and the subtle fragrance of wildflowers sweetened the light breeze. I followed the men up the narrow path, the distant sound of voices and a faint, high-pitched hammering carried from somewhere beyond. I wondered vaguely if Joan of Arc had walked this same path once upon a time. Had she smelled the wildflowers, too? Had she turned her face to the sky to better catch their scent? To feel the breeze across her skin?

The tapping sound grew louder, and we turned at a bend in the path, stepping into an open area where we could see the mouth of a cave in the side of the mountain. Dr. Moreau signaled us to follow him, and it struck me again how fortunate I was to be here. This was like a dream come true, exploring the caves of heroes long gone, with the stale, dusty air closing in around me. *Surreal.*

The tapping sound paused as Dr. Moreau greeted the group in French, one of whom was using a tool to chip away at a piece of rock. Dr. Moreau indicated that we were just there to see where the documents had been found and to observe for a moment. They nodded to us in greeting and went back to work.

I looked around the space, the rock walls, the dirt-packed floor, stepping farther inside and noting the quiet sound of dripping water underneath the murmur of voices and light banging of what I could now see was a chisel. "There are no indications as of yet that anything more than the ancient writings will be unearthed, but it's still essential that all due diligence be followed, so they're collecting some of the rock and other natural elements to test for dating purposes."

"Dr. Moreau, are there any theories about why the writings were found in this particular spot?" Ben asked.

"Not yet, though only a few of the pieces were roughly translated when we were first establishing what they were. I'd like you to go over those pieces again, as the original translators didn't have any particular specialties. They may have missed things we will not. I'm hoping we'll understand from the writings themselves how they came to be here."

Ben nodded, and we all took a few minutes to wander around the cave, to get a feel for where the fragile documents we'd be working on had been hidden for hundreds of years. Why had they been left here? Were they hidden or just...lost somehow? I couldn't wait to begin.

I ran my palm over the rough wall of the cave tentatively. The floor was clear where there were no workers, no equipment, just tightly packed dirt. The voices faded away, the knocks and bangs becoming background noise as I breathed in the smell: dust and earth and a distant mineral-type scent. Without the lights that had been brought in, it would be dark and cool in here. Those conditions were what had preserved so many of the writings.

As I wandered away from the rest of the workers and scientists, a strange feeling came over me, a shiver of awareness that there was something...happy about this place, as if something momentous had happened here that had created a lingering feeling of calm. I shook my head at myself. Silly. I was letting my imagination run away with me. But Callen had been right when he'd said I liked history because of my love of stories and real-life fairy tales, and I found it difficult to stop myself from pondering what might have happened in this small enclosed space hundreds of years ago.

We didn't stay at the site much longer, as we'd only be in the way. We got back in the SUV, dropping Dr. Roskow off at the building that housed the lab and returning to the château.

Once we were back at the château, Dr. Moreau led us to a room next to the one we were using, where he pulled a large portrait away from the wall. It swung out on squeaky hinges, revealing a steel vault set into the wall. "Cool," Ben said, adjusting his glasses. "Is that where the owners of this place kept their jewels?"

Dr. Moreau chuckled. "Among other things as well, I imagine. This château has a rich history. They've loaned us the use of this fireproof vault so we can store the documents here as we translate them. Plus, it's nice and cool down here and the moisture in the air is low."

Once we were back in the conference room, Dr. Moreau threw a box of gloves on the table and collected three laptops from a cabinet near the door. "As you're aware, you'll need to wear these if you take the documents out of the protected coverings. I had to do so a few times to get a better look at a word or paragraph, and you may have to as well." Ben sat down across from me and Dr. Moreau handed us each a laptop and a document encased in a plastic sleeve, much like the one he'd shown me in his office the week before.

"I'll want to check your translations, so e-mail me your file, titled with the number indicated on the sticker at the top of each plastic case, after you've finished." We both nodded and got to work.

I was immediately immersed in the words of a young woman traveling with the French army and apparently disguised as a boy. The other soldiers called her Philippe, though as I'd told Dr. Moreau in his office during my interview, it was obvious from her phrasing that the author of the writings was female, even without her disclosing that fact. She'd settled into the tent of "Jehanne," and the first few writings were descriptions of the camp and information about military strategy she'd overheard. It was all interesting, but I was particularly engaged by her personal observations and the fact that she was obviously having trouble living the life of a common soldier when she'd come from an aristocratic existence.

"She refers to Joan of Arc as Jehanne," I said.

"Yes," Dr. Moreau answered. "The signatures that appear on the few surviving documents from that time say 'Jehanne' as well. It's the medieval spelling of Jeanne, believed to be her first name. These writings seem to further support that is what she went by."

"Interesting," I murmured, feeling a buzz of excitement over the confirmation that these documents were very likely written by someone who knew Joan of Arc.

After a little while, Dr. Moreau excused himself to attend a meeting in one of the upstairs conference rooms, and for hours, the only sound in the room was the clicking of Ben's and my fingers on our respective keyboards and a question or two uttered to the other when we became stuck on a word or phrase.

"Ben, a 'veuglaires' is referred to here. Is that a gun?"

"Uh, no. It's like an English Fowler."

"Yeah, still no idea."

"A sort of wrought-iron cannon."

"Ah, thank you."

"Jessica, have you ever heard of this phrase about a red rag...?"

"Let's put it this way, Ben—there was no Kotex in the Middle Ages."

"Oh God..."

Mostly we worked in silence, but there was a pleasant, comfortable atmosphere in the room, and it felt like before I'd even blinked, there was a soft rap on the door and lunch was being delivered. I brought the bags to the conference table and stretched my back. "Do you want to eat in here?"

"I'd like to get some sunshine, actually, before I start getting seasonal affective disorder from being in the dark so long."

I laughed. "I don't think it sets in that quickly, but good idea. The set of back stairs leads to a courtyard. If I'm not turned around, I think I walked past it when I was looking for the gardens a couple of days ago."

"Let's find out."

We found the sunny courtyard easily and ate our lunch on one of the stone benches, chatting about what we'd read so far and the theories we each had about who the girl named "Philippe" was, though we knew that reading further might solve at least some of those mysteries. It was wonderful to talk to someone who was as intrigued as I was by talk of ancient French culture, and the hour zipped by.

We returned to the basement conference room and continued as we had before, when I came across an excerpt that I read aloud to Ben:

In the year of our Lord 1429, on the twenty-seventh day of April

Everything is dusty and dirty and foul-smelling, the men even worse than the animals, and I find myself longing for nothing more than a tub of steaming water and a cake of lavender soap. Jehanne caught me murmuring to myself about the lack of hygiene in the camp, and though I wanted to die of shame for being caught complaining so, she only laughed and told me to follow her quietly and to stay among the shadows.

We snuck to a nearby river, where the horses had appeased their thirst earlier that day, and Jehanne taught me how to scrub my dirty skin with sand from the river's floor and to use the crushed rose petals at the water's edge to wash my hair. It was simple but heavenly.

Jehanne spoke of her plain peasant upbringing and described the house of her girlhood and her father's beautiful garden. It was there, she said, that she first heard a voice from God at thirteen years old. I asked her if she had been afraid, for if a voice had come out of the clouds and spoken to me, I daresay I would have perished of fright. She laughed and told me that she had been so afraid, she ran into the house and didn't go out for days.

"Then how did you come to ease your fear?" I asked.

She smiled so serenely, her hand swirling across the water as she said, "I have learned that my soul rejoices when I listen to God's wisdom, difficult though it may be." She paused then, and I waited as she seemed to gather her thoughts. "A wise and devout man once advised, 'Live fiercely and without regret.' He did not impart the wisdom to me personally, and yet I find myself repeating the sentiment in my own head. And it is my belief that to follow the path laid before me is to live in such a way."

As I watched her, the words echoed in my own head: Live fiercely and without regret. I must admit, my heart beat with longing to feel such joyful freedom as she described. For I have experienced nothing of the sort. I have known only trappings and rules, and followed the paths others have laid before me, never questioning my own calling in the world.

"What is it you want from life?" Jehanne asked.

The question confused me, for I had never been asked of my own desires. Indeed, I had never dared to ponder such a thing. "I don't know," I answered honestly. "God does not tell me of his mission for me. Only my father does that and with great authority," I added, not able to disguise the displeasure in my voice. "God does not speak to me at all," I said, watching my hand make movements in the cool water of the stream.

But Jehanne only smiled. "God speaks to everyone in some way, if you know how to listen." I vowed to think about that later, for I confess, I do not understand her meaning.

Our conversation turned to lighter matters, and we spoke of the men at camp who are the most insufferable heathens—particularly Captain Olivier Durand, who is the biggest horse's backside of all—and I don't think I've ever laughed so much, nor was my heart so grateful for levity. And though I'm almost afraid to say it, I think that in Jehanne I have not only a soldier to serve, not only God's chosen to follow, but a sister to call a friend.

"She definitely lived a pampered life previous to that," Ben said. "Maybe Charles the Seventh wanted to protect Jehanne's virtue by having another girl in the tent? Perhaps their main priority was to have this girl report on Jehanne? That part's not totally clear."

I nodded. Ben's forehead furrowed in thought for a moment. "Why do you think the girl posing as Philippe was directed to dress like a boy, even though the French army knew Joan of Arc was a girl?"

"Probably for her safety more than anything. Joan of Arc was assigned a bodyguard by Charles, but this young girl was not. A woman traveling with an army in the Middle Ages would have faced danger from both the soldiers surrounding her and from the enemy. Joan of Arc herself reported that the saints had told her to dress as a boy to protect herself from the possibility of rape as she carried out God's mission."

"Yes, I do remember reading that. There were several men assigned to Joan of Arc in various roles. It would have made the most sense that the male"—Ben raised his hands and made air quotes—"assigned to be closest to her was an unassuming, probably slight, teenage boy. At least as far as the appearance of propriety went."

"Yes, exactly. I wish all the entries had been preserved so we didn't have to piece so much together. What is clear is that this girl was directed to do this duty, but seems to have questions and doubts like anyone would." I smiled. "She and Joan both had a mission, though this girl's wasn't exactly in the same league."

"And hopefully things turn out better for her than they did for Joan." Ben grimaced.

"I hope so, too." I paused as I considered the scope of what we were translating. "Without these writings, history would never have known about this girl. It's fascinating, Ben."

"It really is."

We worked for a little longer, and when I leaned back in my chair to stretch my back, Ben looked up. "It's almost six and I'm starving. Dr. Moreau's already left for the day, and he gave me the code for the safe. What do you say we pack it up for the day?"

I was hungry, too, and was fortunately at an opportune stopping point. "Okay, sounds good." I handed Ben the plastic-covered writing I'd been working on, and after gathering his own work, he told me he'd be right back. While he was locking up the writings, I straightened up the conference room, bringing our coffee cups to the coffee station and scooting the chairs in.

Ben and I took the stairs together, entering the back hallway and walking into the lobby. We stopped, chatting and laughing about some of the things we'd needed clarified from the other, namely that I'd mistaken a type of gun for a comb. Ben took my hand, mimicking me brushing my hair and then shaking as the gun went off. I laughed, and he let go, his eyes seeming to linger on someone behind me. When I turned, I saw Callen walking toward us, a bemused look on his face.

"Hi," I said, my heart leaping.

"Ah, hi." He ran his hand through his hair, glancing at Ben.

"Oh, sorry, um, Ben, this is Callen Hayes, an old friend of mine. Callen, this is Ben Roche, my coworker."

They both nodded at each other, and there was an awkward pause. Ben jumped in first. "Well, nice meeting you. Jessica, see you tomorrow."

"Okay, see you tomorrow." Ben turned and headed toward the elevator and Callen put his hands in his pockets, looking sort of unsure.

"I was hoping you'd be getting off work about now and you might want to have dinner," he said, and my heart fluttered at the unusual vulnerability in his stance and expression. Then again, how did I really know if it was unusual? It was strange. In some ways I felt like I knew him based on the recent interviews I'd watched and magazine articles I'd read. But I realized that wasn't true, or if it was, then the whole world knew him, too.

"Dinner sounds perfect."

He smiled. "Great. Do you mind if my friend Nick joins us? I dragged him along on this vacation with me, and he's holed himself up in his room working. I need to make sure he eats once in a while. I made reservations in the dining room."

I ran a hand self-consciously over my hair. I wanted to freshen up, but I was also hungry, and sitting down with a glass of wine sounded heavenly. I decided to put on my best smile and hope I only looked slightly wilted. "Sounds good. I'd love to meet your friend." We walked toward the dining room. "So, what'd you do today?"

"Not a lot, actually. I went back into town and walked around, looked through a few shops."

I glanced at him, and he had a frown on his face. "Not as much fun without me, huh?"

He chuckled. "No. Not even close."

We turned into the château restaurant, already filled with guests, the delicious smells of rich French cooking wafting in the air and the soft sounds of classical music overlaid by the chatter and laughter of the people dining. A man sitting by the window waved. "There's Nick," Callen said, taking my arm and leading me toward him.

Nick stood when we arrived, smiling and holding out his hand to me. "Jessica, nice to meet you. I'm Nick, Callen's only upstanding friend." He had light brown hair and bright green eyes that seemed to sparkle from behind his glasses. He was almost as tall as Callen, but much less solid, bordering on skinny. He was cute, and his smile was warm and sincere.

I grinned, glancing at Callen, who had one brow raised. "It's true. I can't deny it," he said, motioning me to a seat and taking the one next to mine.

"It's very nice to meet you, Nick."

"Callen told me you're here on business and you two knew each other briefly as kids and even more briefly as..." He raised his eyebrows.

I narrowed my eyes, not providing the description he was clearly asking for. *Two people who kissed in a bar? Strangers who groped each other on a rooftop patio?* No, I wanted to hear his version. Clearly Callen had told him *something.*

"...cocktail waitress and patron," he finally finished.

I laughed, and Nick did, too. I liked him. "Nice save. Accurate enough." Grinning, I glanced at Callen, thinking of what Frankie had said. "Yes, fate seems intent on throwing us back together again and again."

"What's meant to be will always find a way," Nick offered.

"Deep. Isn't that a country song?" Callen asked sarcastically, picking up the menu.

Nick laughed. "Probably." He eyed Callen's menu and picked up his own as I took a sip of the water in front of me.

"The, ah, special looks good," Nick said. "If you're in the mood for beef in a burgundy sauce."

"Sounds perfect," Callen said, setting his menu down. A moment later, the waiter came up to our table and took our wine order.

"So, Jessica, what kind of work are you doing here?"

I explained a little bit about the writings that had been discovered and the connection to Joan of Arc, and then told him about my role as part of the team studying them.

"Wow, being fluent enough in French to translate such important documents is really impressive, not to mention you must be a master at it to do the work you do."

I smiled, acknowledging the compliment. "I don't know that I'm a master, but I've always been good with languages. I went to a French school growing up, so I've been studying it for a long time."

"Jessie used to translate her French books to me when we were kids." Callen smiled. I thought back to that, the way he'd listened so raptly, the way he'd seemed mesmerized by the stories. I'd loved watching his enjoyment and delighted in the closeness we'd shared huddled together in that boxcar—our own secret world. The memory caused tenderness to flicker in my chest.

The waiter showed up with our wine, pulling me back to the present, and then he took our dinner order, me the white fish, Nick a chicken dish, and Callen the beef special. "Excuse me," Nick said, glancing at his phone when a text message came through, making a soft *ding*. He began typing something in reply, and I took a grateful sip of my wine, sighing as I set it down on the table. This was nice, and I didn't need to overthink it. What would I have done if Callen wasn't here? I'd be eating alone, probably in my room, and that would have been okay, but this was better. People had vacation affairs all the time and then went back to their normal lives. Not that I was going to have an affair with Callen, per se, or rather, we might kiss, but it wasn't going to go further than that…probably…I meant definitely…

"Are you all right?" Callen asked softly, bumping my shoulder with his. I realized I was staring off into the distance, excited nervousness skipping through my body, my mind running away with itself. I crossed my legs, a surprising burst of pleasure making me very aware of what even *thinking* about getting physical with Callen did to me.

I took a long sip of wine, taking a moment to pull myself back to the present, and smiled. "Yes. Just thinking about today. It was intense."

"Good intense?"

"Yeah. There's just so much to do, and we're all trying to get the work done before the project wraps up."

He nodded. "The guy with you downstairs, is he a translator, too?" He took a sip of wine and appeared only mildly interested, but his jaw ticked once, and I wondered if he might be a little…jealous? Surely I was imagining things. Of course I was. What in the world did Callen Hayes have to be jealous about when it came to any other man on earth?

"Ben? Yes. He's the other assistant working under the head translator, Dr. Moreau. His specialty is medieval French weaponry."

"Sounds smart." His voice was clipped, and Nick looked up from his phone, placing it back on the table.

"He is…yes. He's very smart. I'm lucky to be working with him. The whole team is very impressive."

"Including you," Callen said, smiling at me.

I laughed softly. "Well, I hope I can keep up."

"I have no doubt."

Our food came, and we talked about Nick's company and how he and Callen had met. I was only vaguely surprised that Callen had been a troubled teen. Even when I knew him, I could see the darkness within. The *hopelessness*. Interesting how both Nick and Callen downplayed that aspect in the telling of their story. Filling in some of the gaps of Callen's life had me enthralled, and I listened to it all intently, learning of their initial meeting and of the few hand-to-mouth years before either had achieved any success. Callen was tenacious, a fighter, driven. And I'm sure that contributed to his incredible success.

Callen talked and even laughed, but something seemed to be weighing him down, sort of an underlying moodiness that I'd seen in him years ago as well. That sense I'd always felt when I knew something was wrong but he wasn't sharing it with me. Now I wanted to ask what brought that troubled look to his face sometimes, or what cast that vulnerable expression in his eyes, the one I was sure he thought no one noticed. And maybe no one did. Well, no one except me. And I thought perhaps Nick as well.

In the light of the dining room, I also noticed that Callen had dark smudges under his eyes, as if he hadn't slept well.

Once our meal was over and the table cleared, Nick glanced at his phone again. "Shoot. I have to go. A client in the States is having a website meltdown."

"That doesn't sound good," Callen said.

"Nope. Will you have the waiter put my dinner on my room tab?"

Callen waved his hand. "Yeah. I got it."

We said our goodbyes and Nick left, so focused on his phone he almost collided with a server carrying a tray of food. I winced at the narrow miss and then smiled over at Callen. "I should get going, too. I'm exhausted and I have another early day."

Callen moved a piece of hair away from my face, that troubled look back on his face. "Do you have to?"

I stifled a yawn. "Yeah. I do. We could do dinner tomorrow night?"

"That seems so far away."

"I know. I'm sorry. This job is just..."

"Intense," he supplied, smiling a tiny smile.

I breathed out a short laugh. "Yeah."

A frown flickered across his face, and then he smiled again. "I really am proud of you, Jessie...of all you've become. You're exactly who I thought you'd be."

I smiled. "Thank you. And you, I'm so proud of you, too. Your success is so well earned."

He shook his head, a grimace skating over his features, as if what I'd said had embarrassed him somehow. It confused me. Surely he couldn't doubt his own talent? "Thanks, Jessie." He ran a hand through his hair, looking off into the distance behind me for a moment and then smiling when he looked back. But it didn't meet his eyes. The waiter appeared with the bill, and Callen signed for it, looking back at me. "I'll walk you to the elevator."

"Okay. Aren't you going up? You look tired, too."

"Yeah, I never sleep great in new places. I'm going to take advantage of the piano in the ballroom. I'm supposed to be here writing a composition that's overdue."

"Oh, I didn't know. Well, then, I won't feel bad conking out on you."

We both stood, walking to the front of the dining room. He took my hand, and we made our way to the elevator and stopped in front of it. The lobby was mostly deserted, but I could hear the voices of the diners down the hall, drifting to where we stood. "Will you text me tom—"

Callen pulled me into a small alcove, cutting off my words as I laughed, but then that died as well when his mouth crashed down on mine, his tongue pressing between my lips as I let out a breathy moan. He responded with a groan, almost pained, and pressed himself against me. My arms came around him, threading into his hair as arousal shot through my veins, fast and hot. Immediate. I'd never felt this kind of sudden sexual excitement and I wanted *more*. Oh God, I wanted to wrap my legs around his hips, to press into him and feel his skin on mine. I wanted—

Almost as quickly as he'd begun the kiss, he ended it, stepping back, his chest rising and falling rapidly, his lips parted and wet from our kiss, and his expression...distressed, or maybe desperate. "Good night, Jessie."

"Good night," I murmured, watching him walk away and feeling confused, foggy. Standing against the wall where his body had pressed against mine only moments before, I wasn't sure what to do. I thought about the way he'd looked as we'd stood at the church ruins the day before and he'd been humming softly to himself: peaceful, happy. And I pictured the way he'd looked only moments before: upset, troubled. *Like my broken prince*. I suddenly wasn't very sleepy. I had a feeling Callen needed me. Perhaps his need wasn't simply physical, but he didn't know how to ask for more than that. So he hadn't asked for anything at all.

CHAPTER ELEVEN

CALLEN

I was an idiot. What the fuck was wrong with me?

Idiot. Idiot. Idiot.

I leaned forward and rested my forehead on the top of the piano where I was sitting in the empty ballroom. Opening my eyes and tilting my head, I brought one finger up and played the melody of "Heart and Soul," laughing, a choked sound that turned into a groan.

I wanted a drink so badly. But a drink would turn into two and two would turn into six and I'd end up in bed with some random woman whose name I'd never remember two days from now even if my life depended on it. And fuck, the real problem was that none of that sounded so bad now that I was thinking about it. I was so goddamned tired. Without the numbing effects of alcohol and the release of sex, I'd barely slept the last few nights. The oblivion called to me, and I wanted to answer that call, was desperate to shut down the words ringing through my skull.

Useless. Half-witted. Disappointing.

My finger tapped out a natural minor scale, the saddest and most depressing of all the scales. It fit my mood. Hell, it fit my damn life at the moment. *Except for Jessie.* But she was only temporary, and far too busy to indulge me just because I wanted to spend every waking second with her. But I'd learned long ago that as much as I hated the contrived schmoozing with *friends* night after night, I hated the silence of my own company more. Too much time in my head. Too much time alone.

Because I was lonely.

I'd spent the day in a state of impatient anticipation. The hours had seemed to tick by as I waited for Jessie to be done with work. I'd even—pitifully—stationed myself in a sitting area with a view to the lobby so I'd see her as soon as she came upstairs.

I'd heard Jessie's and her coworker's voices as they approached, animated and full of excitement. For a moment I'd remained where I was as they stopped and discussed things so far over my head, I wouldn't be able to reach them with a ten-foot ladder. Jessie had broken into French a time or two, and the coworker had transferred easily into the same language, their words volleying back and forth, not only on a topic I would never fully understand, but in a language I'd never grasp with any proficiency.

The coworker in question looked like some young professor, a Clark Kent type, and obviously a genius—probably perfect for Jessie. From the jealousy I'd felt when I'd seen him touch her hand, you'd have thought I walked in on them twisted around each other naked. It was immediate and overwhelming, and it scared the living hell out of me.

Then I'd listened as Jessie and Nick had talked about their careers. They were both so full of excitement and passion for what they were building, and though I'd felt proud of both of them, I'd also felt a prick of shame. Because though they were both hungry to succeed, I knew down in my gut that neither one would sacrifice their integrity like I had. Their big break would come from raw talent and a strong work ethic—they'd deserve every ounce of success that came their way. *Not like me.* And sitting there, I'd felt like an outsider in so many ways, someone who wasn't even worthy of their company.

And yet despite the roiling insecurity, dinner had been far too short and I wanted more time with Jessie and—

"What do they call that piece?"

My finger came to an immediate halt as I turned to see Jessie standing behind me. I hadn't even heard her enter the room.

She moved toward me. "Because it sure is depressing."

I breathed out a laugh, turning fully on the bench. "I thought you went to bed." My words came out in a rush, and even I heard the faint ring of desperation in my tone.

She used her finger to indicate I should scoot over, so I did. She sat down next to me and hit my knee lightly with hers. "I decided I wasn't as tired as I thought. And the work I was going to do can wait. Truthfully, it's probably better if I rest my brain a little. Translating takes a lot of focus. I was hoping you were still available."

"So what you're saying is, something mindless sounds appealing. I can provide mindless. It's what I do best." I was attempting a joke, but it was too close to the truth for my own comfort and the words faded away, my mouth turning down into a frown before I'd even realized it.

Jessie's head was turned toward me and she was watching me closely, so I forced a smile. She didn't return it. She seemed to see something about me I hadn't intended to show her. Hadn't that always been the case? Then. Now. "I think you sell yourself short, Callen Hayes," she said very softly, very seriously.

I sighed, running a hand through my hair. "Ah, you always thought far too much of me, Jessie."

"I don't think so." She paused for a moment. "However, if by mindless, you're referring to some bad reality TV? Well, I could go for that."

I glanced at her. "You want to watch TV with me?"

"Sure."

That was a first. I didn't think I'd ever watched TV with a woman. Not that I watched much of it myself, but curled up somewhere private with Jessie? That held some promise. "My room or yours?"

"I'd love to see how the high rollers live."

I chuckled. "What? Do they have you stuffed down in a corner of the basement along with your dusty work space?"

She grinned, and my heart flipped. God, she was the prettiest thing I'd ever seen. Even after spending the day in said dusty workspace, she looked beautiful, if not just a little bit mussed—her hair coming loose from the twist she'd had it in and her eyeliner smudged under her eyes. The effect only added to her appeal though—it made her look as if she'd just been rolling around in bed. My blood heated at the thought, and I forced myself to take a deep breath. Jessie was suggesting we watch TV and nothing more. "No, they don't have me sleeping in the basement, but pretty close. My room's nice—just a bit small."

"Ah. Then, allow me to escort you to my castle on the hill." I stood, offering my hand, and she grasped it, standing as well and giving me a curtsy.

"My prince, returned for me at last."

Her look of amusement and the twinkle in her eye made me smile, but something about her words also had me on guard. I was nobody's prince. But Jessie wasn't asking for that, not really, so I pushed my fears aside, took her arm, and escorted her to the elevator and then down the hallway to the double doors that led to my suite.

The doors opened into a luxurious sitting room with a fireplace, and Jessie whistled softly, causing me to laugh. "Now, this is living," she said.

"Want a tour?"

"Of course."

I opened the door to the bedroom, seeing that the maid service had turned down the bed and left two chocolate mints on the pillow. Jessie wandered inside, trailing a finger along the mahogany armoire and then touching the gold, patterned fabric gathered at the corner of the canopy bed, something heavy and silken that I was only now really noticing. She kicked off her shoes and wiggled her toes on the thick carpet, looking over her shoulder at me and smiling. My heart did that strange thing again that seemed to happen every time her eyes lit up with joy. And she had no clue. She had no clue how beautiful she actually was and how those smiles lifted my heart.

I followed behind her as she entered the en-suite bathroom, and I heard her intake of breath before I turned the corner. "Oh my God, how have you even made it out of your room with a tub like this?"

I glanced at the huge Whirlpool tub, surrounded by marble

tile. It did look enticing now that Jessie was standing next to it and I was picturing her naked with bubbles barely covering her pink nipples. Or would they be brown? She was a brunette with hazel eyes, but that creamy skin and sprinkling of freckles threw me. Suddenly it was a question that seemed as important to answer as any of the world's great mysteries. "Bathtubs are no fun alone."

Jessie scoffed. "A bubble bath, a good book, and a glass of wine? Sounds like the perfect Friday night."

"Oh, Jessie." I sighed. "I have so much to teach you."

She laughed, a genuine one that lit her face and caused an answering grin on my own. "I bet. Come on, show me where the TV is."

The TV was in the bedroom, hidden in a vintage-looking trunk at the base of the bed, and I used the remote control to raise it to viewing level.

There was really nowhere else to sit except the bed, and I wondered if Jessie was going to decide this wasn't a good idea. Surprising me, she turned and asked, "Which side is yours?"

"Uh, the right, I guess."

She nodded and went around the bed, fluffing the pillows on the left, taking her blazer off and tossing it on the chair near the window. I definitely liked seeing her sitting back against the pillows on my bed. I took off my shoes and sat down on the other side, turning the TV on. I handed the remote to Jessie, not caring what we watched, and she flipped around, finally stopping on a show that looked like a French version of *The Housewives of Beverly Hills*. "It has English subtitles," she said. "Is this okay?"

"Yeah, whatever you want to watch is fine with me."

"This isn't boring for you, is it?" she asked, biting at her lip.

"Not at all."

She smiled, and we settled in, Jessie moving over toward me, our legs almost touching. I tried to tune in to what the characters were doing on the screen, but I was so aware of her. I was having trouble focusing on anything other than the heat of her body next to mine, her soft laughter, and the way she smelled—a delicate perfume that was sort of lemony, the same scent that had captivated me on the rooftop in Paris.

I didn't know if I had unconsciously moved closer to her or if she'd moved closer to me—maybe both—but our arms were suddenly pressed together, and it seemed to me that all the heat in my body had traveled to the patch of skin that was now touching Jessie's. It reminded me of the way we'd once lain together in that train car, shoulder to shoulder, hip to hip, as Jessie's sweet voice took me with her to foreign lands, aboard sea vessels, and to deserted islands. Yes, this reminded me of *then*, but the *now* was also new and different. The electricity coursing between us was not a product of childhood, but of the man and woman we'd become.

I turned toward her, and she moved until she was facing me as well, and for a moment we just stared at each other. She looked slightly nervous as she blinked and pulled her bottom lip between her teeth. *Purity.* That's what was in her expression. So unlike the looks of calculated lust I'd come to know. "This reminds me of when we were kids," she said softly, and it surprised me that she had been thinking the same thing I had a moment before.

"I'm not feeling kid-like, Jessie," I said, my voice raspy with the desire I felt for her, my brain cloudy as the blood drained south and seemed to gather and pump heavily between my legs. Her eyes widened slightly and then moved to my mouth and slowly back to my eyes.

"Oh," she whispered. I wasn't sure who moved first, but our lips were suddenly touching, her fingers had threaded into my hair, and I moaned as she took initiative, though slowly, tentatively, her tongue moving along the seam of my lips. I opened, and our tongues met, the soft sweetness of her causing my blood to pulsate hotly through my veins. I tilted my head and our kiss went deeper, Jessie sighing into my mouth as she wrapped her leg over my thigh. *Oh God.* The movement brought our pelvises together, my erection pressed firmly against her. For a moment I simply continued to kiss her, trying not to move, attempting to find the control that seemed to have abandoned me.

Jessie liked to kiss. She liked to explore slowly—it felt guileless rather than seductive, seemingly for the pleasure of kissing alone, without any thought about where this might be going. Something about that was so damned arousing. I was completely lost in her. Lost in this kiss, in her touch. I felt like a horny teenager experiencing sex for the first time, when the opposite was true. I was a man who had done everything there was to do ten times over. So why did this feel different?

As if Jessie had been waiting for me to move and refused to wait any longer, she let out a frustrated moan and rubbed her hips against mine. She tilted her body so my hardness fit into the V of her legs, moving her leg down and up slowly so I slid against that sensitive part of her. The friction was a blissful torture that directed my hips to move and thrust—to *take*—though I held back, trembling with the effort. Jessie broke from my mouth, letting out a gasping breath, and tilted her head back on a moan, rubbing herself against me and causing my own arousal to notch up about a hundred levels. "Callen," she moaned, and I almost came in my pants.

I breathed against her neck, taking her scent into my body,

holding back a laugh of utter surprise at my own response. Maybe this was what sober sex was like. Had it been so long? Although we really weren't even close to having sex. We hadn't even removed a single item of clothing.

Fuck, I want her. I wanted to strip her clothes off and crawl under these covers. I wanted to solve the mystery of the shades of color on the most intimate parts of her body. I wanted to fuck her in every position I knew and then invent a few more. I wanted to watch my cock as it plunged between her legs, coming out slick and wet with proof of her arousal. The vision swirled through my lust-fogged brain, and I wasn't able to hold back the groan that seemed to pulse from my groin to my throat and out from between my lips, a tortured sound of desperate need.

Jessie's hands slid farther up my scalp, and her eyes met mine. Her expression was a mixture of drugged and shell-shocked, and she seemed uncertain what to do next. A spear of pure tenderness shot through me. I'd thought before she was inexperienced, and I was even more sure now. I kissed the side of her mouth. "Are you a virgin, Jessie?" I asked in a strained whisper.

She stilled in my arms, blinking, the slide of her pelvis against mine coming to a slow halt. "I...Is that...? Can you *tell*?" She looked embarrassed, and though some illogical, primal part of me rejoiced, I mostly felt frustrated. Even if Jessie wanted me, she deserved better than having her virginity taken by a man who would walk out of her life in less than two weeks. She deserved the prince she'd always dreamed about.

I sighed, using every ounce of willpower to rein in my body. I kissed her softly and smoothed back a piece of hair. "It's not a bad thing. I just don't want to lose control." *Lie. I desperately want to lose control in her body.* "And you make it far too easy."

Her expressive eyes moved over my face, and whatever she

saw there made her smile. I leaned forward and kissed the freckles I could barely see in the dim hotel lighting, and she laughed, gripping my cheeks and bringing her lips to mine, rolling on top of me. I smiled against her mouth and allowed the kiss to go deeper for a moment before pulling away. The soft weight of her over me, along with her taste on my tongue, was going to cause any semblance of self-discipline to spin away just when I'd gathered it back. I groaned, rolling her onto her back and looking down into her face. "Why haven't you been with anyone?"

Her gaze slid away from mine momentarily. "I—I mean, I've dated. I've just never let things go that far. I guess I made my studies my priority in college and then the move to Paris and…" She shrugged, the tiniest movement of one shoulder. "I haven't found anyone who…tempted me to get that involved."

I stared down at her for a moment, a strange fluttering inside me. Some stupid part of me *wanted* to be that man, wished I could be, but I wasn't, and it would be wrong to pretend I was. She was Jessie—*Princess Jessie*—pure and sweet and *good*. Even if the man I'd become didn't have a valiant bone in his body, the boy she'd once known *had*, and I needed *that* small particle of me to take the lead. I nodded, rolling away and standing quickly. "Do you want some water?"

Her eyes moved to my still-tented pants and then quickly back to my face. "Uh, no, I'm good," she said. I went into the bathroom and took a long couple of minutes at the sink, downing a glass of water and willing my body to cool down. I heard Jessie moving around in the room, maybe getting ready to leave. Thoughts of the long, lonely night in front of me, of knowing I was going to wake up and spend the day just waiting for her again, assaulted me. I was so tired but unable to sleep…I looked at myself in the mirror, my tousled hair, my lips reddened from kissing. I wasn't going to have sex with Jessie, but I didn't want her to go.

Returning to the room, I was relieved to see Jessie perched against the pillows. She'd taken her hair down and was running her fingers through it in an attempt to fix what our make-out session had done. She looked at me and stifled a yawn as I sat back down on the bed, turning toward her. "Will you stay with me tonight?" I shook my head. "Just to sleep. I know that sounds like a line, but I swear, it won't be anything more than sleeping. I just get…" I took a deep breath. "It's hard for me to sleep some-times." *All the time.* "If I'm alone I mean." I sounded pathetic. *Because I fucking am.* "I understand if you can't—"

Jessie had been watching me closely as I rambled, and she sud-denly put her fingers on my lips, halting my word vomit. Thank God. "Do you have a T-shirt I can sleep in? And I'll need to set an alarm."

Relief flooded my body. "Yeah." I smiled. "Thank you."

She nodded, and I grabbed a T-shirt from my suitcase, tossing it to her as she smiled and closed the door to the bathroom. I turned off the TV and riffled through my clothes, wondering what I should sleep in. Thinking that what I normally slept in— nothing at all—wouldn't work tonight. I finally decided on a pair of boxers and a T-shirt. Hopefully Jessie would be okay with that, too.

When she came out of the bathroom, she paused in the door-way, pulling the T-shirt down and looking uncertain. She opened her mouth to say something but then closed it, hesitating again before pointing at her cell phone sitting on the bedside table. "I'll set my alarm now so I don't forget."

"Okay."

She nodded as our eyes lingered, something flowing between

us, but spoken in a language I didn't know. It was like hearing a French song drifting from a shop as I walked by. The melody was elusive, the words foreign, and even as I was drawn to it, the music faded before I had time to turn around. She walked past me, and I paused, feeling confused, unsettled, yet still incredibly relieved she was staying. I ducked into the bathroom, where I brushed my teeth and changed clothes.

She was already under the covers when I emerged, the TV and all the lights except one turned off. I got under the sheets and turned my body toward hers. She smiled sleepily. "Tell me about the music you're working on right now."

A lump settled in my stomach. "I'm having a little bit of a hard time with it actually." I let out a breath. "Not a little, a lot."

"Oh," she whispered. She regarded me, her gaze sympathetic. "I guess composers get writer's block just like any other writers. What do you usually do to overcome it?"

Fuck. Drink. Anything to shut out his words. I shook my head, feeling disgusted with myself. "Nothing that's been helping recently."

She reached out and moved a lock of hair away from my eyes. It felt intimate, unfamiliar. Something about being in bed with Jessie this way almost made me feel shy. Laughable. I'd done things far more intimate with women I didn't even know and had never felt shy, not once. Yet lying here in the darkness with her, whispering to each other felt warm and...right, different, but good. *Because it's Jessie. Because she's safe.* "How does it work exactly? The process for writing a film score?"

"Usually I read the script or watch an unedited version of the movie, depending on where the filmmaker is in the process. Then I write the music to fit the feel of the film."

"Ah. And what's the feel of this film? What type of story is it?"

I paused for only a moment. "A story of redemption...love." Not that I knew anything about either of those things. Yet I'd faked it before. *Fake. You're a fake.*

"Hmm," Jessie hummed, her eyes searching my face for a few moments. "Can I tell you the way I felt the first time I heard the theme song you wrote for *Un Amour Pour Tous Les Temps*?"

I nodded, loving how the French title flowed so effortlessly from her mouth. It had been the piece that'd gained me notoriety, my first big break. Back then, his voice had been a whisper, but now it was a shout. It was as if the more my fame grew, the more success I attained, the louder his words became, drowning out the music. *Why? Why can't he leave me alone?* But right now Jessie's sleepy voice was a calm murmur and it was only her words that filled my mind.

"When I was a little girl, I had this swing in the backyard. That's where I would go before I met you, before I was old enough to play outside my own yard. The swing had been hung by the previous owners in this huge peach tree right at the edge of our property. When I swung high, I could almost touch the branches, and I could see the rosebushes over the fence in Mrs. Webber's garden.

"When I first heard the song you'd written, it made me feel the same way I had swinging under that peach tree. It was like I'd gone so high I felt the leaves brush against my cheek, and my heart soared so quickly that my body didn't have time to catch up. The breeze rushed over and through me, and I swore I could smell the faint scents of peaches and summer roses. It was like every good and beautiful thing in the world came together all at once, and you'd found a way to express it in one single song."

There was a pinching feeling in my chest that was making it

hard to breathe, and I felt full and empty all at once. Full with the knowledge that Jessie believed in me, at least in my ability to write music. And empty because I was scared, so scared. I feared that if I *had* done what she'd described—*once*—it was only because it was an accident, or some strange bout of luck I'd never be able to re-create.

She smiled, cupping my cheek and running her thumb over my cheekbone. She looked so adorable sleepy. "Maybe you could try to think of something beautiful you've experienced—something that engaged all your senses—and put it to music. I know you can." In her eyes I saw belief. *In me.* Her eyes fluttered and closed, her long dark lashes making crescents on her cheeks, her lips parting as she fell asleep.

Jessie.

I know you can.

I think you're the most wonderful person I ever met.

Yes, Jessie believed in me—at least in my potential. She always had. *Because she doesn't know everything about you*, a voice inside mocked. Maybe…but she believed in me right now, and tonight she was here, asleep in my bed. Warm and sweet and good. The far-off music I thought I'd heard at the edge of the church ruins overlooking the Loire River with Jessie the day before seemed to draw closer. I grasped a note, two, something coming together in my mind. Just a vague idea…not even a full melody, but…something. I pictured that little girl soaring high into the air and then falling quickly as the breeze rushed over her and she laughed with joy.

I know you can.

I waited for a while, watching Jessie sleep, watching the slow rise and fall of her chest, and then slipped out of bed, careful not to wake her. I shut off the light, plunging the bedroom into complete darkness, and tiptoed into the sitting room, closing the bedroom door behind me.

I think you're the most wonderful person I ever met.

The music drew even closer, rising inside me, the melody taking form, the *feeling* of it washing over me. Jessie was right about what she'd said earlier—what else was music but emotion put to sound? And the emotions inside me right now felt pure and happy.

I grabbed for a sheet of ledger paper, my hands trembling with doubt, expecting the melody to fall apart at any moment, for the music to stop. But it didn't. I glanced at the door to the bedroom, wanting to get something written down—anything, please anything—but also wanting to crawl back into bed with Jessie, to feel her warmth against me, to breathe in her scent, and to know her in the dark.

My hand captured the music that swelled inside my mind, maybe even my heart, though I'd never been able to tell the two apart. I wrote, crumpling up pages, but keeping others, and before I knew it, the light of the rising sun was creeping through a gap in the curtain, casting the room in pale shades of gold, growing brighter than the lamp I'd been using on the desk.

My hand felt cramped and my back sore as I blinked and looked around. My God, I'd written all night. My heart beating quickly, I riffled through the pages in front of me and saw that I had the entire beginnings of a composition. I scanned through the pages, humming the notes as they danced between the staves. And I thought it was...decent. I swallowed. It was getting there. Maybe. My heart beat faster with fear and with elation and with the desire to keep writing and writing and writing. I almost laughed out loud, or maybe I really did, because a moment later the door opened and Jessie was standing there, looking disoriented and disheveled and completely gorgeous. "What are you doing?" she asked, her voice throaty with sleep.

"Writing."

Her eyes moved to the desk and then back to me, and she smiled. "You artists," she said teasingly, affection lacing her sleepy voice. "I have to go."

"Yeah, okay." I walked to where she stood and took her face in mine, kissing her lips softly. "Thank you for staying."

She nodded and smiled her sweet smile. "Get some sleep, okay?"

"I will."

Jessie pulled her khaki pants and blazer on over the T-shirt she'd borrowed and then made her way quickly to the door of my suite. "Text me later," she called as she pulled the door closed behind her.

I went into the bedroom, flopping down on the bed with a smile. Rolling to the side, I smelled the pillow Jessie had slept on. It smelled like her, and I gathered it to me, clutching it to my chest as I fell asleep.

I dreamed, but not the dreams that haunted me—not the dreams of him. Not the dreams of his words and his fists. I dreamed of a dancing feather, just a wisp of downy white fluff, moving in the breeze in front of me, causing me to laugh out loud. I extended my arm, reaching for the feather as it swirled in the air, guiding my footsteps as I allowed it to lead the way. I was mesmerized—almost entranced—as it dipped and somersaulted, rose and spun, always just out of reach. Teasing, taunting. I hurried to catch up, my own movement increasing the push of air, causing it to fly forward, off the sidewalk, down a trail, over a slope, and along a set of train tracks, where it disappeared.

Inside an abandoned boxcar.

CHAPTER TWELVE

JESSICA

In the year of our Lord 1429, on the twelfth day of June

The moon is full tonight, so bright that one can see the blood still staining the grassy field where the battle was fought this morning. I found myself standing at the edge of that field staring out at it, a million questions running through my tired mind, when Captain "Horse's Arse" Durand happened upon me on his way back to camp and inquired as to my lingering. I made a brief reference to the questions war naturally raises within one's mind, and the impossible duff commented that only a girl would stand about philosophizing while men were injured and dying only a stone's throw away.

I gasped in a breath of shock and said, "A girl? I'm hardly a girl, sir."

He looked at me in that smug way of his with one eyebrow arched. "If God is designing boys who look like you, then our species is in trouble," said the insolent scoundrel. Then he continued by saying, "Now, make yourself useful and go assist Jehanne rather than standing by uselessly contemplating the universe." And with that he rode away.

The arrogant fool! With his big muscles and superior countenance. The way he struts through camp as if he himself owns the world and makes all the rules. Well, he does not rule me! I had been waiting in our tent all day and had assisted Jehanne from her uniform, cleaned and repaired it, and had but taken a moment to step outside for some air.

I stormed back to the tent, and though she was exhausted from the battle, Jehanne asked what was wrong, and I shared my brief run-in with the captain. She laughed, which served to smooth my ruffled feathers, and for a moment I was able to see the mirth in his ridiculousness.

"It is near impossible for a man who's seen so much dying to understand God's role in any of it," said she.

"And you?" I asked softly, for my doubts are the same, much to my own shame. Why would God allow such suffering?

"Yes, me too," she whispered, her voice fading with sleep. "But I must put my questions aside and answer the call nonetheless. That is what faith is. Knowing *that though I do not have all the answers, God does, and he stands only for good."*

My heart aches to believe it, and yet how does one do so with the stench of death all around, with the blast of cannons ringing in your ears long after the fight has ended? I thought she'd fallen asleep, when a smile curved her lips and she said on a whisper, "And you, my friend, like that horse's arse far more than you're willing to admit just yet."

A smile curved my own lips. I sensed a love story buried in the papers in front of me and wondered if we'd find out what became of Captain Durand and the girl dressed as a boy, traveling with an army and a saint.

I stretched my arms and legs and picked up my coffee cup, taking a sip and blanching at the cold, bitter taste. Ben had left an hour before, and I was alone in the conference room, with instructions for locking the papers up when I was done.

My brain was starting to feel fuzzy, so I began gathering my things in preparation of calling it a day. The ring of my phone broke the silence in the room, and I started, digging it out. "Hello?"

"Hey there." My heart did a strange little flip at the sound of Callen's smooth, rich voice.

"Hey yourself."

"How was your day?"

I stifled a yawn. "Good. Long. I'm hungry."

"Good. I'm planning on feeding you. I thought we could drive into town tonight and try a different restaurant. Nick has a website crisis, so it'll just be you and me."

"I didn't realize website maintenance was so full of mayhem.

But dinner sounds good. We can bring something back for Nick." Truthfully, I was glad to be getting out. As delicious as the food here was, I would like to try something new.

"Meet me upstairs in ten?"

I smiled. "Yeah. See you then."

As I gathered the documents I'd worked on that day and made my way to the office next door, I couldn't help but recall my time with Callen last night. I'd eaten dinner with Callen and Nick and again slept in Callen's room. We'd kissed, and my body wanted more, but I knew Callen was right when he pulled away, not allowing things to go much further than that. *Wasn't he?* Yes. Yes, of course.

Callen exercised such control when it came to how far we went physically. Part of me was disappointed that he so easily had sex with scores of other women and wouldn't even really *try* with me. Then again, I didn't want him to try, did I? No, because it would be far too easy to throw all caution to the wind and say yes to anything he asked of me. And then where would I be? Well, I guess I'd be in the exact same place I was going to be anyway: alone and mildly heartbroken. Only I'd also be devirginized, which possibly wasn't *such* a bad thing. Maybe I'd made too much of it, waited too long, put far too much importance on something other girls did not. Then again, wouldn't sharing something with Callen I'd never shared with anyone else just cause our parting to hurt all the more?

I made a frustrated sound in my throat, annoyed at myself for my own waffling thoughts. I'd never been a waffler! I was always sure, steadfast. I pictured my goals and I went toward them diligently. Only...love wasn't really like that, was it?

Love?

No, not love. Affection. Sexual attraction. Care. "Oh, good

Lord." I slammed the safe, spinning the lock before carefully clicking the picture hanging over it into place.

* * *

In the year of our Lord 1429, on the seventeenth day of June

I'm writing this entry by the bare flicker of candle-light at the end of another day of battle. More fight-ing will commence tomorrow, and with each passing minute my fear grows for the lives that shall be lost, for the blood that will surely be spilled, and mostly for the agony of dread that lies within my heart as I watch the army depart for battle. A battle for which my only role is the waiting, a certain torture in itself. Alone in our tent at night, Jehanne speaks her fears to me as I do to her. And strangely, though I would deign it to be the opposite, I find it comforting that she is as afraid as I. Though her insides quiver in fright—for this she has told me—she does not hesitate to lead the men straight into the fray, where they claim victory again and again. So strong is her faith, so devout is her belief, that de-spite her terror, she continues to live fiercely. Is this the true definition of bravery: being afraid but acting anyway? Following the dictates of your faith and your heart straight into the battle for which you've been called? It seems to me to be so. For how is there bravery if there is no fear?

I read the passage to Ben and he paused, looking at me thoughtfully. "It's really profound, Jessica, because what we know of Joan of Arc tells of her extreme bravery on the battle-field, of her unfailing faith, but no one's ever spoken of or known about her private thoughts and fears…until now."

"Exactly. She was a military leader who led an army of men, but she was also a teenage girl." She believed her calling so strongly that she did what few would have done, yet how could a peasant girl who'd only known a safe, provincial life not be afraid to charge straight toward enemy swords? Not be afraid that she was *wrong* and leading men directly to their deaths? Deaths that might be for a faulty cause?

I wandered upstairs later, the picture of the dim interior of a tent in the middle of an army camp where two young girls lay whispering together running through my mind. Two girls who were about the same age and yet played vastly different roles in the course of history—one a peasant, one nobility, one canonized, and one forgotten. And yet both were brave in their own right. I wondered what had happened to Joan of Arc's camp assistant and if the writings would enable us to identify her and provide a clue as to her fate.

Fate.

I trailed a finger over the rough plaster wall as I walked slowly down the hall, feeling the bumps and divots beneath the pad of my index finger. Was it fate that pulled the strings, that led us to our destiny? And what happened when we didn't fol-low the path we were meant for? What if we were too blind to *see* it? What if we ran inside our house as Joan of Arc did that first day the voices came to her, but never went out again? What if we stayed locked up, safe, but avoided our calling? Did it only affect us, or did it end up altering the entire world?

And if only *all* callings could be as clear as a voice ringing down from the clouds with a specific mission.

"You look deep in thought."

I jerked my head up and laughed when I saw Callen leaning against the door to my room, his hands in his pockets, so casually handsome it caused my heart to leap.

"Slumming it?"

He chuckled. "Not even close. You of all people should know that, given you literally met me on the wrong side of the tracks."

I grinned over my shoulder, stepping inside my room. "Funny, I remember meeting you over a sparkling river in the mouth of a rocky cave deep in the Enchanted Linden Forest."

Callen laughed, closing the door behind him. "You're right. My memory is so unreliable sometimes."

"That's because of that—"

He backed me up against the wall, my breath hitching as he put both hands on the wall next to my head and smiled down at me. "You were saying?"

I cleared my throat, distracted by the solid press of his body, the scent of him right up close, and the beauty of his face looking at me as if I were the only person in his world. "That, um...spell the wicked—"

His lips came down on mine, and I could feel his smile as he began kissing me. He dragged his lips down my throat as he pressed his pelvis into mine, shooting sparks between my thighs. "The spell the wicked..."

"...Lord Blackshadow cast on you." I moaned at the feel of his lips nipping at the tender skin of my neck, bringing my arms up and wrapping them around his shoulders so I could pull him even closer. His muscles bunched under my hands, the hard feel of his male body such delicious wonder.

I felt his lips tip into another smile against my skin. "The wicked Lord Blackshadow *did* cast a spell on me, and now I'm as wicked as him." He brought his head up, looking right into my eyes. "And there's no cure for me, Jessie."

For some reason his words sent a shiver of hurt through me, though I wasn't sure why. We stared at each other for a moment, something thick in the space between us. A warning? A statement? Or maybe a question. Whatever it was, I wasn't sure how to interpret it, much less form an answer.

He broke the spell as he looked away and glanced around briefly, apparently taking in the tiny size of my stone-walled room for the first time since we'd stepped inside. "They really do have you in a dungeon, don't they?"

"Will you rescue me, Callen?"

His expression sobered, and for just a moment we stared at each other yet again, but then Callen smiled and pulled away. "Come away with me this weekend."

I stood straight, smoothing my hair. "Come away? We are away."

"No, I mean from here. Let's see a little more of the Loire Valley."

"You want to sightsee?"

He shrugged. "Yeah. It'll be our greatest adventure yet." He smiled, a twinkle in his eye.

I thought about it. There was really no reason I needed to stay here this weekend. No one else was working; in fact, Ben had told me he was going on a sightseeing tour himself and would be away from the château. He'd even asked to leave a little early on Friday, and Dr. Moreau said he'd be using the basement conference room for meetings during the afternoon and so that worked fine. And I needn't be afraid of spending the night with Callen. We'd been sleeping in the same bed for almost a week now and evidently he had little trouble resisting me. I was…resistible in that sense, it seemed.

That depressed me just a bit, but I *was* happy that he'd apparently found a way to move past his writer's block. Each night I'd been with him, he'd slipped out of bed and written late into the night while I slept. I'd wake to find him hunched over that desk just outside the bedroom, looking sleepy but content, and it filled my heart with joy. I knew I couldn't take credit, but I hoped I at least had a calming effect on him—one that allowed him to access his inner genius.

Callen and I enjoyed each other's company, and I wanted to see more of the Loire Valley. We had agreed to make the most of what little time we had together, so why not? "Sure. Okay. I can get off a little early on Friday."

Callen grinned. "Awesome. We'll make it one perfect weekend."

One. It would be the only weekend we'd ever have alone together, and that sent a shivery excitement whirring through my body and filled me with a cold despondency.

One.

Just one.

* * *

In the year of our Lord 1429, on the thirtieth day of June

My heart is beating so fast I fear it may explode straight from my chest.

Tonight, Captain Durand and several of his men went to a small village, where they were to obtain food for the army from local farmers. But they returned with pitiable rations. The farmers were not cooperative despite the king's prise. I had been bathing in the nearby creek and joined up with their horses as they entered camp, and I expressed my disappointment that the farmers should choose not to feed their own country's army.

"Why should they?" asked the captain in that testy way he has that brings to mind a porcupine right before it shoots its quills.

"Why should they? Because we fight for them," I returned.

"We?" he asked wryly, and before I could offer a retort, he went on. "And what of the fact that they already pay taxes to fund the king's army? How much more should they give? Should their own family go hungry so we can eat? Should they give us the shirts off their backs as well, perchance?"

"They should give that which they've been ordered to give," I insisted. For should they not?

"Spoken like a pampered girl who expects hardworking men to do her bidding," said the pompous arse, and I felt my own quills rising.

"A girl? Sir, I have explained to you that I am a boy," I nearly yelled. And then he laughed.

The other men had ridden ahead, leaving us to our battle, and I was so angry, I took off my shoe and hurled it at him. The blackguard laughed even harder, so that I thought—hoped—he might fall right off his horse.

"All right, young sir, if you're really a boy, go piss on that tree over there while standing up. Let me see how far you can shoot it," he said.

I was disgusted and told him so. "You are lewd, sir, and no gentleman."

He shook his head, dismounting and picking up my shoe, which he inspected with one arrogant eyebrow raised. I had to admit it looked quite dainty in his large hand, and I scowled and looked away. He brought the shoe to me, and before I knew what was happening, he'd taken hold of me and pulled me from my mount. I stood in front of him, ready to shred him to pieces with my outraged tongue when he ... oh I can barely write it ... he ... kissed me!

And the worst part of all ... I liked it. Oh, help me, Lord, I liked it very, very much.

Once I'd finished with work on Friday, I'd gone back to my room and packed a bag, still distracted by that breathless kiss between the girl and Captain Durand. I'd have stayed to read another entry, but unfortunately, Dr. Moreau had come into the room with a few colleagues for the meetings he'd mentioned, and so I'd reluctantly abandoned the girl and Olivier Durand with their lips locked and my heart beating out of my chest to be left on such a cliffhanger. But they weren't going anywhere, so I'd turned my mind to Callen, excited—and still a bit apprehensive—about what this weekend would bring.

As I stepped out the front door of the château, I stopped in my tracks when I saw Callen leaning against a red convertible sports car parked at the curb.

His smile was slow and easy as he pulled his sunglasses off, pushing himself away from the car and walking toward me. He was wearing jeans and a casual dark gray T-shirt that hugged his chest and showed off his broad shoulders. His stride was smooth and masculine. *Oh, dear Lord.* I swallowed. He was so gorgeous that sometimes it startled me just a bit. He took my bag with a smile, and I laughed nervously. "Where in the world did you get that?" I nodded toward the sleek red car.

"Rental. We ride in style." He opened the passenger-side door for me, and I sank into the soft leather and clicked my seat belt into place. After he'd put my bag in the trunk, he slid into the driver's seat and pulled away from the château, down the long winding drive, and onto the main road.

"So where are we headed?"

"So impatient. Just sit back and let me take the lead this time, Princess."

CHAPTER THIRTEEN

CALLEN

I glanced at Jessie and smiled, taking her hand in mine across the center console. Her hair was pulled back in a ponytail, but a few strands had come loose in the wind and were blowing across her cheeks. A pair of sunglasses that looked far too large for her face were perched on her cute nose. She wore a pair of tight jeans that showed off her slim legs, a blue-and-white-striped shirt, and a light tan jacket. She looked beautiful and carefree, and I couldn't help the happiness that gripped me, knowing I had her all to myself for two full days. I was going to enjoy every second of it—it was the last real time alone we'd have. I'd be leaving the château a week from today, but I refused to think about that now. We had the weekend stretched out in front of us. It was our final adventure together, and I intended to make the most of it.

I'd written the entire first part of the musical score, and

though my heart beat quickly with barely controlled hope, I also breathed an internal sigh of relief that the writer's block had lifted. Not only had it lifted, but I thought the piece showed promise. I wouldn't allow myself to get too excited because I still had such an uncertain grip on the entire score. But if I could just continue with the same inspiration and determine how to bring it all together...it might...it might not just be good, but great.

I had Jessie to thank for what I'd accomplished so far. She was my muse, and I couldn't have done it without her. Something about her drowned out the self-contempt. Whereas awards, accolades, even a million screaming fans couldn't convince me I had talent, Jessie's sincere smile made me feel as if I could do anything. As long as she believed, I could as well.

What will you do when she's gone?

Stop. Don't think about that.

The beautiful scenery whipped by, gently rolling hills, small farms, fields of wildflowers, and quaint towns. Jessie and I chatted about mundane things as the radio played French ballads. I felt a sense of peace, of rightness with the world, and I wondered about the last time I'd felt this way. *Had I ever?*

The GPS led us off the main highway, down a winding road to a vineyard, the rows and rows of grapes stretching into the distance. A gleaming white stone castle loomed high in front of us, its turrets touching the clouds. "Oh my gosh," Jessie breathed, leaning forward and gazing at the ancient structure. "This is gorgeous. A winery?"

I nodded. "A wine tour and an early dinner." Nick had helped me find the perfect spot to take Jessie, something that might appeal to her love of history and love of all things French. I'd made reservations for a wine tour and then booked us into another fancy château an hour away. Nick had laughed, saying he'd never seen this *romantic* side of me, and I'd told him it was a one-time deal. I certainly didn't tell him that I'd felt a thrill of excitement at the prospect of pleasing Jessie, and even more so in the surety that I knew what she liked and had the ability to provide it for her.

Nick had clapped me on the shoulder. "It happens to the best of us sooner or later," he'd said, a mock look of pity on his face.

"What is that exactly?"

He'd winked. "I'll leave you to define it for yourself, *mon ami.*" I could only roll my eyes. The man had barely left his room the entire trip, and yet suddenly he was French.

A staff member at the winery greeted us as we stepped from the car, and we followed her inside the castle, stopping to marvel at the impressive foyer with its antique-looking table in the middle of the space and a grand staircase rising beyond. The rooms to the left and the right had been turned into what looked like a restaurant and gift shop. "Your self-guided tour starts in the courtyard, monsieur and madame. Dinner will be served in the garden, and your tasting will follow."

I took Jessie's hand, and we followed the older woman outside to a bike rack that held numerous bicycles. *Uh.* My heart dropped. I looked around, but the woman was already unlocking a bike, which she leaned toward us. Jessie took the handlebars and sucked in a breath of excitement. "It's a bike-riding tour? This is amazing!"

The woman wheeled a bicycle over to me, and I took it with a tight smile, thanking her. It couldn't be that hard, right? Even six-year-olds figured it out. She pointed off in the distance to where the gardens began, the rows of grapevines in the distance beyond. "There are bike trails all the way through, and you are free to use any of the paths.

Your dinner will be set up in Lumière de la Rose. You cannot miss the sign."

"*Merci*," I murmured, bringing one leg over the bike as Jessie had done and walking with it until I made it to the edge of the stone patio area where the bikes had been stored. The gravel under my feet crunched softly as I rolled/walked over it, and I felt even less sure about attempting to balance on what felt like an unsteady surface.

As the woman turned toward the building, Jessie was looking back at me curiously, the bike balanced between her legs and one foot on a pedal, obviously ready to hop on and go.

I attempted an easygoing smile, but it felt more like a grimace. Jessie turned more fully and tilted her head. "Don't you know how to ride a bike?"

I ambled closer to her. "Not exactly."

Her brows came together. "You *never* learned how to ride a bicycle?"

My chest tightened, and I felt embarrassed, or maybe ashamed. I didn't know what the fuck I was feeling because the truth was, I hadn't been raised in the sort of household where a dad took his kid out on the sidewalk and clapped for him when he finally teetered shakily ahead on two wheels for the first time. My dad had never thought I deserved more than a smack upside the head and his everlasting disappointment. "No."

She must have sensed the underlying emotion in my tone because her eyes softened, and she swung her leg off the bike and smiled. "Let's just walk, then. It's a beautiful day."

I looked at her and knew she was being nice, trying to accommodate for my lack of experience. But I'd also seen the genuine excitement in her eyes when she'd realized we were going to take a bike tour. I couldn't take that from her. "No. I can do this."

She studied me for a moment. "Of course you can. But do you want to?"

"Yeah. I mean, how hard can it be?"

"It's not hard. It just takes some practice. Here, watch me." She showed me where the brakes were on the handlebars, and then she got back on the bike and pushed off with her foot on one pedal. When she'd gained a little bit of movement, she put her other foot on the pedal and took off. I tried to do as she'd done, and after several miserable tries—that made me want to wrestle the bike to the ground until it was a bent and broken heap of aluminum—I finally managed to balance and gained some speed, steering shakily to where Jessie was waiting.

She grinned. "You got it. Come on. We'll go slow."

I followed behind her as she pedaled, and after a few minutes I felt more in control, getting the hang of both balancing and steering at the same time. I couldn't help the grin that spread over my face as I pulled up alongside her, and she glanced over at me and laughed. Just like the kite, this felt like another form of flying: the breeze in my face, the rich scent of earth and the sweet scent of flowers in the air, and my own pride at having accomplished something. I thought of the way Jessie had described her childhood swing—*like every good and beautiful thing in the world coming together all at once.*

We rode slowly through the flourishing gardens, stopping here and there to look at something or another, chatting easily, Jessie's laugh floating back to me as she pedaled ahead. And I felt that same mindless elation that I'd only ever achieved at the bottom of a bottle or through momentary physical pleasure. But *this* wouldn't bring the eventual shame and self-hatred. This would bring memories I'd want to revisit again and again.

Because memories would be all I had.

The realization made my stomach clench, but I pushed the thought away again, reminding myself that this weekend was ours, not for regrets, but as something happy to hold on to.

"Hey," I called ahead. "Are you hungry yet?"

Jessie glanced back and pulled to a stop at the side of the path, where I joined her. "Starving."

"We're supposed to look for a sign for the loom whatever garden."

She laughed. "Lumière de la Rose. It means Light of the Rose. It was back there." She started turning and I followed, and we made our way back to the turnoff for the garden where I'd arranged dinner to be set up.

I smelled the roses long before we arrived at the garden, a sensual smell that filled the air with a light, spicy sweetness. "Mmm, do you smell that?" Jessie asked, tipping her head up and inhaling deeply. "Nothing smells better than real garden roses."

"Look over there." I pointed. "I think that's where we're eating." There was a round table set for two shaded by a willow tree on the edge of the garden. The table was adorned with a white tablecloth, two place settings, and a vase of roses probably freshly picked from the garden.

Jessie followed my gaze and stood staring at it for a few moments before she looked at me, her expression full of so much pleasure, my throat constricted. "You did this for me?"

"Well, the vineyard did it. I just ordered—"

"Thank you," she said, her eyes alight with joy. "It's beautiful."

I smiled, and we propped our bikes against the opposite side of the tree and took a seat at the table. There was an ice bucket with champagne between the table and the tree, and I picked up the bottle, popping the cork and holding it out over the grass as it bubbled over. Jessie laughed and held out her glass, the bubbly liquid rising to the top before falling. After pouring my own, I held up my glass. "To what?"

"To never being too old to learn new things," Jessie said, winking and clinking her glass to mine. I smiled, inclining my head in agreement. After taking a sip, Jessie sat back in her chair and sighed, looking around. "This is perfect. One perfect moment in time," she murmured. There was something in her expression I wasn't sure how to read, but I agreed with her words. It *was* perfect. Here there was nothing but us, nothing except the earth beneath our feet, the sky over our heads, the deep serenity of nature all around. It felt as if we'd traveled back in time to where no troubles, no mistakes, no past existed. Only now.

The rose garden where we sat butted up to the back of the castle. A moment later, a waiter in a white apron appeared at the doorway carrying a tray and then moved toward us. When he arrived he greeted us in French and set two covered plates on the table, removing the lids as a waft of something rich and savory greeted my nose. "*Bon appétit*," he said, bowing. Then he turned and left.

"Wow. This looks amazing," Jessie said as she dug in. It was some sort of chicken dish in a rich cream sauce, and I almost moaned when I took a bite.

"Goddamn, this is delicious," I said, and Jessie laughed. Just as I took another bite, I felt a drop of rain and set my fork down, holding up my hand as another few raindrops touched my skin. A glance upward showed storm clouds previously hidden by the tall castle moving in quickly.

"Monsieur, madame," I heard, and the waiter reappeared, walking swiftly toward our table. "Rain is coming. I suggest you come inside to the restaurant and you may finish your dinner there."

I looked down at my plate regretfully, not wanting anything to interrupt the delicious meal but deciding he was probably right. "Okay," I said, and he nodded, clearing our plates and the other dishes from the table quickly and hurrying back toward the castle. My heart sank with the knowledge that our day had been interrupted by bad weather.

"Do you want to hang out inside until this passes and then we can still try to see the vineyards and do the tasting afterward?" Jessie asked.

I looked up, assessing the clouds, trying to determine what direction they might be heading. Maybe it would just be a brief rain shower, over as quickly as it seemed to have begun. For a minute there were only a few drops here and there, and I looked at Jessie, about to agree with her suggestion. Suddenly, the heavens opened up and it began to pour.

We both jumped up, Jessie letting out a shriek as we fumbled for our bikes, pulling them away from the tree and running for the path. The rain increased, drumming noisily on the ground around us as Jessie screamed but then laughed, ducking her head against the onslaught as she jumped on her bike. "Come on!" she called, her voice practically lost in the sound of the rain pounding all around. Holy fuck, it was a torrential downpour.

I got on my own bike, feeling wobbly and unsure, as if I might steer myself into a wall of rosebushes, practically blind, sheets of water obscuring my view. I saw the watercolor shape of Jessie riding in front of me and followed her outline. We turned out of the garden and onto the main path, and I pedaled quickly to catch up with her. I wobbled precariously, catching myself and letting out a huff of relief right before my front wheel slipped on the side of the path. I let out a yell as my bike went down, me underneath it, sprawled in mud. *Oh Christ.*

For a moment I just lay there, the rain pummeling me as I sputtered and brought one muddy hand up to shield my face. This was the most ridiculous fucking thing that had ever happened to me, and I'd been in a shit ton of weird situations.

"Callen!" Jessie was suddenly standing over me, reaching her hand out to help me up, and I noted distantly that this was the second time in less than a week that I'd landed flat on my back in front of her. *Jesus.* I started to get up, but I was partially under my bike and when I turned to push it aside, Jessie lost her balance and slipped, sprawling facefirst into the mud next to me.

I pushed the bike away. "Oh shit, Jessie! Are you okay?" I rolled toward her, and for a second I thought she was crying and my heart started hammering along with the rain, but when I turned her toward me, she was laughing so hard that it was silent.

I stared, the rain causing the mud to streak down her face in dirty rivulets, exposing stripes of her pale skin beneath. And I couldn't help it. Laughter exploded from my chest as I leaned forward, attempting to rein in my sudden hilarity while simultaneously helping her to her feet.

She took my hand, still laughing, and when she tried to stand, her foot came out from under her again and we both toppled over, me on top of her, her breath exploding out of her mouth in a soft "oof" between bursts of laughter. "Oh shit, Jess. Christ." I choked out a few more bursts of laughter before pushing myself up, my hand becoming momentarily stuck in the thick mud next to her. "Come up to your knees." I reached my hand out to her again and she took it, getting to her knees next to me before we both stood slowly and carefully. I gripped her hand in mine as I took a few squidgy-sounding steps through the mud to the bike path. Jessie stepped up next to me, and we stood there for a moment getting our bearings, the rain sluicing off *some* of the mud. We both reached down and pulled our bikes up, facing them forward on the path.

"Do we even bother to run for the car at this point?" she asked.

The car. *Oh fuck.* Guess who didn't put the top up on the convertible? It had to be a bathtub by now. As if she'd followed my line of thinking, her mouth opened into a shocked O—which was more comical than anything with those streaks of mud still rolling down her face—and she shouted, "Oh my God! The car!" We started running, as quickly as possible while holding on to the handlebars and wheeling our bikes next to us.

The rain drummed on the ground as we made a wobbly dash back through the gardens and toward the front of the castle where I'd parked the car. We barely stopped at the bike storage racks, leaning our bikes against them and continuing on. As we rounded the corner and ran quickly to the car, Jessie let out a defeated sound in the back of her throat. Water pooled on the floor and sat in puddles on the leather seats. *God fucking dammit.* Still, I couldn't help the helpless chuckle. How the fuck was this happening? I opened the driver's-side door and jumped out of the way just in time to avoid the stream of water that came pouring out.

"Should we see if there's a room we can rent in there?" Jessie asked, pointing at the castle. The rain was letting up, and I would have been thankful, only more rain couldn't really have made anything worse, so what did it matter at this point if it stopped?

"It's only a restaurant, a gift shop, and some tasting rooms,"

I said, remembering what Nick had spouted about the online description of this place and what it featured. I leaned in and started the car, bringing the top up. At least the car still ran.

"The château I booked is only an hour away. We'll blast the heat, and then you can take a long swim in the huge spa tub I made sure was in the room I booked."

Jessie groaned with pleasure. "Will they even let us into their hotel looking like this?"

"I'll tip someone a lot of money." I came around the car and signaled her to step back and then opened her door, too. Water came pouring out, and I wiped the puddle off her seat as best I could and then inclined my mud-caked arm inside. "Your carriage, milady."

A burst of laughter erupted from Jessie, and she curtsied and stepped inside regally, the seat making a squelching sound as she sat down.

I got in and adjusted the dials so the heat was blasting. I glanced over at Jessie, her hair wet and caked with mud, plastered to her skull, and her teeth blindingly white against her mud-streaked face. She looked alarmingly awful. So why the hell did I want to kiss her so badly?

I shook my head, chuckling as I pulled out of the lot and headed for the main road, thankful I'd prepaid for the food, tour, and tasting. Yet I couldn't help feeling disappointed we didn't get to finish the delicious meal. I was hungry. My clothes were soaked yet stiff, and I'd never felt dirtier in my entire life. I was sure I'd be scrubbing grit out of my hair for the next two years.

We'd driven only about five miles up the road when we came to a barricade, a couple of gendarme vehicles positioned in front of it with their lights on, blue swirling slowly in the dimness of the late afternoon, made darker by the storm clouds gathered overhead. I pulled to a stop and rolled the window down, leaning my head out. The gendarme standing next to his car looked briefly startled when he saw me, and I remembered I probably looked just about the same way Jessie did: scary. The officer came over to the car and looked inside, his eyes widening further when he saw Jessie.

He said something in French and Jessie laughed, putting her hand on my arm and saying something in rapid French to which the officer laughed back. He pointed to the barricade and said something further, and Jessie answered, nodding. They spoke again for another minute, and then the officer walked away with a quick backward wave and gestured to indicate where I should turn around. "There's a mudslide up ahead because of the rain," Jessie explained. "He said they should have it cleared by tomorrow afternoon."

"Tomorrow afternoon?" I leaned forward and rapped my head twice on the steering wheel. "This trip has sort of gone to shit, huh?"

Jessie smiled sweetly, tenderly, something sparkling in her mud-rimmed eyes. "Oh, I wouldn't say that just yet. The officer said there's a town about half an hour back down the road with an inn that should have a room available."

I sighed. "An inn? Sounds…quaint."

Jessie smiled. "I guess we'll see, right?"

Yeah, I guess we'll see. Despite Jessie's hopeful tone, defeat settled in my chest, the feeling that this storm was a sign that I could make all the plans I wanted—try as hard as I could to make Jessie happy and meet her in her world—and something would still come along to remind me that it wasn't enough. That *I* wasn't enough.

And I never would be.

CHAPTER FOURTEEN

JESSICA

We followed the signs to the tiny town—more a village from the looks of it—and drove slowly through the center of what seemed to be the downtown area, if it could even be called that. It was really six ancient-looking buildings centered around a town square.

"Where do you think this inn is?" Callen mumbled, leaning forward and peering through the fogged-up windshield. The combination of the damp interior and the heat was making it almost impossible to keep the windows clear. It felt like we were in the dirtiest steam bath on the planet. My skin had begun itching from the mud almost immediately, but I was doing my best not to scratch. I didn't want to make Callen feel any worse about the direction his perfectly planned day had taken. "I doubt there'll be a flashing vacancy sign to look out for. And I...don't read French."

A part of me wanted to giggle again at this situation, at the absolute mess the two of us looked like, but Callen's expression was a mixture of shattered and cranky, his tone defeated, and I thought it best not to dissolve into another fit of laughter right now. "No, there probably won't be a flashing sign. It looks like a small enough village though. If we take a loop through, we'll probably spot it. We're looking for the word '*auberge*,' or '*hôtel*,' '*résidence*' maybe…" I murmured, squinting out the rain-streaked glass.

We were literally the only car driving through the cobblestone streets, and though lights shone from some of the windows, it looked as if the entire populace of the town had gone indoors with the rain. "There," I said, spotting a stone building with a hand-painted sign that read, NUIT DES RÊVES. *Night of Dreams.*

Callen parked the car across the street, where two other tiny European cars were parked, and we both got out, dried mud cracking and falling from my clothes as I stood up. Ugh.

I stared across the street at the pretty three-story building, window boxes at the top-floor windows featuring cheerful red geraniums. They made me smile. How perfectly French. The awning above the door was black and white striped, and the door itself was painted the same red as the flowers. I was instantly charmed. Callen joined me where I stood, our bags in hand, and we crossed the street, climbing the stairs and entering the inn.

It was dim inside and smelled of dusty ancient wood and some type of citrusy furniture polish. The entry was small but elegant, with a plush carpet of reds, purples, and golds. Damask patterned wallpaper on the walls clearly showed the seams but was otherwise in good shape. The counter had a large gilt-edged mirror above it reflecting a set of stairs that must lead to the rental rooms. We rang the bell and waited.

After a moment I heard a door open and close somewhere near the back, and a few seconds later an older woman wearing a white apron came bustling into the foyer. "*Bonjour, bonjour*," she called, her words dying as she caught sight of us. I stood still, not wanting any mud to fall off me while she stared. I didn't have to imagine the sight we made—the mirror behind the counter had already told me I looked as bad as, if not worse than, Callen. *How embarrassing.*

"*Bonjour.*" I gave the woman a smile that felt more like a grimace. "Please excuse our appearance. We, uh, got caught in a rain shower... There was mud and... We'd like to rent a room," I said in French, figuring the woman would be more accommodating of our grime if I spoke in her native tongue.

She laughed, placing a hand on her round belly. "I'd say there was. My goodness! You poor things." She glanced at Callen, who was looking around at the portraits on the wall. "Your husband does not speak French, *oui*?"

I hoped she couldn't see the blush under all the grime streaking my face. "No. And he's not my husband. We, ah, well..." I glanced at Callen, my eyes lingering on him for a moment as he looked around, unaware we were speaking of him. He was dirty and muddy, his hair stiff and sticking in every direction, and still he was the most handsome man in the world. "We are..."

She hummed as a smile appeared on her face. "Ah, but yes you are." She sighed as if with affection and clasped her hands in front of her. "*Oui, oui*, I see perfectly." She moved around the counter and began flipping through her book. After a moment she frowned. "I only have one room available. It's our smallest one, but I hope that will be okay?"

Only one room available? The place seemed utterly deserted. "Oh, that's... fine. As long as there's a shower?"

"Ah, *oui*. But of course."

I turned to Callen. "She has a room available, but it's the smallest one."

A look of confusion came over his face and he glanced around quickly, as if he were thinking about the deserted feel of the place just as I had moments before. "If that's all she has." He took his wallet out. "How much?"

"You don't have to pay for everything—"

He gave me a disapproving look. "This weekend is on me, Jessie."

I sighed and quoted the price to Callen, and he handed the money to the woman. She put it away in a drawer, from which she also removed a key. "Here you are. Room 301 at the top of the stairs. I'm Madame Leclaire. Just ring if you need me."

"Merci, Madame Leclaire." We turned and climbed the narrow set of stairs, passing the first floor and rising to the second and then the third. There was only one room on the top floor, and it appeared to be an attic room. Callen used the key and pushed the door open slowly, as we both peered inside. The room was tiny, but it looked clean and rather lovely. Callen closed the door behind us as I looked around. My eyes caught on the bed, and though it looked comfortable and inviting, the linens white and fresh, Callen and I would practically have to sleep on top of each other if we both slept there.

I swallowed. "Uh…"

"I can, ah, take the…" He looked around, but the room was so small there was barely even a place on the floor where he could comfortably lie down.

"No. That's silly. We can make this work. Anyway, I'm more concerned with a shower."

There was a closed door on the other side of the room, and I peeked my head in. The bathroom was cramped, too, but again, it looked clean, the white tile gleaming, thick towels hanging from the towel bars. There wasn't a tub, but we couldn't really take a bath in the state we were in anyway.

I turned back around and smiled. Callen was standing in the middle of the room looking sullen and awkward, and I had a brief flash of him as a boy. He'd worn that same look then—regularly—and it made my nerve endings tingle in recognition. We stared at each other, the silence between us growing heavier, the room around us seeming even smaller. Callen blinked, starting to run a hand through his hair in that familiar gesture. He cringed when his palm hit the stiff strands. "How about I take a really quick shower first and then try to find food while you get cleaned up?"

I nodded, a jerky self-conscious movement. Why did I feel so unbalanced all of a sudden? "That sounds good." Now that I thought about it, I was hungry. I'd taken only a bite or two of what would have been an early dinner before the rain had come.

"Great, ah, I'll just..." Callen moved toward me, indicating that he needed to get into the bathroom, and I realized I was blocking the door like an idiot. I scooted out of the way, the heat of his body moving past me before he closed the door. I heard the shower start and took the time to look at the room's furnishings. As dirty as I was, I didn't dare sit on anything. Other than the bed, there was only a wooden bureau of drawers, a night table, and an upholstered chair by the window. I leaned over the chair, pushing the curtain aside as I glanced out at the rainy street. From my vantage point, I could see that a few shops were open, but the town still looked quiet and mostly deserted. I was high enough to see that beyond the buildings, miles of French farmland stretched out around the town. I could see neat rows of orchard trees—apples maybe? Cows grazed, their forms dotting the rolling hills in the distance. What a beautiful, peaceful life.

I turned quickly when I heard the shower shut off, my heartbeat accelerating as Callen came out, a towel wrapped around his narrow hips and water still glistening on his skin. *Oh.* I'd kissed him, slept in the same bed with him, felt the intimacy of his arousal through our clothes, but I hadn't yet seen him naked— or nearly—and his male beauty made me feel weak in the knees.

He smiled, grabbing his overnight bag and placing it on the bureau. "It's all yours. The shower's small, but the water pressure's great. I think I feel human again."

I laughed softly. "Good. I'll just"—I pointed to the bathroom, grabbing my own overnight bag—"see you when you get back, then."

"Yeah, maybe they have food downstairs. Madame Leclaire was wearing an apron, wasn't she?"

"I think so. But there's also a restaurant across the street." I pointed to the window. "I can see it from here, and it looks open."

"Okay, great. Enjoy your shower."

I nodded and closed the bathroom door behind me, exhaling. What was this sudden awkwardness between us, this hesitation? This strange sense of intimacy that made me feel breathless and nervous? Was it only the close quarters creating this feeling?

I peeled off my damp, muddy clothing and left it in a heap on the floor next to Callen's. Maybe we could wash it in the shower later and hang it to dry. Or maybe Madame Leclaire had a washing machine she'd let us use.

The shower's warm spray was incredible, and I groaned in pleasure as I soaped my hair and watched the muddy water run clear. The inn's shampoo and shower gel was scented like roses, and I smiled. When I remembered this weekend, it would forever be scented with the fragrance of roses. And it would always bring to mind a mud-caked Callen.

After lathering my body and my hair several times, I finally felt squeaky clean and emerged from the shower, wrapping my body in one of the soft, thick towels. There was a blow-dryer under the sink, and I used it to dry my hair.

I riffled through my bag, looking at the jeans and the one dinner dress I'd packed. My eyes finally landed on the long, white cotton nightgown. I bit at my lip. It might be a little early for pj's, but the thought of putting on another pair of jeans made me cringe, and clearly I couldn't put on a formal dress to eat a takeout dinner in our hotel room. Callen had already seen me in nothing other than his long T-shirt. Would he really care if I wore my nightgown? It wasn't like it was sexy, so he would know I wasn't trying to send some "take me now" message. In fact, if anything, this was the opposite of sexy. Frankie made fun of my nightgowns, but I liked the feel of the soft cotton from head to toe. Callen would understand my need to be comfortable. Settled, I pulled the nightgown over my head, sighing as the material caressed my skin like a hug.

I opened the bathroom door cautiously, unsure if Callen was back yet, but the room was empty. Sinking into the upholstered chair, I noticed a magazine rack next to the window that held a few French magazines and a couple of paperbacks. I picked up one of the paperbacks—from the cover it appeared to be a cozy mystery—and began reading the first few paragraphs. I attempted to focus on the story, but my mind strayed and my eyes were pulled to the rain-streaked pane of glass.

My thoughts wandered to the girl whose name I still didn't

know and Captain Durand, the "horse's arse." I smiled, thinking of their kiss, wondering if love found a way, even in the midst of a military camp in a war-torn country, as a girl hid her identity and a man faced battle. My fervent hope was that it did, that if anything could thrive under those conditions, it was love. I wanted to believe that love was the rarest of all flowers: it delighted in the sunshine but did not *require* it to grow and flourish.

My thoughts turned to Callen and the memory of him riding unsteadily on a bike that had looked both too small for him and too large as he wobbled and careened toward me on the garden path. And then the expression on his face when he'd finally gotten the hang of it: cautious joy, the same expression he seemed to adopt when anything brought him happiness. As if he *wanted* to embrace the elation of the moment, but was too afraid to fully do so. I wondered if he even realized that he always held a part of himself back. And I wondered what it would take to finally see him surrender completely to the happiness of any one moment. *Or whether he even could.* I imagined that if he found a way, the resulting music would be stunning.

I glanced at the tiny bed, my body flushing with warmth at the thought of lying there with Callen, our bodies pressed against each other's, his heat surrounding me throughout the night. If the girl whose writings I was translating was teaching me anything, it was that our stories were so fleeting, left rarely on paper for others to read and learn from, and more often only in the hearts of those we were brave enough to love. We had one chance, one life, and then it was gone. *Live fiercely and without regret.* I had no assurances from Callen about anything except the temporary nature of…*us.* But what would happen if *I* didn't put limits on what occurred between Callen and me this weekend? What would happen if I simply let my body and heart lead the way, without overthinking, without letting fear guide me? Not because I wasn't scared of the consequences, but because life was short and moments were small windows of opportunity that might never, ever come again.

I had the strange sense that fate had been leading us to this attic room on a rain-swept day in France. I knew it didn't make sense, that it might even be my imaginative mind creating fantasies, yet the feeling persisted.

The truth was, Callen had always been my prince, and I realized now that no one since had ever measured up. Perhaps it wasn't as I told him after all. It wasn't that I hadn't found anyone who *tempted me to get that involved*. Perhaps I simply hadn't allowed anyone into my heart—*or body*—because *my prince* already resided there.

And for tonight at least, he was mine.

CHAPTER FIFTEEN

CALLEN

The door opened on a quiet creak, and I paused as I caught sight of Jessie curled up in the chair by the window, the light of the lowering sun soft and muted through the gauzy curtain. She raised her head, and our eyes met. I pushed the door closed behind me, the sight of her tugging at my insides in some way I wasn't sure how to define.

I set the brown paper bags on the table by the door. "Sandwiches," I said, my voice sounding strained, as if there were something caught in my throat. "Madame Leclaire said we could order food to our room next time if we want."

She smiled. "Sounds perfect." She continued to study me, an expression on her face I was unfamiliar with, and I wanted to ask her what she was thinking. But for some reason, I also wasn't sure I wanted to know.

My eyes moved down her body, and I realized that what I had first assumed was a blanket was really a nightgown. A really long nightgown with lots and lots of fabric. There wasn't one inch of skin showing anywhere. I'd never seen anything quite like it. "That looks"—I raised one brow—"warm."

She laughed, biting her lip and glancing down at herself. When she looked back at me, her smile was sweetly demure, and it made my heart speed up in my chest. *God, she's beautiful.* She pulled her feet out from under her, balancing her heels on the edge of the chair, and for a moment the only thing showing were her ten pink toes. I'd never once, in all my life, noticed a woman's toes, and suddenly the sight of Jessie's peeking out from beneath her nightgown seemed incredibly intimate. I swallowed as she placed her feet on the floor and rose slowly. As she stood before the window that way, the pale golden light behind her, I could see the outline of her naked body beneath the white fabric, the shadow of her areolas and the V between her legs. My breath hitched. I had teased her a moment before, but I suddenly realized how overrated lingerie was. I'd never seen anything as erotic as Jessie standing in a white cotton nightgown with the last glimmer of daylight behind her, unknowingly revealing all her secrets. I swelled and hardened, feeling achy and full, my mouth suddenly dry.

I felt as stripped as this small, plain room. There was nothing fancy here. I hadn't been able to give Jessie the biggest or the best. Without the cover of my wealth, of the things I could provide with the money I'd earned, the finery, the luxuries, I was just…me, standing before her without any pretense—or at least none that I could manage in that moment. Right then I was just the same kid she'd come upon in the boxcar that day so long ago. Since then I'd hidden behind so many things, gotten lost in the lifestyle I'd chosen, felt like I was all smoke and mirrors for so, so long. Looking at Jessie in front of me now, the beautiful woman staring at me with such honesty in her eyes, I felt overwhelmed with possibility, with the hope that she saw *me* and liked what she saw. Maybe—*God, maybe*—she'd even find a way to accept the things I was so terrified to let anyone know. "Jessie," I breathed, the word a plea, a question, a prayer.

We both moved toward each other at the same time, meeting at the foot of the bed, our bodies colliding gently. I took her face in my hands and realized I was trembling. *Am I scared?* I wasn't sure what I felt other than an all-consuming need for her. "Jessie," I repeated, her name anchoring me somehow, as if I had fallen somewhere deep and unfamiliar and she was the only thing holding me steady. *Rescuing me.*

For several heartbeats, we quietly studied each other up close in the pale yellow light of the room. I'd made promises to myself, set boundaries, and yet suddenly it felt as if none of them mattered. They felt far away, unimportant, made in a place where all the rules were different and where I was not free to follow my heart. We'd have to return to all that later. But here…*here…*

My breath hitched as my gaze moved over Jessie's arched brows, to those sensitive hazel eyes, across the light dusting of freckles that made my heart careen wildly in my chest, down to that beautifully pouty top lip. My own lips parted, a question floating in the air that I didn't know how to voice.

Jessie's eyes met mine, and she seemed to know what I was thinking because she answered the question I'd been too afraid to ask. "Yes, I want you, too."

I let out a harsh exhale, bringing my mouth to hers, first running my tongue across that delectable upper lip. *Mine.* I delved my tongue into her mouth, tasting the sweetness of her as she moaned and pressed her softness against me. I broke from her lips to trail mine down the silky skin of her throat. "Are you sure, Jessie?" I murmured. I wanted this. I wanted it so much I thought I'd die if she changed her mind, but I had to give her the opportunity to do just that. I had to know she wouldn't regret this, that she wouldn't hate me for taking something so precious. *Her.*

And yet the harsh pounding of my heart was as much fear as it was desire. The fear was an aphrodisiac, too, the knowledge that this mattered in some way sex had never mattered before. My blood hummed with the thrill, my senses utterly and completely *aware* of every gentle brush of her fingertips, every soft inhale of breath, the smell of this room—orange-scented furniture polish and old wood—and Jessie, bathed in the subtle fragrance of roses. "You smell different," I murmured. "Like the garden at the winery. Did you bring the roses back with us?"

I felt her lips move into a smile. "I think so, yes."

Her fingers threaded through my hair, the scratch of her nails on my scalp delicious bliss, and I moaned, hardening even more and pressing my aching groin against her. Jessie met my moan with one of her own and dropped her hands from my hair, stepping back. She gripped the material of her nightgown at her hips and pulled it up slowly, her gaze remaining locked on mine until she pulled the fabric over her head. Her hair cascaded around her shoulders and over her breasts as she tossed the garment aside.

My blood thrummed hotter as I allowed my gaze to move down her naked body. She was a masterpiece. I used my finger to brush one side of her hair back, exposing a perfect breast, pale pink areolas, and her already hardened nipples. I leaned in and took one in my mouth, running my tongue around it slowly as

Jessie let out a groan, bringing her hands back to my head and pressing her breast more firmly into my mouth. I sucked gently, and Jessie let out another sweet moan. "Oh, Callen, yes."

Leaning back, I moved her hair off the other breast and licked and sucked at that one as well, until I felt her hips lift slightly, seeking relief. The heavy buzz of electricity pumped furiously between my legs to the same rhythm as my heart.

Jessie's hands pulled at my T-shirt and I leaned back, yanking it over my head quickly and taking her hand, leading her to the side of the bed. Reaching around her, I pulled the heavy comforter back, exposing crisp white sheets. She sat down, gazing at me with so much trust that my heart nearly beat out of my chest.

Her hair spread out around her as she lay back, and for a moment my eyes drank in the sensual beauty of her: the shape of her curves against the white background of the sheet, the peachy tone of her skin, the roundness of her breasts, capped with pretty, pink nipples, down to the patch of brown hair between her legs.

Her breath shuddered, and I kicked off my shoes, removing my pants and boxers and kicking them aside before I slid into bed. The feel of our naked skin pressed together was almost too much, and I wondered if I would even be able to hold out long enough to bring her pleasure. I felt like an overeager boy, so filled with lust my body vibrated with it.

What are you doing to me, Jessie?

Music pulsed inside me, not a melody but a harmony, a deep, slow-moving, primal tempo that played in time to the blood pumping through my veins. I held on to it, though loosely, somehow knowing I only had to recall this moment, the dreamy, blissful expression on Jessie's face, the scent of this day—roses and rain—for the refrain to return.

Struggling to rein in my pulsing desire, I ran my hands down her body, learning her intimately, the velvety texture of her skin, the way her belly clenched when I touched it lightly, the firm smoothness of her thigh, the birthmark on her hip, the things that made her *her* and no one else. Possessiveness coiled inside me, and I brought my lips to hers, kissing her slowly—marking her maybe—as I brought my hand between her legs. I groaned when my finger slid into the already slick wetness of her tight opening. "Jessie," I moaned. She pressed her hips upward, silently asking for more, so I breathed in a deep, steadying breath, bringing the silky liquid up and over the tiny swollen bud at the apex of her thighs, circling it slowly. She let out a strangled moan, pressing herself toward my hand as I attempted to cool my own raging desire.

Her moans became loud gasps when I brought my mouth back to her breasts and licked at her nipples in time with the circling of my finger.

I wanted her to lose her mind with arousal, to go halfway insane with lust, to feel heaven and earth colliding as she came on my hand. I didn't have to wait long. Several seconds later, she arched her back, screaming my name as she climaxed.

A short sob came from her throat as she came down, her body relaxing all the while her legs circled my hips, bringing me closer to her.

"Now," she breathed, a desperate note to her voice, moving her pelvis to line up with mine. I laughed shortly, a strangled sound of humor that turned into a hiss when she succeeded in bringing the tip of my penis to the wetness of her opening.

"Wait, Jessie. A condom."

I reached blindly for my pants, locating them and fumbling for my wallet with one hand, holding myself off Jessie with the other. I finally managed to extricate my wallet from the pocket of my jeans and removed the condom. Leaning back, I ripped it open and slid it over my length, the brush of my fingers causing me to suck in a breath. I was so hard I felt like I was going to explode with the merest touch.

Jessie watched me with lazy eyes, reaching toward me in a silent request to move back into her arms. I did, bringing my lips to hers, leaning one elbow on the bed next to her to hold my weight and using my other hand to bring my erection to the soft, sweet warmth between her legs. I held myself there for a moment, suddenly afraid, worried not only that I was going to hurt her, but that this somehow was going to hurt me as well. "Jessie—" I started, intending to ask her again if she was sure, if she was certain she wanted to give this to me.

"Callen, *yes*," she said before I could form the question. And then she lifted herself, bringing me deeper into her. I groaned out in bliss at the tight squeeze of her around the throbbing head of my arousal. She tensed up. I'd never been with a virgin before, but I figured the best way to do this was quickly. I pressed inside her, feeling the tearing of the delicate membrane. She cried out, her thighs clamping more tightly around my hips.

"I'm sorry, Jessie. I'm sorry," I said, kissing her face even as my hips demanded that I move. It felt so fucking good to be inside her; I felt half-crazy, the need to thrust and pound so overwhelming that I could barely hold myself back. But I didn't want to hurt her any more than I already had, and so I waited.

"It's okay," she whispered. "I'm okay now." She brought her lips to mine and kissed me sweetly, tenderly, her fingernails running down my back and over my ass, causing my whole body to shudder. "You can move," she said, obviously feeling the effort I was exerting in remaining still. "Let me feel you. *All* of you."

With her permission, the last thread of control broke, and I began to thrust into her, my breath coming out in small bursts of sound. She was so deliciously tight, so wet, her body gripping me snugly in a silken clasp. She clung to me, trusting, and in that moment I *did* feel like a prince. *Her prince.* My heart beat to the music that began to rise inside me once again. Pulsing. Sultry. Both dark and beautiful, speaking of this thing between us: her leg sliding up my hip to allow me deeper, my muscles tensed with pleasure, our bodies dewy with sweat as we slid together, the scent created by our mingled pheromones driving me higher...higher. I dropped my face into her neck, letting out a short yell that ended on a shuddery groan as I came, the pleasure tightening my abdomen and shooting all the way down to my toes. "Ohhh, Jessie, Jessie." I slowed, one final shiver moving through me before I stilled, the stars diminishing before my eyes as I turned my head and breathed in the scent of her skin.

The light outside the window was all but gone and the rain had started again, a soft pitter-patter on the roof right above us that seemed to be the perfect end music to the slowing of my heart, the loosening of muscles, the dreamy afterglow of lovemaking. I turned, pulling Jessie so she was facing me, and for a moment we just looked at each other. Her smile was soft and her eyes held no regret. "Jessie," I whispered, trailing a finger down the side of her cheek, her skin so smooth, so soft. She turned into the touch, closing her eyes on a sigh. "Was it okay?"

Her eyes opened, and she nodded. "It was the most wonderful thing I ever experienced."

You're the most wonderful person I ever met.

But she had that wrong. *She* was the most wonderful person *I'd* ever met. Smart, beautiful, gentle, fierce, joyful, and kind.

I leaned in and kissed her, then remembered there might be

blood. At the very least, I should take care of her in the aftermath of her very first time. *Her very first time.* It belonged to me. No matter what happened, that could never change. The thought filled me with a possessive happiness that I didn't let myself look at too closely, at least not now.

Pulling away and stepping out of bed, I said, "Let me get something to clean you with. I'll be right back."

I walked quickly to the bathroom, where I flushed the condom and wet a washcloth with warm water. Back in the room, I sat on the edge of the bed and gently washed the trace of blood from between Jessie's legs and then brought the washcloth back to the bathroom, rinsing it out.

I pulled the sheet and comforter over us as I slipped back into bed beside her, gathering her close. For a few minutes, we simply watched the rain on the windowpane, Jessie's fingers running lazily up and down my arm, our legs twisted together, my body heavy with satisfaction. "It feels like we're in a different world," I said.

I felt her smile against my shoulder. "I was just thinking the same thing."

After a moment she tilted her head back so she could look at me. The pad of her index finger moved up my arm and circled slowly around my nipple. "Did you know you hum when you're relaxed or happy?"

I chuckled, realizing I'd been doing just that. "I do?" I paused, considering. "Yeah, maybe I do."

She nodded, her smile increasing.

"No one's ever noticed that."

"Maybe you're not relaxed and happy often enough." She kissed my shoulder, biting softly at my flesh.

"Ouch."

She laughed, snuggling down into the blankets. She was right, though. It had been a long time since I'd felt happy and relaxed.

I felt her limbs grow heavier and her lashes flutter against my skin. "Do you think we'll be able to take any part of this back with us, Callen?" she whispered, a note of hope lacing her soft, sleepy voice.

I hesitated. I knew what she meant because I'd thought it myself. Here there was no baggage, no worries, no barriers or regrets. Here there was only us and nothing else, just feeling and honesty. But that wouldn't be the case when we got back to the château where she was working. There—in *that* world—I would have to pull on the cloak of lies I wore and once again become the mess I'd arrived as. Only...that wasn't totally true, was it? She'd changed me, *saved* me, at least as far as the music went. I was hearing it again, not just bits and pieces, but long strings of melody that shook me, moved me, and compelled me to get them down on paper. But what happened when I left? Would the music die again? Would I revert to the life I'd been leading—the life of meaningless vices—in order to quiet my own mind long enough to hear the notes?

I exhaled and pulled Jessie closer. I didn't want that. I wanted *her*. I was desperate to hold on to the only good thing I'd ever had. But it wasn't possible. If she knew how little I really had to offer, she wouldn't want me, *shouldn't* want me, and I couldn't do that to her. Trap her in a way she'd come to resent, cause her to look at me with shame and embarrassment. I couldn't bear that. It would kill me.

"I don't know," I answered honestly. I could hear the regret in my voice, and my chest tightened with pain. But she'd gifted me with so much, and I owed her the truth.

CHAPTER SIXTEEN

JESSICA

I blinked, disoriented, as my eyes grew used to the low light in the room. Memory swept in, bringing with it a warm surge of elation as I recalled the way Callen had looked as we'd made love, his mouth parted and his skin flushed with arousal, the muscles of his arms tensed as he held himself above me. I squeezed my legs together lightly, feeling the tinge of achiness where he'd been, smiling despite the slight discomfort. Where was he? I was in the bed alone.

Pulling myself up so I could see over the puffy comforter, I spotted Callen sitting in the chair by the window in only his boxers, his tanned skin smooth in the low light, a notepad on his knees as he hunched over it. His lower lip was pulled beneath his upper teeth and his hand moved rapidly as he used a pen to scrawl something—musical notes, I assumed—on the page.

"Hey," I said softly. His head snapped up, and he released his lip. I smiled at the look of intensity on his face, the focus. "Sorry. I didn't mean to interrupt."

He shook his head, standing and setting the notepad and pen down on the bureau next to the empty bag of food we'd consumed hours before, sitting cross-legged on the floor wrapped in blankets. My lips tipped up at the memory of the intimate floor picnic and how no food had ever tasted more delicious. Callen moved to the bed, clicking off the one lamp that had been on, and got back in next to me, bringing the covers over us and pulling me close. "I didn't want to wake you."

I snuggled into him. He was so solid, so hard everywhere, and yet somehow the perfect pillow. "Mmm." I sighed. "You didn't. It's just sleeping in a new place. For a minute I didn't know where I was. What were you writing?"

"The harmony of the piece I've been working on. It came to me tonight."

I lifted my head. "Really? Is that how it works? You hear music in your head first and then write it down on paper?"

"Yeah. Sometimes."

We were silent for a minute before I said, "I'm glad the writer's block has lifted. Why do you think you were so stuck?"

He paused for so long, I glanced up at him, wondering if he was going to answer at all. "I'm sure you remember from when we were kids that I didn't have the best home life, Jessie." My heart clenched painfully, and I nodded. "My dad, he liked to throw punches, but he liked to hurl insults even more. The worst things he could think of, the things he knew would hurt the most..." Silence again, as if he was struggling to find the right words, maybe even skirting around some, though I wasn't sure why I got that feeling. "I hear his words sometimes, even still.

They run through my mind and they, I don't know, it's like they paralyze me, make me feel that same worthlessness I did as a kid."

I leaned up. "Oh, Callen. But you've found so much success in your life. You've proven him wrong on every level."

He exhaled a big breath. "Maybe. But I hear the echoes of his words, and it's like they get stuck on repeat and I can't make them stop."

"Except with alcohol and…partying," I said. *Women*. A thought I pushed aside. He was opening up to me, baring his heart, and I wanted desperately to know this part of him.

"Yeah. For a while I could numb myself enough so his words were muted, just background noise. But it's been harder and harder to do that." He kissed my shoulder. "Until you."

I bit at my lip, a surge of hope filling me, the feeling that he *needed* me. The problem was, I didn't want to be needed *only* as some sort of muse for his music. I wanted to be loved. "Do you have any kind of relationship with him now?"

"No."

"What about your mom? You never mentioned her…"

"No." So much pain in that one word. "She died when I was eight. An overdose of prescription meds. They said it was an accident, but…I don't know. She had been depressed for as long as I could remember."

"I'm sorry," I whispered, wishing he'd told me about that when we were children. It would have explained more of the sadness in his young eyes. I'd lost my own mother to illness, and that had been hard enough to deal with as an adult. What would it be like for a sensitive eight-year-old to lose his mother to something that may or may not have been an accident? Especially when the parent he had left sounded like a mean bastard who had probably been little comfort, if any at all.

He was silent for a while and felt sort of tense, so I moved my hand down the ridges of his abdomen, seeking to distract. His muscles bunched, and he drew in a breath. "Did I ever tell you that I hear music in my head sometimes, too? The one that's playing right now goes a little something like this: bow chicka wow wow."

He laughed, the sound deep and sexy right next to my ear, and I tipped my head, grinning at him. "That's good stuff," he said.

"I'm glad you like it."

"Come here, Mozart, and give me that wandering hand before you and that sexy beat give me ideas."

"What sort of ideas?"

"Ideas that your body needs to rest from."

"Hmm," I grumped. "Maybe just for tonight."

"Just for tonight." He pulled me close and his heat enveloped me, the scent of him—warm male skin and some piney-smelling product he'd used recently—bringing security and comfort. I sighed, and after only a few minutes, drifted back to sleep.

* * *

I woke to the feel of something hard at my back and a hand kneading my breast gently. I moaned, pressing my butt back against Callen as he sucked in a sharp hiss. "I want you," he whispered. "Are you still sore?"

I was, just a bit, but I didn't care. I was turned on, and I wanted to feel the fullness as he entered me, the sweet invasion as we became one. "No."

I turned around and gazed at him, the soft midmorning light

bringing out the chocolaty highlights of his hair and the traces of blue in his gray eyes. His jaw was rough with stubble, and his lips looked swollen from sleep and all the kissing we'd done the night before. He was beautiful, my prince finally returned, and I knew I loved him. Maybe I'd never stopped.

"I had planned to get up early and take you to a museum near the château. The château we never made it to," he murmured, biting softly at my ear.

I smiled, running my hand down his chest. "You're my museum," I whispered, pushing him gently so he rolled to his back. I threw a leg over his and kissed his neck as he groaned. "So much to see and experience," I murmured against his skin, my hand grazing the ridges of his stomach, moving down to trace a finger along the hollow at his hip. "The art offered here is a study in form and"—I went lower, wrapping my hand around his hardness as he hissed in a tortured breath—"function."

I slid my hand slowly up and down, glorying in the hot throb beneath my fingers, and he arched his back, a burst of garbled words rasping from his mouth. I held back a grin. "Hmm. Do you offer studies in antiquated languages, too?"

He laughed, though it was infused with a groan. He put his hand over mine, stilling it momentarily so he could roll me to my back, taking charge, leaning in and flicking my nipple with his tongue. "Only one, and it's as old as time itself. Want me to teach it to you?"

My smile turned to a sigh of pleasure. "Oh yes."

We made love slowly, a leisurely quality that hadn't been there the night before, when we'd both been greedy with the newness of discovering each other's bodies.

He kissed down the curve of my neck to my shoulder and ran his hands up my inner thighs, before flipping me over, causing me to laugh, a chuckle that turned into a moan as he ran his fingernails over my backside and nuzzled his prickly jaw on my shoulder blades. It seemed as if he wanted to explore all the places he might have missed the night before, to see every part of me in the morning light. *We have time*, I wanted to say. *We have all the time in the world.* But I knew that was a lie, and I didn't want to think about it, so I pushed it away. The feel of his hands on my body became my focus, and I lost myself in the earthy male smell of his skin after a night's sleep and how it spoke to every feminine part of me.

We lay together afterward in satisfied repletion as I snuggled into him. A goose feather from the duvet spiraled upward with my movement and then floated lazily downward in a gossamer shaft of muted sunlight. Callen reached up and tried to grasp the fluttering piece of down, laughing when it danced away. He turned to face me, his hand running down my back as he pressed a quick kiss to the side of my mouth. "Do you know how I found that boxcar? The day we met?"

"No. How?"

He glanced upward, a smile playing over his mouth. I reached up and let my thumb glide over the perfect indent in the center of his bottom lip, unable to resist touching anywhere and everywhere that drew my interest. I felt hungry to experience him in every way I could...while I could. He kissed my thumb once, then pulled back. "I followed a feather." He paused, taking a piece of my hair between his fingers and rubbing them together, feeling its texture. At this point he must know the feel of every single part of me, and yet he sighed as he watched his own fingers move, seemingly captivated by the strands, perhaps as hungry as I was. The thought made me warm and content. "I'd had a run-in with my father, and I'd left the house. This feather...caught my attention, and I followed it." His gaze met mine. "I followed it to that boxcar, where you found me only a few hours later. I didn't even remember that until recently." He leaned in and kissed me, and I was lost in him once again.

The day went by in changes of light and the steady rise and fall of pleasure, his fingernails grazing my skin, his mouth seemingly everywhere. He called downstairs and ordered croissants and coffee and then later, more sandwiches and an upside-down fruit and pastry dessert called tarte tatin, which we again ate on the floor picnic-style.

Callen leaned forward and kissed me, licking the bit of caramelized apple on the side of my mouth as I laughed. He groaned. "We'd better take a shower. I don't have any more condoms with me."

I raised a brow. "I'm disappointed in your lack of preparedness."

He smiled, and it was sweet. "No, I wasn't prepared for this, Jessie. For you. But somehow..." He kissed me again.

"Somehow what?" I whispered.

"Somehow I got lucky, far luckier than I deserve." He seemed pensive as he sat back, beginning to gather the wrappers from our lunch.

I didn't want this day to end, not the intimacy of the small bed, the whispered words, eating picnic meals naked, wrapped in blankets, and so I smiled, nudging him. "Well, I guess your luck has run out." I stood, letting the blanket drop at my feet. "I'm going to take a shower and think about all the things we might be able to do without a condom." I put my finger on my chin in feigned consideration. "There probably aren't any, though I'm pretty inexperienced—"

Callen stood so fast, he startled me and made me yelp out a laugh. "I'm feeling lucky again."

We used far too much hot water before we emerged, pruney and laughing and me educated on the delights of shower benches and mouths, body wash and naked skin.

"Let me take you to dinner tonight. We can't spend the entire day in this room."

"Can't we?"

"Maybe we already did. Let me feed you properly, at least one meal where we use utensils."

I smiled, thinking utensils were overrated. The rain had stopped earlier in the day, and out the window, the street was dry, the sun lowering. I thought of the backless Clémence Maillard dress I'd packed and was suddenly excited about the prospect of getting dressed up and going out for dinner with Callen. "Okay."

I blew my hair dry and put it up in a twist, leaving a few wisps loose around my face and neck, applied some makeup, and then slipped the dress on, smoothing it down my hips, making note once again of the fact that Clémence's creations miraculously resisted wrinkling. I slipped on the strappy black sandals I'd brought to go with it and emerged from the bathroom.

Callen was standing at the window, gazing out. He was humming, and it was sweet and melodic, beautiful. For a moment I simply watched him, listening to his music. But he must have sensed me standing behind him because he turned around and smiled, handsome in a pair of dark slacks and a pale gray button-down shirt. "Wow, you look great."

Callen looked from my face slowly down to my feet as he walked to where I stood, something almost reverent in his eyes. "You...I don't even know what to say about you.

You're stunning. You're the most beautiful woman I've ever seen."

I smiled, biting my lip. I knew that wasn't true. I'd seen the women he usually spent time with. He'd obviously been with women far more beautiful than I was, but the way he was looking at me right then made me feel as if he really did believe his own words.

When we walked down the stairs, Madame Leclaire was at the front desk. I asked about a restaurant close by, and she gave us directions to one a few blocks over. She beamed at us as we waved goodbye, winking as we smiled back.

The cozy family-owned restaurant was charming and intimate, the white wine I ordered rich and buttery, the food delicious, and the music soft and romantic. We sat by the window and chatted easily about our lives, about me living in Paris, about what he liked and didn't like about Los Angeles. My heart overflowed with the love I felt for him, the ease with which we talked about everything and nothing, and the magical feel of this weekend, in this village where fate had somehow delivered us. And though I'd given myself to him knowing it wouldn't last, I allowed myself to pretend it might, just for now. Just for tonight.

CHAPTER SEVENTEEN

CALLEN

The letters blurred and changed positions, moving on the paper as if they were running from me.

"What's this?" he demanded, his index finger pounding on the open textbook in front of me, his voice gruff with fury.

I wanted to please him. I wanted to make him proud of me so badly, but I didn't have the answer, couldn't even begin to guess. My lips started quivering, and I felt tears burning the backs of my lids.

Please, God, please help me.

My dad flipped the book over roughly, letting out an angry growl as he rose to his feet, causing me to startle and sit back abruptly. "What the fuck is wrong with you, you little retard? Jesus Christ. It's a fucking W!"

"I'm sorry," I squeaked, my shoulders sagging with humiliation and defeat.

"Try again," he barked.

I stared down at the paper, the black ink smearing before my eyes, the tears finally spilling over and tracking down my cheeks.

"Are you crying, you little bitch? Are you fucking crying?"

I shook my head, denying it, despite the obvious evidence. I tried to stop, tried to pull the devastation and shame back inside me. But I wanted my mom, and thinking of her made me cry more, made me want her back so badly it felt like a pit in my stomach that would never, ever be filled. She was dead, and she'd never come back. Never protect me again. It was only us now—him and me and the never-ending reminder that I was a disappointment. The tears came faster, a small sob rising from my throat.

The smack was sudden and unexpected and caused me to jerk backward, the chair I was in falling over with a clatter. I scrabbled backward as he loomed over me, reaching down and grabbing me by the shirt and backhanding me again.

At the surprise of the slap, the tears dried on my cheeks, a shocked numbness taking the place of the pain inside. My dad had shoved me a couple of times, had slammed his fist on the table, even punched a hole in the wall one time, but he'd never hit me in the face before.

"You want me to give you something to cry over, you fucking idiot?"

My cheek stung and my hip hurt where I'd hit the floor, but the physical aches felt better than the hurt inside my heart. I spit at him and watched as his face contorted with rage, and he brought his hand back to strike me again. He didn't realize that wasn't what made me cry. The words made me cry, and I'd just figured out how to make them stop. Now I knew how to make him stop.

"Callen, you're dreaming. Shh, wake up. It's only a dream." Her voice came from far away, and I started awake, a cry of anguish on my lips, the wet feel of tears on my cheeks. I was breathing harshly, and I didn't know where I was. I blinked, moving my head around, the vision of a small, ratty kitchen fading as the tiny attic room came into focus. Reality settled in. I had been dreaming. I wasn't back *there*. I was here. With Jessie.

"Jessie," I rasped. Her arms came around me, the warmth of her body such sweet comfort I wanted to drown in her and never come up for air. "Jessie, Jessie."

"I'm here. It's okay. What were you dreaming about?" She wiped the tears off my cheeks with such tenderness, her eyes pools of concern in the dim moonlit room.

"Him, I guess. I don't know," I lied. I didn't want to talk about it. I needed to push the memory of him far, far away and not think about the way it'd felt to be that little boy. My breathing slowed. I was here with Jessie in the warm circle of her arms. I wanted—*needed*—to lose myself in her, to bury myself in her body and soak in the peace—the healing—she offered.

"Jessie." I sighed, bringing my hand to her cheek and turning so I was leaning over her. For a moment I just stared at her, her pretty face soft with sleep and a look in her eyes I thought might be love. It scared me—*terrified* me—but it also filled me with an aching wonder. I took the feeling inside myself, storing it deep in my heart. Even if I couldn't keep it, I could take it out and look at it, remember what it felt like. And in that way it would always be mine.

I leaned in, kissing her and drinking in the familiar taste of her mouth, moaning with the way it caused my heart to leap and my body to tighten. She brought her arms around me, and when my mouth moved to her breast, she wove her fingers into my hair and wrapped her legs around my hips.

I guided myself inside her, lifting my head from her nipple

momentarily as I hissed out the bliss of her body's tight grasp. Pinpricks of light exploded in my mind, clearing away thoughts of anything other than her as I began to move and thrust.

I brought my mouth to hers again and we kissed, our tongues dancing as we moved together, slowly at first, gently, and then faster, almost frenzied. Our skin slickened and the room filled with the wet sound of sex, of Jessie's moans and my panted exhales of breath. It was *life*. It was beautiful and primal and euphoric, and I gloried in it, in her touch, her smell, the way our bodies fit together as if we'd been made for only each other.

The pain, the doubts, the echoes of the words that had once sliced like knives, the scabs that still bled so easily, all that hurt faded away and there was only her. Her heartbeat, her scent, the sweet clench of her inner muscles as they massaged me with such warm, delicious friction.

"Jessie, oh God, the things you make me want," I panted.

"Take them. They're yours," she said breathlessly right before she cried out, her inner muscles contracting around me and bringing on my own orgasm, almost shocking in its intensity. I thought I called her name, but I couldn't be sure as my head reared back and I pressed myself into her, milking every drop of intensity from my climax, circling my hips and then falling forward on a strangled moan of pleasure.

Take them. They're yours.

Goddamn, that had been...incredible. Mind-blowing. I'd never felt anything like that. I...I stilled.

I didn't use a condom.

Ah, fuck. It was the first time I'd ever had sex without one, even during my far-too-frequent drunken interludes, all the poor choices I'd made, I'd never gone without a condom—at least...at least that I could remember. I shut my eyes in self-disgust, thankful I'd received a full bill of health right before I'd left for France and sickened that I even had to think about that in reference to my pure, sweet Jessie. I blew out a harsh breath against Jessie's neck, trying to expand my lungs, trying to calm my racing heart. I could feel hers pounding, too, and I put my hand over it, her life blood pumping beneath my palm, our bodies still connected intimately. "I didn't use a condom," I said, and her fingers, which had been running down my arm, stilled. "I'm clean, Jessie, I promise." I couldn't hide the shame in my voice. "The timing...is it okay?"

"Yes, I think so," she whispered.

Jesus, I hoped so. Didn't I? For the breath of a moment, I felt a burst of powerful euphoria, but I forced it down, extinguished it before it could grow and spread. No, I'd decided the day before that to trap Jessie in any sense would be wrong, the most selfish thing I could possibly do to her. But to trap her *this* way would be the worst of all because she couldn't ever extricate me from her life even if she wanted to. She wouldn't only be trapped, but she'd be trapped forever because she'd be the mother of my child. *Our* child.

I pulled out of her, regret filling my chest over the possibility that I'd just gotten her pregnant, that even now life might be blossoming inside her. I rolled away, but I couldn't help reaching for her and pulling her back to me. I wasn't ready to let go. Not yet.

* * *

The Sunday morning air was warm and fresh, and everything smelled clean the way it does after days of rain. We'd woken early and showered, dressing and packing up the room somewhat somberly. There was a sort of quiet awkwardness between us, and I wasn't sure if it was just the fact that our weekend was wrapping up or if Jessie had regrets about what we'd done.

"It feels like saying goodbye to a magical place we'll never see again," she murmured as she turned back toward the room one last time. I let out a breath, happy to know what her morning reticence had meant. She was going to miss this room as much as I was.

I smiled. It was magical, and we wouldn't return. The sadness of that thought swept through me as I picked up our bags and closed the door to the room where I'd first made love to Jessie Creswell. *My Jessie*. We had only a handful of days left now, and they wouldn't be here. They'd be back in the real world, where things were not the same.

Madame Leclaire checked us out, smiling warmly as we said goodbye. As we were opening the door, Jessie looked back and asked a question in French. Madame Leclaire laughed, her chest shaking with her movement as she answered. Jessie grinned and said something else, and then we left.

"What'd you ask her?"

"I asked if there were really any other guests staying at her inn."

"And?"

"There weren't."

Huh.

Jessie glanced at me and smiled bashfully. For a moment it looked as if she were deciding whether or not to enlighten me, but then she said, "Madame Leclaire said sometimes the beginning of love is just a simple matter of proximity."

Love.

Was it possible? Could Jessie really love me? For a second,

just one quickened heartbeat, I let myself question the possibility before forcing my mind to move on. I couldn't let myself hope for that. I couldn't. Still, I smiled, thinking of the small room, the tiny bed. Close proximity had made for an amazing weekend. Good lighting hadn't hurt either. I pictured the way the dwindling twilight had shone in the window, showcasing Jessie's slender curves beneath the white nightgown, the way her skin had glowed like satin in the yellow light of dawn. The visions of her that way would stay with me until my dying day.

The car had mostly dried out in the few days we'd been at the inn, but it had a slightly mildewed smell that made Jessie scrunch her nose up. I laughed and put the top down. Hopefully the fresh air would help dry it more completely. Either way, I was glad I'd said yes when the man at the rental company had asked if I wanted the insurance.

Jessie sighed. "I'm excited to get back to work, but I don't want this weekend to end."

I took her hand, squeezing it. "I actually planned one more stop on the way back."

"Where?" she asked excitedly.

"It's a surprise." I followed the voice of the GPS to the sign for the turnoff to Domrémy-la-Pucelle, the town where, I'd learned, thanks to Nick's help once again, Joan of Arc had grown up. Jessie obviously knew, too, because when she saw the sign, she sucked in a breath, squeezing my hand.

"Oh my gosh, how did you know?"

"I did my research." I grinned, pleasure radiating through me to see the delight on her face. "But if there are bikes involved, I'm out."

She laughed. "Deal."

We made a series of turns through the town, parking and

walking hand in hand to the small, slope-roofed farmhouse where Joan of Arc had been born and raised. The main room was the largest, featuring a fireplace, tiled floors, and wood-beamed ceilings. I glanced around with minimal interest, mostly just wanting to watch Jessie as she wandered, trailing her finger over things in that way she did and leaning close to study the details. Every once in a while she would look up and smile with such joy, and it made my heart wrench with happiness. For now I'd enjoy every look of wonder that crossed her pretty face.

When we left, Jessie seemed to be reflecting on something, but I left her to her own thoughts, figuring they were focused on the work she was doing, the history surrounding her area of study.

We made one final stop, an ancient-looking church a short drive away from Joan of Arc's birthplace.

"The Church of Saint Rémy," Jessie said, a note of reverence in her voice. "This is where Joan used to come and pray. She was baptized here."

We went inside, the interior silent, the scent of candles and some sort of pungent oil in the air. Jessie looked up at the high, arched ceilings, and I took in the dark, hand-carved pews and the colorful stained-glass windows. I wasn't a religious man by any stretch of the imagination, but there was something in the air here, something... weighty that I could feel pressing on my chest when I closed my eyes. Here I could almost believe that a *place* could contain centuries of prayers, confessions, joy and grief, that pieces of those calls to God still hung in the air and had taken on a life of their own.

"It feels... different in here, doesn't it?" Jessie asked, voicing what I'd been pondering.

I almost said yes, but I didn't want to talk about a god I couldn't believe in, a god who, if he did exist, had abandoned me when I'd needed him most. "I think it's that smell, whatever it is, going to our heads."

Jessie glanced at me, her eyes lingering on my face for a moment before she smiled. "Chrism oil," she murmured, looking away. "It's the balsam you smell."

I put my hands in my pockets and followed her as she made her way to the front, where there was a stand with tiers of small candles. She lit a match and leaned forward, igniting one of the candles. She looked over her shoulder at me. "Do you want to say a prayer for someone?"

I shook my head. "No."

She nodded and then walked toward one of the panes of colored glass nearby. "Hard to believe, isn't it?"

"What?" My voice sounded strained, and I cleared my throat.

Jessie tilted her head, still staring at the colorful glass featuring a woman in armor, who I assumed to be Joan of Arc, astride a horse and holding her battle standard. People gazed up at her in prayer, a mother holding her baby toward the warrior saint. "That a little girl who came here to pray once upon a time would one day be depicted in the stained glass. That a young, illiterate peasant girl inspired a nation."

"Illiterate?" I asked, my voice cracking again, my heartbeat sounding loud in my ears.

"Mmm," Jessie hummed. "Farmers' children weren't generally taught to read in the fourteen hundreds."

"Oh."

At the single utterance, she turned her head, her expression concerned, as if she'd heard something in that one word that gave her pause. "It's why stained glass became so popular in the Middle Ages. So the people sitting in the pews—many of whom were illiterate—could understand biblical stories."

"Huh. Interesting."

Jessie nodded. "Yes, and that's why the writings I'm translating are so fascinating. Joan of Arc had a few letters transcribed at different points, but she wouldn't have been able to keep a diary, would have no way to record her personal thoughts back then; nor would she likely have had someone else write them down for her. And so to see her through this girl's eyes is…just an amazing window to the past and an incredible insight into the mind of a young woman who couldn't have left behind her own story. We're very lucky she had someone to help her do what she couldn't do herself."

Her eyes had lit up as she spoke, the passion for her work obvious, and I loved seeing her that way. But it also caused a lump to settle in my throat because it confirmed what I already knew: there was no place for me in her life. She was a woman who deserved everything good life had to offer, including a man she could look up to and feel proud of.

That man wasn't me, and damn if I didn't feel a small piece of my heart crack every time I was reminded of that fact.

"I've never, uh, been much for the church."

"No?"

"No. I prefer to confess my sins to the bottom of a bottle of bourbon."

She laughed softly. "I'm not much of a churchgoer either. My family wasn't religious."

I studied her as she gazed at the window again. I'd noticed the reverence in her eyes as she looked at the statues, the pews, the etchings in the wooden pictures hung on the walls. She might not be religious, but she seemed to be spiritual. "Do you believe in God, Jessie?"

She tilted her head, not answering for a moment. Finally, she said, "There's this story I heard once about a religious man who got caught in a flood. He climbed onto the roof of his house and trusted that God would rescue him. A neighbor came by in a boat and said, 'The water is rising. Get in my boat.'

"But the religious man replied, 'No thanks. I've prayed to God, and I know he'll save me.'

"A little while later, a rescue team came by in a boat. 'The water is rising. Get in our boat.'

"But, again, the religious man said, 'No thanks. I've prayed to God, and I know he'll save me.'

"A short time after that, a police helicopter hovered overhead and threw down a ladder. 'The water is rising,' they said. 'Grab the ladder, and we'll fly you to safety.'

"But the religious man replied, 'No thanks. I've prayed to God, and I know he'll save me.'

"All this time the water had continued to rise, until soon it reached above the roof and the religious man drowned. When he arrived in heaven, he demanded to see God immediately. When he was standing before him, he said, 'Lord, why am I here in heaven? I prayed for you to save me. I trusted that you would rescue me from that flood.'

"'Yes, my child, you did,' replied God. 'And I sent you two boats and a rescue helicopter. But you sent them away.'"

I stared at her, a strange feeling swirling inside me, the sensation that tiny ants were crawling on my skin. I gave Jessie a wry smile.

"Anyway," Jessie said, smiling back, giving a bashful chuckle. "That's sort of my spiritual belief summed up in a story. Maybe there's such a thing as God or fate, but ultimately, I believe that if there is a God, he helps those who help themselves."

I didn't comment. God had never helped me. God took my

mother away and left me with a monster. God had always left me to drown. "Should we go?" I asked. "I'm sure you have things to do to get ready for your day tomorrow."

"Yeah. I do." She walked the few steps to where I stood and took my hand. "Thank you, Callen. Thank you for this weekend and all the thought you put into it for me." She glanced down, her lashes fluttering against her cheeks, and my heart flipped slowly. "I'll never forget it."

"I won't either, Jessie." And no truer words had ever been spoken.

CHAPTER EIGHTEEN

JESSICA

My heart dropped just a bit when Château de la Bellefeuille came into view. As magnificent and breathtaking as the structure was, it signaled the end of this glorious weekend, and even more heart-breakingly, the dwindling time we had together in France. Five days and Callen would be gone. Was there any chance at all that he'd want to make our relationship more permanent? And if so, how would that work exactly? I hardly wanted to allow my mind to try to work out solutions, but somehow it kept wandering there. He could work from France as well as anywhere, couldn't he? He'd have to uproot his entire life to do so, but—

"Here we are," Callen said, pulling up to the curb. I wasn't sure if I imagined the disappointment in his voice or if I was merely transferring my own emotions onto him and hearing things in his tone that weren't actually there.

The valet opened my door, and I stepped out, meeting Callen on the sidewalk after he'd collected our bags from the trunk and tipped the valet. We entered the château and walked toward the elevator. I wasn't sure what to do. Was this where we parted, or should I ask him if he'd like to go to dinner? I did need an early night so I'd be well rested for work tomorrow, but Callen and I had so little time, and I wanted to take advantage of every moment we had. And I'd grown used to his body next to mine as I drifted off to sleep, the scent of his skin as he held me tight against him.

Oh, Jessica, you're in for so much heartbreak.

"Jessie," Callen said, stopping as we stepped inside of the main foyer. "I know you have things to do and that you have to work tomorrow, but...stay with me tonight. I'll let you sleep. I promise. I—"

"Yes." I nodded, exhaling a relieved breath. "Yes."

The relief that washed over Callen's expression made my heart jump, and I gave him a kiss.

His body seemed looser beside me as we walked the short distance to the elevator and then rode to the top floor. The hallway carpeting was soft beneath my feet, and I could hardly wait to use that tub of his and soak my muscles after being in the car half the day. Maybe Callen would join me. A secretive smile tilted my lips, and Callen glanced over at me, raising his brows as we got to the door of his suite and he set our bags down to root in his pocket for the key. "What exactly are you thinking right now?"

I leaned against the wall, watching him as he put the key in the lock. "I was just thinking about that big tub of yours."

His eyes flared, and he grinned as he pushed the door open, picking up the bags and nodding toward the suite, indicating I should enter ahead of him. "I like where that thought is going.

Let's talk more about it," he said as he closed the door behind him. I just grinned, heading toward the bedroom, where I stopped suddenly, inhaling a shocked breath of air.

There was a half-naked woman lying on his bed.

My blood chilled in my veins as she sat up and lifted one thin blond eyebrow, her full red mouth raised in an amused smirk, the skimpy black bra and panties she wore leaving nothing to the imagination.

"What the hell are you doing in my room, Annette?" Callen growled from behind me.

My limbs felt frozen, and yet my heart was beating a mile a minute. Who the hell was Annette? And why was she practically naked and lying in his bed as if she had every right to be there?

A dozen images ran through my mind, because this felt all too familiar. How many times had my mom stormed into hotel rooms where half-naked women had sat up in shock, pulling sheets around themselves? How many times had my brother and I trailed behind her, cheeks flaming and eyes stinging?

"What are you doing in *France*? How the fuck did you get into my room?" Callen demanded.

Annette leaned back on Callen's pillow and ran her hand idly over her perfectly round breast, flicking her nipple through the lace of the bra. I looked away. My face felt hot, and I knew it must be flushed with shock and humiliation.

"I distracted the man at the front desk and swiped a key. I didn't know hotels still used *keys*. It's charming. Oh, stop looking at me that way. You're usually so much happier to see me, Callen darling. Your enthusiasm is usually"—she glanced at his crotch—"bigger. Is it because of her? She can join us. We've tried everything else, but not that. I'm game—"

"Shut up, Annette," Callen growled again, grabbing a throw

blanket from the end of the bed and tossing it at her. "And cover yourself up." Callen glanced at me, his cheeks flushed, his eyes filled with shame. "Jessie...I'm sorry..."

I just stared at him, wide-eyed. I didn't know what to say. I didn't fully understand what was going on other than that this woman was apparently a regular part of his life in Los Angeles. My head was swimming, and I realized she looked vaguely familiar. Had she been with him at the lounge that night in Paris? I'd only really had eyes for Callen, but now that I was taking a good look at her, I thought she had been there. But hadn't he been with the French blonde? The one who'd told him to finish with the help?

The happy bubble I'd just been in hadn't only burst; it had exploded.

Annette sighed, swinging her legs to the side of the bed and standing. She laughed. "The look on your face, Callen. As if you've never seen me naked before."

I blanched, feeling as if I might vomit, and reached for the wall to steady my shaking legs just as footsteps sounded behind me. I caught Annette's face draining of color as well, her mouth opening and closing before I turned to find a short, balding man standing in the doorway behind us, his eyes moving between the three of us.

"Oh Christ," I heard Callen utter.

"What is this?" the man asked.

"Larry..."

"You're fucking my *wife*?" The man stared at Callen, his expression tense with anger and what looked like horrified surprise.

Annette let out a small cough, grabbing the blanket on the bed and wrapping it around her body. "Larry, darling, it's just a misunderstanding," she started, but he cut her off with a venomous glare.

"Of all the disgusting, immoral things you've done," Larry said, directing his words at Callen. "I thought even you had some standards."

Callen closed his eyes for a brief second, his expression pained. He looked at Larry and then glanced at Annette, and I recognized the look on his face. I'd seen it often on my father's. Callen was deciding whether or not to lie. He ran a hand through his hair and let out a huff of breath. "Yes, I have slept with Annette in the past. I'm sorry. I have no excuse. Not anymore." So in the end he'd decided on the truth. My father had never gone that route, and yet I realized maybe it wouldn't have mattered. Standing here now, I still felt sick and humiliated. Was *I* the other woman in Annette's eyes? It felt like that in some sick, twisted way. I wanted to bolt from the room, or better yet, just disappear.

Larry shook his head, his gaze still full of disgust. "I left you a voice message to let you know we were coming to spend a few days with you, figured you could use some company." He glanced at me. "But you never have lacked for company, have you? One fucking distraction after another."

"Don't. Not her." He looked at me, his jaw tensed, his eyes blank. "Jessie, go back to your room."

I gaped, blinking at him. *What the hell?* He was dismissing *me*? After the beautiful weekend we'd spent together, after we'd made love? Why wasn't he throwing *them* out? I glanced back at Annette wrapped in a blanket, her breasts barely covered, the lines of her perfect body easily seen with the material wrapped so tightly around her.

Oh God, this is his life.

She is his life.

Of all the disgusting, immoral things you've done... That was his life. Disgusting. Immoral.

Jessie, go back to your room.

If I had momentarily forgotten I was temporary, *this* was a clear and brutal reminder. I turned without a word, grabbing my overnight bag still on the floor by the door, and practically ran out of the room. I didn't allow the tears to fall until I was back in my room. I dropped my bag on the floor, pressed my back against the closed door, and sobbed.

* * *

The knock on my door startled me, and I sat up on the bed. "Jessie?" I heard called softly.

Callen.

I had vowed not to go to him after what had happened earlier—after he'd dismissed me. I would not chase him. I would not beg for an apology. For some reason, I hadn't even considered that he might come after me. It confused me, set me off-balance. I swiped my fingers under my eyes, though my tears had already dried, and tiptoed to the door. I placed my hands on it and rested my ear against the wood, not sure what to do. Not sure I even wanted to see him right now.

"Please, Jessie." His voice seemed to be directly on the other side of the door, as if he, too, was leaning against it. "Please open the door. We need to talk." I stepped back, biting at my lip. "Please," he repeated.

I sighed, the lock making a sharp clicking sound as I turned it and pulled the door open. He took up the doorframe, his big body filling the space, his face weary and regretful. "I'm sorry. I'm so sorry."

I shook my head, pressing my lips together, moving back so he could enter. For a second we just stared at each other, the space between us full of tension. "Those people, they were with you that night in Paris at the lounge where I worked."

He nodded. "He's my agent, and she's his wife."

"Oh." The word was a whisper, laced with the intense disappointment I felt.

"I didn't ask her to come to my room. I didn't even know they were coming to France."

"He said he left you a message," I said, closing the door and leaning back against it.

"I was with you, Jessie. I practically forgot I *had* a phone..." His words faded away.

I closed my eyes for a moment. I had, too. It'd felt like we were in our own world, a place meant just for us. I'd been afraid to come back to the real world and been smacked with the reason no more than ten minutes after setting foot back in the château. If I hadn't been there, would he have taken her up on her offer? "You're...having an affair with her?"

He grimaced. "No, that's not...It's..." He massaged the back of his neck, looking utterly miserable. After a moment he shook his head. "I've done so many things I'm ashamed of, Jessie. I hate the things..." He shook his head again, as if he was at a complete loss for words.

The moment stretched between us. *I have no excuse*, he'd said before. At least he'd realized it. Still, the whole episode had felt so...low. *Tawdry*. Immoral, just as his agent had said. I didn't want to see Callen that way. I knew he'd slept with lots of women. I knew he drank. He'd even told me why, and I'd tried

to understand. But this...It made me feel ashamed of him—
disgusted—and it hurt. He had always been my prince, first in
my imagination, then in my memory, and now in my heart. I
loved him. *But this?*

"Do they have children?" I asked, glancing away. My voice
sounded flat.

He paused, studying me, his expression so sad it made my
heart lurch. I didn't want to feel bad for him. He was the villain
here. "No."

Did that make it better? Did it matter? Or was I just making
this about me? About my own painful memories?

"God, don't look at me that way, Jessie," he rasped. "I never
lied about the life I led. I never promised you anything I couldn't
deliver. You agreed to this. No promises. No regrets."

"I know," I said softly. "It's just..." I shrugged, a self-
conscious gesture. I felt so very tender and raw. "You've always
been my prince, Callen," I admitted, voicing the thought I'd just
had, letting him into my heart. "It hurts to see you as anything
else. After this weekend I'd hoped—"

"Stop. I can't be your prince, Jessie. You have to see that."
Callen swore softly, turning away.

My heart contracted in pain. Did I see that after what I'd
just experienced upstairs? Maybe. But I was having such a hard
time separating the man I'd spent the weekend with from *this*
man. I couldn't merge the man who had brought me to an empty
church in the middle of nowhere simply because he knew it
would fascinate me with this man who seemed without morals
or a conscience, a man who could hurt people so easily and so
selfishly. "I guess...I...I hoped you'd decide you don't want to
live that way, surrounded by shallow people, becoming one yourself, making choices that leave you feeling ashamed, the way I

see you do now. I know you felt what I did this weekend, Callen. I was there. I saw *you*. That man upstairs a few minutes ago, that wasn't you. Or at least…it doesn't have to be. Not anymore." I reached for him, but he didn't reach back.

"You're wrong," he said, his voice a choked whisper. I let my hand fall, pain radiating through me. "God, Jessie, if I could change for anyone, it would be you. I don't want to be that man. But it's who I've become. It's who I have to be."

He backed away, the look on his face filled with such agony, I could only stare in dismay. If he felt as upset as I did, if he didn't *want* to be that person, why was he doing this? "What…? Why? Why do you have to be someone you detest?"

Callen sighed as he turned from me, moving toward the window, where he pulled the curtain open and stared out at the garden. His stance was rigid, his shoulders tensed, and he was quiet for so long, I almost went to him. But something held me back. I felt a heavy anticipation, as if he was weighing whether he should share something with me, as if he was attempting to gather some inner strength. And so I waited, barely breathing.

"I can't read," he said, the words so quiet, I almost questioned whether I'd heard them correctly. My heart began beating quickly, and my mind filled with confusion. He turned to me, such naked vulnerability in his eyes that I sucked in a gasp. "I can't read books, or menus, or signs. I can't read texts or e-mails. I couldn't leave you a note at the train tracks when we were teenagers because I can't write a fucking letter, not even one."

Wait…what?

I felt frozen with shock, my mind whirling to try to gather any clues that might have told me. I couldn't think of any. "I…I didn't know."

"I'm good at hiding it. I've made hiding it my other career, Jessie."

I stepped forward, drawn to him, to the pain on his face and the way he looked so lonely standing there in front of the window. The light created a halo around him, his dark hair falling over his forehead. "How, though, Callen? I don't understand."

He looked to the side for a moment, shoving his hands in his pockets and shrugging, the movement barely noticeable. "I struggled a lot in school when I was a kid. The letters...I couldn't grasp them. I was finally diagnosed with a learning disability, but"—he pulled his hand from his pocket and brushed his hair back from his forehead—"still, it was so hard. The school paid for this tutor to come to the house, but my dad would watch, and it made me so fucking nervous, so I wouldn't try, and then I would act out later." He sighed, the sound full of such weariness it made my heart catch.

"Pretty soon I figured out that if my dad got frustrated enough, he'd end the lesson and then lash out at me physically. I preferred the physical abuse to the humiliation of not being able to understand the letters."

"Oh, Callen," I breathed, tears springing to my eyes. "That's what you meant, all those years ago, when you said you didn't mind being hit."

His nod was shaky. "Yeah. Being hit was better than the names he called me. *Idiot. Retard. Disappointment.* Being hit was better than constantly feeling like a worthless failure."

"And...the words you hear on repeat in your head, it's him calling you names because you can't read? All the praise, all the accolades, yet it's only him you hear." I paused for a moment and looked at his forlorn expression. "He steals your magic."

"Yeah." The word came out on the whisper of a breath. "It's

why I can't be alone. Why I'd do *anything* not to have to be alone. Because when I'm alone, he is all I hear in my head."

I went to him, unable to hold myself back, even though many things still weighed so heavily on my heart. To leave him standing there alone after he told me the secret he'd held on to for so long was unbearable. I wrapped my arms around his waist, laying my head on his chest and squeezing him to me. His hands came up, threading through my hair, and he laid his chin on top of my head. "Jessie," he sighed.

After a minute he raised his head, and I tipped mine back to look at him. "I'm sorry about today. I'm sorry you were confronted with the worst of me. I'm so fucking ashamed. But do you see, I'm not your prince and I never can be. I couldn't write you a love letter if my life depended on it. I can't even write my own name. I'd just…embarrass you."

"You'd never embarrass me, Callen, and you can learn. You're a man now, not a scared little boy afraid of disappointing his father. You could hire a private tutor if you wanted. You read musical notes and symbols. If you can read those, you can learn how to make sense of letters, too."

He took my arms from around his waist and stepped away, shaking his head. "No. It's not the same."

"How?"

"I don't know for sure. Maybe it's a right brain/left brain thing. Maybe I'm an anomaly. I have no idea. It's not like I can research this kind of stuff." He looked away for a moment. "That day in the boxcar when you showed me the music in your book, it was like…" His face screwed up as if he struggled to explain it, even to himself. "It was like the notes had actual weight, with their round, heavy bottoms and the light little staff on the top. Their shape…anchored them to the paper, and they didn't

twist and turn and fly away like letters and numbers did. Do."
He shook his head. "I can't explain it, Jessie, but I read those
notes. They stuck in my brain, and when I looked at them the
next day, they looked the same as the day before and I remembered their names."

Emotion clogged my throat so that I could barely speak. *Oh,
Callen.* "That's...I mean, I wish I had known. I wish I had understood how important that music book was to you. I would
have brought you every single one I could get my hands on."

He smiled, and it was soft, sweet, a little sad. "I know you
would have. The keyboard, though, it helped even more, especially once I could put a sound to the note. Somehow hearing
what the symbol sounded like cemented it in my brain. I became
obsessed with music, with how the notes fit together, how they
complemented each other, how a string of them changed their
feeling. I..."

I shook my head in wonder. God, did he think just anyone
could have taught themselves to read music, to play on an old
keyboard, to compose music that went straight to people's souls?
"You're a genius, Callen. You're a musical genius."

He laughed, but it didn't hold much amusement, more pain
than levity. "I'm hardly a genius. I'm a—"

"Don't." I moved forward, putting two fingers against his lips,
halting his words. "Don't you dare say it. Don't you repeat what
he said to you." I let my hand fall away, shaking my head. "It's
not his voice you hear in your head, is it? It's *yours.* It's your voice,
repeating the words he once said to you, reinforcing them. You
still believe they're the truth, so they still hold so much power."

He opened his mouth and then shut it, his eyes moving over
my face. He let out a shaky breath. "I don't know. I don't even
know anymore."

"They're lies, Callen, and they always were. Lies told by a cruel, heartless man to a scared, impressionable little boy. You have to believe that before they'll go away."

He ran a hand through his hair, sighing before dropping his arms to his sides. "I'll still never learn to read, Jessie."

He was wrong, but I let it go for the moment. He'd have to find the courage to try. I couldn't do that for him. I stepped forward again, placing my palms on his chest, tilting my head to look into his face. "Then write me love letters with your music. Write me songs that make my heart ache and my soul feel full. If you... If you have feelings for me, express them through your songs. I don't care. But don't live a life you don't want to lead. Don't become something you don't want to be. Don't throw away what we have because you don't feel worthy of me."

"I'm *not* worthy of you. How will you feel when you have to constantly read things *to* me? How boring will it be for you to be with a man who can't discuss history, or any politics other than those I see on the evening news, or, hell, even the meme everyone laughs at except me because I have no fucking clue what it says?"

I sighed. "Callen, there are books on tape, or documentaries, if you're really interested in history. I think you probably know that, and you would have listened or watched before now if you really wanted to. If you're not compelled to learn about history, don't do it for me. I don't care about that. I want to hear what you think about the colors of the sunset coming in our window and what your ideas about fate are. I want to hear about the things in your heart and the way you see the world around you."

"Ah, Jessie," he breathed, his eyes soft as he gazed at me. He pulled me to him, and for a few minutes we stayed just like that, my ear to his chest as I listened to the steady beat of his heart, his lips on the top of my head.

When we finally pulled apart, he sighed. "I just...I don't know. You deserve everything, and I want to be the man who can give it to you, but I...I'm not."

My heart beat dully in my chest. He was wrong. I loved him, and I didn't care that he couldn't read, didn't care that he'd lied about it. I understood my broken prince so well now. It had all fallen into place. But none of what I felt mattered. What I knew, what I believed, didn't make a whit of difference if he didn't believe it himself.

"Please don't look so sad, Jessie. We still have a little time. Let's not waste it."

A little time.

We were back to that. It was all he was willing to give us, and I wanted more. I wanted *him*, but I was suddenly so confused. I'd hoped we could work something out, but now I couldn't see the picture clearly. It was misty and full of roads that suddenly ended, fading into nowhere. Oh God, how would I say goodbye when I didn't want to, when I wanted him in my life and he still didn't believe he belonged there?

A little time.

A handful of days.

It wasn't enough.

It was all I had.

CHAPTER NINETEEN

CALLEN

The burn of the liquor was a welcome distraction from my thoughts, if only a momentary one. If I drank enough, it would dull them completely, but that would mean I'd likely pass out and miss a whole night with Jessie when we had so few left: four to be exact.

I was still completely sickened by myself, by the up-close view Jessie had into the life of debauchery I'd been living. *Annette. Fucking Christ.* I felt like I'd sullied Jessie's purity just by her witnessing that horrific scene. Not only that, but I'd stuck a knife into the very spot she'd confided to me was the most tender place inside her. I knew what that felt like, and I hated myself for doing it to Jessie.

I sighed, raking my hands through my hair, going over what we'd said to each other in her room the night before. Jessie knew

I couldn't read, and she hadn't immediately rejected me. The knowledge sang in my soul and yet…the familiar shame *still* clanged in the background, drowning out the relief. I had lied for so long, I didn't think I had the courage to live the truth openly, couldn't even imagine what it would feel like not to have to cover for myself in a million small ways that I could never anticipate until they actually happened.

I'd become a master at deception, had honed my ability to lie on the spot, to distract, to deflect. And it was fucking exhausting. I'd grown used to the lies at this point, but now that Jessie knew, what would it feel like to lie in *front* of her and know she understood what I was doing? What kind of shame would that inspire? To constantly lie in front of someone you respected who *knew* you were lying? And if she saw the skill with which I did it, would she understand, or would it eventually whittle away any trust she might be able to have in me? How could you trust in someone who reminded you of the person who had hurt you the most?

I took another sip of alcohol, frustrated and confused by my own aimless thoughts.

I'd been tempted to stay in my room for the day, waiting for Jessie, but I'd felt cooped up. The music wasn't playing in my head. No writing would get done, and I'd wanted a drink. I'd called Nick, and he'd been working, but he'd said he'd meet me at the bar at five. I'd come down at four and had been nursing the same drink for the past forty-five minutes. Someone laughed loudly from the other side of the bar, and I glanced up at the older couple and then around, hoping to God Larry wasn't anywhere nearby.

There really hadn't been much to say to him the day before and there wasn't anything to say now. What was the purpose of saying sorry when it didn't erase the betrayal? And as for him, apparently he'd decided there was no reason to waste his time yelling at me or Annette. Who would want the facts of when and how often anyway? *Fuck.*

I knew Annette had left on the first flight out of France, and Larry was leaving the next day. I had no idea of the state of their marriage after what had happened in my room. Of all the revolting moments in my life, that one had to take the cake. I blew out a breath, the memory causing another flash of disgust to reverberate through me.

I didn't even know if I still had an agent at this point, or if I even wanted Larry's representation. Or anyone else's for that matter.

Larry was very good at what he did and had the best contacts in the business, but I'd seen him stab enough people in the back to know I couldn't fully trust him either. *Just as he couldn't trust me, obviously.* Unfortunately, I'd gotten sucked into that whole lifestyle because it was easier for someone like me to hang around people who easily looked the other way, who didn't ask deep questions, who smiled and nodded at flimsy excuses and flimsier behavior. And so I'd become one of them.

On his way out of my hotel room, Larry had told me about an interview with a French TV program, one that I *would be incredibly moronic to attempt to get out of.* The final look of disgust told me that *moronic* was putting it mildly. That he'd scheduled me to work while I was on vacation sucked, but I wasn't in a position to say no. Not after what Larry'd walked in on.

"Well, look who's returned." Nick slid onto the barstool next to me and raised a brow as he glanced at my drink. "I thought it was happy hour. And if it is, why do you look so damn unhappy?"

I bared my teeth in what I hoped was a decent smile. "How's that?"

He shuddered. "Not good."

That elicited an actual laugh. But then I groaned, taking another sip of my drink. The bartender came over, and Nick ordered a beer before turning back to look at me again.

"What's wrong, Cal? I hoped you would return from your romantic weekend with a spring in your step and a smile on your face. All that research into wine tours and museums, French gardens and breakfast spots...All that planning and it didn't go well?"

I stared into my drink, allowing myself to relive the weekend, just for a moment. Jessie and I had never made it out of bed long enough to do half of what I'd planned. And it'd been...incredible. "It went too well. Everything's...suddenly complicated."

Nick's drink was placed in front of him, and he took a long sip. "Ah. I see."

I tipped my head, looking at him sideways. He did. He always had. It was why I'd first begun pushing him away when I'd started bringing people into my life like Larry and Annette. I turned my head, staring down at the bar, collecting my courage. "Nick, why don't you ever text me?" That and a hundred other little things I'd pretended not to notice.

There was only silence, but instead of looking up, I folded the cocktail napkin in front of me over once, and then again, turning it into a small square.

"Do you want me to say it?" Nick asked softly.

I blew out a breath. "No." I'd known for a long time he knew I couldn't read. It'd been an unspoken truth between us. I wasn't sure how he'd first connected the dots, but he'd been with me before I had enough money to hire people to read my contracts, before I had the funds for computer programs and phones that I could download apps to. He'd noticed, and because it was obvious that I was ashamed, he'd never said a word. He'd just helped me when and where he could.

"It's nothing to be ashamed of, Callen."

I didn't answer, and after a moment he asked, "Is that why?"

"Why what?"

"Why things are suddenly complicated? You could tell her, you know."

"I did."

I glanced at him, and he was wearing an expression of genuine surprise. "How'd she react?"

I shook my head. "She says she doesn't care. And right now she probably doesn't, but that's because she hasn't considered all the ways it would affect her, even probably all the ways it affects *me*." She had no way to know what a struggle it was, knowing it'd be easier to tell people the truth, but also understanding that it could be asking to be taken advantage of. No idea how being illiterate not only made me feel stupid, but it made me feel vulnerable. There were things others might believe made it easier—like voice to text—but those were filled with pitfalls, too. I should know; autocorrect had made a fool out of me one too many times. So I'd abandoned certain technology. I'd rather appear rude for not answering right away than like the idiot I was.

"Okay. So you'll…what? Just be alone forever? Drinking way too much, sleeping with any woman who crosses your path, rinse and repeat until your liver gives out or your dick falls off? Sounds like a hell of a plan."

I couldn't help the chuckle that came up my throat. "When you put it that way…"

"Exactly." Nick sighed. "Sad, lonely, and dickless. Not the way to live, or die."

"So what do I do, then? She lives halfway around the world."

He shrugged. "Those are details the two of you will have to figure out. All I know, Cal, is that I haven't seen your eyes shine with anything other than intoxication for a very, very long time. And I was afraid I'd never see it again." I heard the sadness in his voice, and it made me wince. He'd seen the path of destruction I'd been on for a while now and had tried to head me off. I hadn't listened. I'd done everything to push him away, shut him out.

I took a sip of my drink. "You didn't have time to come on this trip with me, did you?" He'd been working almost the entire time we'd been here.

"I always have time for you, Cal."

I smiled at him. Yeah, he always had. Even when he really didn't, he *made* time. The only one who truly did. "I'm sorry I've been such a lousy friend lately, man."

Nick took a swig of beer. "Get the next round and I'll forgive you."

I laughed, but it ended in a grimace. I owed him a lot more than that. A hell of a lot more. "Thank you."

We shared a drink and chatted, the mood growing lighter, and after fifteen minutes, I felt someone slide up next to me and glanced to my right. The girl smiled and for a second I couldn't place her, but then I remembered her from the first night I'd arrived, the same night Jessie had shown up in this very bar. The girl smiled coyly. "Hello again."

"How are you?"

"We're good." Her friend leaned around her and waved at us, and seeing the vacant seat next to Nick, walked behind us and scooted into it. She held out her hand and began introducing her-self to Nick.

"I hoped I'd see you again this week," the girl said. Fuck, I couldn't remember her name. The bartender came by, and she ordered a chocolate martini as I searched my brain for her name. Had it ever even registered?

"Yeah," I said after the bartender had turned away to make her drink. "I've been working a lot, and spending time with friends." Friends. That felt wrong. But if Jessie wasn't a *friend*, what was she?

"Working? I thought you were just here on vacation. Are you composing something new?"

"Yeah. I'm working on a score for a movie." Who would have guessed that I'd show up here, suffering from a terrible case of writer's block, and a week later I'd be in the middle of a piece I suspected—*hoped*—might be one of the best things I'd ever writ-ten? *Jessie*. It was because of Jessie.

"That's so exciting!" the girl said, putting her hand on my arm, the signal I knew meant I could take her back to my room if I wanted to. I didn't.

I pulled my arm from beneath her hand just as the bar-tender set her drink in front of her, and she held up her glass to me. "To your latest masterpiece." She took a sip of her martini.

"I appreciate that." Well, this was awkward. I knew she had an agenda, and I wasn't interested. *And I never had to bother with small talk before.* I opened my mouth to excuse myself, but she started talking before I could.

"My friends and I have been doing a lot of sightseeing," she went on. "There's so much to do in the Loire Valley. It's beauti-ful." She took another drink of her cocktail and then tilted her head, smiling flirtatiously. "I still haven't had a chance to enjoy the hot tub."

I released a breath on an uncomfortable smile. "Listen, ah—" I looked up and saw Jessie standing in the doorway of the bar, staring over at me with a look on her face that was simultaneously surprised and hurt. I hadn't expected her to get out of work for another half an hour or so, but I was so happy to see her, I was on my feet in an instant. She began walking toward me, her body held stiffly, as though she felt unsure. "I gotta go," I muttered to the girl next to me.

"Wait? Already? I was hoping we could—"

"Sorry." I turned to the bartender. "Charge all these to my room," I said, indicating Nick and the two girls. The bartender nodded, and I threw down a tip. "Nick, see you at dinner?"

"No. Can't tonight. Breakfast?"

I nodded at him and scooted out from between the barstools, noting the pout on the face of the girl I'd been talking to, and walked toward Jessie. She gave me an awkward smile and waved to Nick. "Hey," I said, "how was work?"

Jessie glanced behind me at the bar. "You don't have to leave if you were—"

"I was waiting for you. *Only* for you, Jessie."

She gave me a brief smile. "Okay. Well, then, shall we?"

I took her hand as we turned. She shot a quick look behind us, her expression troubled for a moment before she flashed me another smile that didn't quite meet her eyes.

CHAPTER TWENTY

JESSICA

In the year of our Lord 1429, on the twenty-first day of July

We are returned from the coronation of King Charles VII, made victorious much in part due to Jehanne's bravery as she led our troops to victory. The celebration was a sight to behold, and though I dressed as myself with all the fineries of which I am familiar, I felt somehow... not myself at all. I've changed, and I'm not sure how to change back, nor if I even desire to.

My father made my introductions to several gentlemen of the court and told me that he is simply waiting for the most advantageous offer for my hand. My heart sank at knowing this is what I will return to when my

*duties have ended—a loveless marriage and a lifetime
of pretending.*

*I spotted Olivier skulking behind pillars and partaking of far too much wine as he watched me dance with
one aristocratic gentlemen after another. I danced and
laughed, yet I was unable to stop thinking about that
kiss the captain and I shared before he released me and
returned to camp, leaving me angry that he'd taken
such liberties and somehow dissatisfied that our kiss
had ended. And so when he pulled me behind a column and pressed himself against me, planting his lips
on mine again, I did not stop him. Indeed, I must admit
that I encouraged it and returned his kiss with much
fervor. I will be utterly ruined if it is found that I have
conducted myself in such a manner, and with a member of the military no less, and yet I do not seem to
care. What am I doing? Olivier and I have no hope for
a future—none at all—and yet I crave his hands on me
in a way that both terrifies and thrills me.*

*I am almost thankful to be back at camp now, where
the rules are different, where I am still playing a part
and yet I am somehow more free. The focus has turned,
once again, to the strategy of war and whether it is best
to press our advantage and take Paris. Olivier says he
agrees with Jehanne's assertion that we should, though
Charles wavers, swayed no doubt by the opinion of his
court. Sometimes I grow so weary of all this war, I
think I might scream. Why should God care about our
victory? Aren't there English soldiers in their tents right
now praying to the very same God? Why should he
answer some prayers and not others? Jehanne says I*

ask the wrong questions, but I don't know what the right ones are. Perhaps if I could cease questioning as she does, my mind would find peace. Perhaps God is attempting to lead us all to peace, but if no one but Jehanne has faith in his calling, we are destined to fail. For one girl cannot save an entire nation by herself, no matter how devout she may be. Indeed, one girl cannot save anyone—not a country, nor a man—lest they believe as strongly as she.

He was dreaming again. This time I knew what he was dreaming about as he whimpered softly, the sound a child would make, and clenched the sheets in his hands.

I'd been dreaming, too, of the translation I'd worked on earlier that day. Dreaming of coronations and secret kisses, war troops and military camps, and a young girl trying to navigate it all. But his cries had woken me, and now my dream faded away like late-morning mist.

"Callen," I whispered, shaking him gently. "Callen, wake up. You're dreaming." He flailed slightly, his head turning as if he'd taken a sudden smack on the cheek, his eyes springing open. He blinked at me in the low light of my room, reality dawning, the shadows in his eyes fading as he released a long breath and pulled me close.

I ran my hand down his cheek, feeling the roughness of his jaw. It had to be close to morning. I'd have to roll away to glance at the bedside clock, and I didn't want to turn from him, even for a second. "Same dream?" I asked.

"Yeah. Same dream."

"He can't hurt you anymore," I whispered. Only he *was* hurting him, wasn't he? How could I help him stop allowing his father's words to poison his mind? "His words are lies." I scooted closer, pulling him tight, feeling the quick beating of his heart against my shoulder. After a few minutes, it slowed, his body relaxing.

"Come live with me, Jessie," he whispered against my hair.

My eyes blinked open, and I tilted my head back. "Live with you? In L.A.?"

"Yes."

A shimmer of happiness ran through me, but so did a jolt of uneasiness. Move to Los Angeles, where the life I'd been confronted with in his room upstairs was everywhere around him?

"Why are you so quiet?" There was vulnerability in his voice, and I realized how difficult it must have been to ask the question. Was he suggesting he'd change? Change his lifestyle altogether for me? It's what I wanted, right? Only why did I feel so unsure? Because his words from yesterday were still so fresh in my mind. *"God, Jessie, if I could change for anyone, it would be you. I don't want to be that man. But it's who I've become. It's who I have to be."* *If* he could change…

"It's just…my job is here."

"It's temporary, though, isn't it?"

"Yes. But I was hoping it would lead to something permanent."

"I understand how much you love your work. But couldn't you work in Los Angeles, too? Aren't there translating jobs there?"

There were things I could do there, I supposed. I could teach, maybe, or translate books perhaps…I sighed. It just wasn't exactly my dream. But Callen *was* my dream…He always had been.

"I'd feed you French chocolate," he whispered, leaning down

and rubbing his lips over my forehead. I could feel the smile he wore, and I could feel when it faded. His breath misted over my skin. "The music plays when I'm with you."

"And if it stops again? Even when I'm there?" I asked. *Please don't want me just for that reason alone. Love me, Callen. Love me and I might follow you anywhere.*

"I... What do you mean?"

"I mean, will you turn back to other women if I can't make the music keep playing for you?"

He was quiet for several long moments. "I haven't looked at another woman since we've been together, Jessie. I haven't even *thought* of another woman. Not once."

That wasn't exactly a denial. "I know," I said softly. Something inside felt like it was squeezing, a familiar ache, the same discomfort I'd felt every time one of those hotel room doors would open and the sound of my mother's sobs would fill my ears. Oh yes, I had my own ghosts, too. And maybe Callen's hesitation was because of his shaky trust in *himself*, but how could I hang all my hopes on him—move back across the world—when he wasn't able to reassure me of his faithfulness. If he couldn't trust himself, wouldn't I be a fool to trust him, too? "You could move to France," I said, the hope clear in my voice. "You can compose from anywhere."

He was quiet another moment. "It's not that. It's...I *know* L.A. I know the streets and the stores, how to get places, where to go for things. I have people who read contracts for me and restaurants where I know what to order. I work with conductors who know my style, what they consider my quirks, and are comfortable interpreting the things I don't write on my scores. It'd be...starting all over again in so many ways. I'd be dependent and working with two languages I can't read, instead of just one."

He feels safe there. Safe from the discovery of being illiterate. Safety can be a type of prison, though, too. A wall to hide behind. "You did great when we went away for the weekend, though. You'd never been to any of those places."

"I did well because Nick helped me."

"Nick...he knows?" I asked.

"Yeah."

I was surprised. I'd gotten the impression he hadn't shared it with anyone except me. But of course there would have to be a few people who knew...his trusted friends, perhaps even his secretary, the people he hired who knew to be discreet...Still, to have to depend on so many people instead of yourself, what a burden to carry.

"You can learn to read, Callen. You are not hopeless because your father said you were. Stop repeating his words. *Prove* he was wrong." *Fight. Go to battle even though you're afraid.*

"And if I can't? Will that prove he was right?" He rolled away from me, turning onto his back and staring at the ceiling.

I watched him in the low light, the beauty of his profile, the tense way he held his jaw. So that was it. That was the rub. He was terrified to try, terrified all those words that rang in his head would be corroborated by his inability to learn, even now. *Oh, Callen.*

"He was wrong," I whispered. "I wish I could prove it to you."

He sighed, turning toward me again, his fingers running through my hair until I sighed as well. "What have we gotten ourselves into, Princess Jessie?"

"We find ourselves in a treacherous land," I whispered, teasing. He chuckled, leaning his forehead against mine. "Fraught with swamps to swallow us up and quicksand that can suck a man under in three minutes flat."

"What will we do?"

"Have faith, Prince Callen."

He let out another gust of breath, pulling me close again. "That was the part I was never very good at."

* * *

In the year of our Lord 1429, on the twenty-seventh day of October

I am shaking as I write this, and yet the most profound sense of peace fills me.

Olivier and I stole away for a time, and as we were walking back toward camp, the subject of Jehanne came up. "You don't like that she's here," I accused. He denied it, saying that he is happy for any and all inspiration for his men. "But you don't believe that she is divinely led?" I asked.

He faced me and said, "No, I don't. But if they do, does it really matter?" I had no answer for that, though my heart felt heavy and troubled.

We walked in silence for a short while, each deep in our own thoughts, when the captain suddenly pulled me back and put his finger to his lips, as if he'd heard something or someone. We paused, and when we both peered through a break in the trees, we saw Jehanne, her head tipped back and her eyes closed. I was stricken with a sudden sense of... stillness, of something which I find difficult to explain. I could tell Olivier felt it, too, for he was watching similarly, with a look of stunned bewilderment on his face. It was as if the area where she stood was filled with a light that held no brightness, no glow, only... serenity, a deep, loving calm. It felt like a blessing, and it made me want to step forward, to

bathe in it, to become part of it. And yet I didn't under-
stand it either, and I held tightly to the captain's hand
as he held tightly to mine. Jehanne's lips were moving
as if she were talking to someone, and she smiled, turn-
ing and walking back toward camp.

My mind felt foggy with awe, but strangely, I didn't
feel like I required answers. I knew we'd witnessed
something miraculous, but there was no proof other
than the faith in my heart. And that was enough.

The next day, time seemed to move at a turtle's pace. Before
now, I had found it so easy to lose myself in my work, fascinated
by the story unfolding in front of my eyes, by the questions it
posed, by the wonder it invoked. But though Callen and I had
spoken about one of us moving to be closer to the other, neither
of us seemed courageous enough to take that leap. And so we
were left with mere days together.

I was so scared that once Callen left and we were apart, any
feelings he'd developed for me would fade. It caused my heart to
ache because I knew my own feelings would be far, far less fleeting. And yet, if that were the case, if Callen's feelings for me *were*
quick to dim, I guessed that would answer whether he did actually care about me *enough*.

I'd been thinking more and more about my mother lately, that
old wound surfacing as I wrestled with my insecurities about
Callen. When she'd told us she had cancer, I pictured that tu-
mor inside her to be the product of all the pent-up anguish she'd
carried for years over my father's affairs. It was like the physical
representation of all his sins, yet *she* alone had carried them and
took them on as her own.

I would never live that way. Not again. I wanted a man who

would fight for me, who would slay dragons for me, and whose love I could count on to be as steady and unchanging as the stars.

I was desperate for Callen to be that man, but I wondered if he was too damaged, too bent on self-destruction. If he wasn't willing to fight for himself, his own battles, perhaps he wouldn't be able to fight for me either.

In the year of our Lord 1430, on the fourth day of March

Today's battle was expected to be an easy victory but, in fact, it was a horror. I was needed outside camp, where the injured and the dead were being carried— a seemingly never-ending parade of blood and misery. The nearby blasts and screams rang in my ears so that I thought I might go insane with terror. A victory was secured, but by the time the battle had ended, my heart was so battered by fear that Olivier and Jehanne would not return that I could hardly bear it.

I waited at the edge of the road for them, and when I saw Olivier on his horse, I was not able to disguise my relief, and sobbing, I ran to him. He swore savagely as he scooped me onto his horse, turning immediately onto a side path that veered off the main road. I was crying and he was cursing and we were both kissing, and I do believe perhaps our minds were lost for a time, so desperate were we both to confirm the safety of the other.

"You came too close to the battlefield," he said angrily through kisses. "This is madness! I can't worry about you that way. It will get me killed, do you understand?"

I shivered in his arms, crying harder, wanting to

merge our bodies into one so that I knew well and
truly that he was alive and unharmed. "Take me somewhere, Olivier, somewhere there is only us and nothing
else. No war, no battlefield, no blood nor screams of the
dying."

He sounded so pained as he asked, "Are you sure?"

"Yes," I practically cried. I needed this, needed him.

He swore again and then said, "You won't be able to
go back. You'll be ruined."

I laughed, and it sounded crazed. "I am already ruined. This war has ruined me. The terror has ruined
me. The questions that have no answers have ruined
me. Make me whole again, Olivier. That is what I
want."

He held me close as we galloped away, for hours it
seemed, my heart calming as I lay back against him. He
rode us far away, and I knew it was to give me time to
change my mind, but it only made clearer the rightness
of my decision. I loved him. My heart belonged to him.
And here there were no rules except those governed by
God. Here, riding through this field of wildflowers on a
horse that had carried my love to battle, there were no
strictures of society, only the wild beating of our hearts
and the knowledge that if something was done in love
it could not be judged wrong. Here there were no assurances, and yet there were answers all the same.

We came to a stream, where Olivier tied his horse
and left him to drink his fill and graze on the sweet
grass that grew on the bank. From there we walked
to a cave that sat at the top of a hill, almost hidden
in the rock, and he told me, "If we get separated, if

you're lost, come here when the moon is new, just as it is tonight. From this moment, this place is ours."

"Yes," I agreed. "This place is ours."

"What do you want, Adélaïde?" he asked, as if giving me one final chance to deny him.

I kissed him and whispered against his lips, "I want to live fiercely and without regret. I want you, Captain Olivier Durand."

And with those words, Olivier first pulled me tight and then laid down a thin blanket that had been atop his saddle and his jacket over that. And for a time, in the mouth of that cave—our cave—where we could still see the stars, the war paused, the battle cries hushed, and there was only us. There was only that same peaceful stillness. There was only love.

Adélaïde! Her name was Adélaïde. Breathless with excitement, I e-mailed Dr. Moreau immediately and then texted Ben, who was out on an errand. I sat there in the quiet for a few minutes, repeating her name in my head, somehow feeling even closer to her. *Adélaïde.*

Midmorning I went to the courtyard where Ben and I usually ate our lunch together, needing a change of scenery and some fresh air after spending hours inside a windowless room. I thought about the piece I'd translated earlier. *There was only love*, Adélaïde had written, and it had caused a pang of yearning in my heart. I'd moved on in my translating, but I kept coming back to that line. I wanted the same. With Callen. I wanted our boxcar or our small room at the inn, our own version of the cave where Olivier and Adélaïde were able to leave the world behind. But I wanted more than stolen hours or weekends. So much more. *Have faith*, I'd told him, but in truth, I was having trouble holding on to my own.

It wasn't lunchtime yet, but I decided to stretch my legs and clear my head. I'd tried to call Frankie that morning, but she was already at work and likely would be busy all day as she worked around the clock to get samples ready for an upcoming runway show.

I strolled around the perimeter of the space, trailing my hand along the wall. Climbing jasmine grew up the side of the château, and I breathed in its sweet fragrance, closing my eyes for a moment and listening to the birds. I heard footsteps and turned to see Ben coming up the stairs, obviously having just returned. "Hey, you all right?"

I nodded. "I'm fine. I'm just…having a little trouble concentrating today." I gave him a wry smile. "She's describing the landscape in the piece I'm translating now. It's slow going."

Ben smiled. "Hey, it's a momentous day, though. We know her name. Do you think we can discover more about who she was?"

"I hope so. Dr. Moreau seemed excited about it, too, when he e-mailed me back. That one little word buried in an entry and now we know what to call her."

"Yes. Adélaïde," he murmured before smiling again. "Yeah, seems to suit her."

We were both quiet for a moment, and then Ben tilted his head, looking at me more closely. "So, despite the earlier excitement of discovering Adélaïde's name, what you're translating right now is mundane and you needed a break. You sure that's all it is? You look a little…blue."

As I stared into his concerned eyes, I felt my expression crumble. I sat down heavily on the bench behind me. "You're right, I am."

"Is it that guy who's staying here? Callen Hayes, right? The composer?"

"Yeah. I'm sorry. We're here to do a job, and I'm not—"

"We all have lives, Jessica. We can't put them on hold because it would be more convenient. I'm sure Adélaïde and Olivier would say the same thing." He sat down next to me.

I smiled. "Yes, they would, wouldn't they? It *would* be more convenient to press pause for a little while whenever we wished." Plus, it would give me time to figure out a solution. If only life worked that way.

He tilted his head. "I'm a good listener."

"I don't want to bore you."

"Jessica, anything that gets me out of that room for a few minutes is more than welcome, trust me. Bore me, please."

I laughed. The truth was, sitting in that room translating Adélaïde's story these last weeks had brought a feeling of camaraderie with Ben. We worked well together, and there was an ease between us. So I took a breath and gave him the short version of my history with Callen and the general state of our current situation. Naturally, I left out the fact that Callen was illiterate; that wasn't my secret to share.

"I have to admit that I was...surprised to find out you're dating someone, ah..."

"Like him?"

He grimaced. "I don't mean that to sound bad. It's just that he has a reputation as a partier and you seem more like the homebody type."

He wasn't wrong. "I know. On the surface we do seem all wrong for each other."

"I guess on the surface Adélaïde and Captain Olivier Durand seemed all wrong for each other, too."

I glanced at him. "But we don't know how that story ends yet."

"True. Bad example."

I laughed. Ben hadn't necessarily offered any advice, but his listening to my story made me feel better, and just purging some of it was a relief. Ben was a genuinely decent guy, and I appreciated the friendship we'd developed while working together so closely.

"Why don't *you* have a woman who's causing you heartache so I can return the favor?"

He laughed. "Because I spend too much time in dusty, windowless rooms."

I grinned. "Speaking of which…"

"Yeah." He sighed. "We should get back."

He helped me up from the bench, and I gave him a quick hug, thankful for his friendship and that he'd taken the time to listen. As we were walking back toward the steps, I saw movement on one of the balconies and glanced up, swearing I saw a man with dark hair duck back inside.

* * *

In the year of our Lord 1430, on the twenty-third day of May

Oh, dear Lord in heaven. I was on my knees for hours begging you to deliver Jehanne and Olivier to safety, and it does not seem your will. Word came that Jehanne was thrown off her horse during battle and the Burgundians took her captive. The men brought the news back after hours and hours of the torturous waiting and praying. I looked for Olivier in the line of returning soldiers, and he was nowhere to be found, and when I demanded the men take me to where the fight occurred to look for him, they said it was unsafe and insisted I return to camp.

I believe they know of my disguise and I do not feel safe among them without Olivier watching out for me. I found a horse and rode to town despite their warnings, my heart racing to the beat of the horse's galloping hooves, and I walked among the dead and dying still left on the battlefield.

The pain that wrenched my heart and the bile that burned my throat was not only for all the blood spilled in the street, but for the aching terror I carried. I did not see Olivier and know not where he is, or if his body has been carried away. His beloved body. Oh, dear God, please help him. Help Jehanne. My heart is a dark, empty shell to know they are in such peril. And please, dear Lord, shine your guiding light upon me so that I may know my role in this tragedy and act only for your good.

"And so it begins," I murmured to Ben, the sadness I felt inside infusing my tone.

He looked up from his work. "What's that?"

"Jehanne's been captured."

He sat back in his chair. "Ah. Yes, the beginning of the end indeed."

And Olivier...where was he? My heart beat hollowly for Adélaïde's pain.

Ben and I finished up a little later, and I trudged upstairs, tired, saddened by what I'd translated, but energized to see

Callen, too. He had told me about the interview Larry had set up for him in one of the upstairs meeting rooms, and I knew he was getting ready for that. It'd take only an hour at most, he'd said, and then we'd go to dinner, something intimate, something special. Another reminder that our time together was dwindling away, the sand flowing ever faster through the hourglass.

I'd planned to head to my own room and take a quick shower and change out of my work clothes into something a little more special.

As I passed the open doorway to the large bar/lounge area, I was surprised when I heard my name called. And then I noticed Larry sitting in an upholstered chair that was part of an intimate furniture grouping near the window. I hesitated, my steps slowing, unsure if I should simply nod my head and keep walking or if I should enter the lounge and say hi. Hi? *Well, hello. Our first meeting was sort of horrible, with your wife standing there in her underwear and all, but great to see you again.*

Larry smiled and stood, gesturing for me to come inside. I turned, walking slowly toward him. "Jessica, right?" he asked as I approached the seating area.

"Yes." I shook my head, trying not to look embarrassed but having a feeling I was failing. "I'm sorry, Mr.—"

"Larry." He gestured at the blue silk love seat, and I sat as he took his own seat. "We met under very awkward circumstances," he said, shooting me a regretful look. I released a breath, unable to help feeling bad for him. I'd been upset, but he... Well, that whole scene had to have devastated him. I could relate in a sense, having been an up-close witness to scenes like that too many times to count.

"Yes. I'm sorry."

"You have nothing to be sorry for. Callen and I have buried the hatchet. The issue is between my wife and me." A cocktail waitress came by, and Larry looked at me questioningly.

"Oh, no," I said. "Nothing for me."

"One drink?" he asked. "To replace a bad first meeting with a better one?"

I smiled. "Well, all right. Just one. A glass of chardonnay, please."

Larry ordered another drink, and the cocktail waitress turned to fill our order. "Are you going to Callen's interview?"

I nodded. "Yes."

"Good." He studied me for a moment. "He mentioned knowing you as a child. A funny stroke of fate that you met again all these years later."

Fate again. "Yes. Funny." The cocktail waitress brought our drinks, and I took a sip of mine, the cool alcohol spreading through my veins and relaxing my limbs. I sat back on the couch.

"Long day?"

"Yes, actually. A long week." I smiled and told him a little bit about the work I was doing in the Loire Valley. He'd read about the find, rare for someone not in the field, so it was enjoyable to answer his questions. The awkwardness faded, and as I sipped the wine I relaxed even more.

"I can see why you've become Callen's latest muse." *Latest muse.* I definitely didn't like the word *latest*, and I wasn't sure whether I liked the word *muse* either. It implied that I alone was responsible for his creativity, and Larry's words were yet another affirmation that my place in Callen's life would be temporary. "I know his secret, you know."

My head snapped up. *Oh.* Larry took a casual sip of his drink. Well, of course Larry must know. He had to be one of the people who helped Callen manage contracts, read e-mails, business letters... "I, yes, it's very hard for him. He's so ashamed of it."

Larry shook his head. "He shouldn't be."

"I agree. A learning disability is nothing to be ashamed of. Just because he couldn't learn to read as a child doesn't mean he can't learn now. There are so many advancements in..." My words trailed off at the shocked look that passed over Larry's face. Something inside me dropped to my feet. "Weren't you...? Isn't that...?"

"Callen's illiterate?"

Heat flooded my face, and I swayed where I sat, setting my almost empty glass of wine on the table so I wouldn't drop it. "I thought that's what you were talking about," I whispered. *Oh God. Oh no. What did I do?*

Larry looked off out the window for a moment, as if going over something in his head. When he looked back at me, his eyes had lit up with realization. "Yes, it makes sense," he muttered, almost to himself. "I was referring to his writer's block, by the way."

Oh God.

"Please," I begged, shaking my head, "please don't say anything, Larry. He—he trusted me with that information, and—"

"Relax, Jessica. I won't say a word."

I managed a smile and nodded. "Thank you. He would"—I sucked in a shaky breath—"be so upset." *Mortified. Angry. Take your pick.*

Larry smiled, and for some reason, discomfort slithered down my spine. I studied his face for a moment, but worried I was overreacting. "I should go," I said, standing. "I have to get ready for dinner."

"And the interview," he said, smiling and standing as well. *The interview, right.*

I nodded. "Thank you for the drink, Larry, and the conversation. And thank you for your understanding about—"

"Of course. I know how important trust is, Jessica."

I paused, his words, the tone in his voice, causing a jolt of unease, but he turned away from me, so I turned as well, making my way out of the bar. When I got to the doorway, I looked back at Larry, but he was already gone.

CHAPTER TWENTY-ONE

JESSICA

I could hear the buzz from the meeting room all the way down the hall and moved toward it, my heels clicking on the stone floor. I took a deep breath. I'd showered, changed into a navy-blue fitted cocktail dress, and put on a pair of strappy, silver heels. I'd managed to look put together, but inside I still felt a restless panic over having so carelessly spilled Callen's secret to Larry. Of all the irresponsible things to do. Why couldn't I have slowed down and listened instead of just blurting it out like that?

Rather than panicking completely, I tried to consider what I'd read before leaving work earlier. This situation with Callen and my loose tongue was something that would work out. Poor Adélaïde was experiencing something utterly hopeless.

I pulled the heavy door to the meeting room open and stepped inside. There were four or five rows of chairs set up in the middle of the floor, most of them already filled, and at the front of the room two chairs for Callen and the interviewer. I glanced at the cameras set up to the side, where the cameraman looked to be testing the equipment.

"Jessie." I heard Callen's voice and turned, my heart expanding to see his large smile as he moved toward me. He slowed, his head moving up and down as he took in my dress. "Wow."

He was freshly shaven, and his hair was combed back from his face, the angles of his jaw and cheekbones and the golden cast of his skin on full display. He was so beautiful that my breath hitched, and for a second I had the urge to cry. The feeling startled me, and I put my hand to my chest as if to tamp the feeling down. "Same to you."

He smiled. "This shouldn't take long. I made reservations in town." He took my hands in his, his eyes growing soft. "I'm looking forward to getting you alone."

"Me, too."

"Hey, guys," Nick greeted, walking up to us. "You ready?" he asked Callen, nodding toward the camera.

Callen shrugged. "Oh yeah. I've done a thousand of these. Same questions every time." He pretended to hold a microphone to his mouth. "Where *do* you get your inspiration?" He tilted his head, raising his eyebrows. "Tell us about your writing process."

Nick laughed. "You'd rather them ask if you were a tree, what kind of tree would you be?"

"I'd take anything to mix it up a bit. Japanese cherry by the way."

A man came up to Callen and tapped him on the arm, and he turned. "Ready?"

"Yeah." He turned back to Nick and me. "See you afterward."

I followed Nick to two chairs near the front, and we took

our seats. Final adjustments were made with the cameras, and I watched as microphones were clipped on Callen's shirt and the interviewer's jacket. The interviewer was an older man with graying hair and a small, round pot belly that strained the buttons of his shirt. Having lived in Paris for the last year, I recognized him as the host of a tabloid-type show that I'd watched once or twice but ended up tuning out because of the smarmy feel to it. He liked "gotcha" questions that left the interviewee floundering for answers. A brick settled in my stomach, and my hands turned icy.

Please ask him about being a tree. Please, please.

"You okay?" Nick asked, glancing at me worriedly.

I nodded. I was being paranoid. Later, when Callen and I went to dinner, I'd confess my slipup so he was aware that Larry knew. It was the right thing to do. I prayed that even if he was mad and upset, he would understand it was an accident. I'd never hurt him on purpose.

"*Bonsoir, mesdames et messieurs,*" the interviewer said, turning to the camera. "*Je m'appelle Cyril Sauvage, et voici Le Grand Soir.*" He gave a crooked grin to the camera and waited a few beats before nodding to Callen and giving a short introduction in English. I knew from the time I'd briefly watched him interview an English-speaking guest that subtitles would appear at the bottom of the screen for the French viewers.

"Callen—may I call you Callen?"

"Of course." Callen looked so handsome sitting there under the stage lights behind him, his posture casual, an easygoing smile on his face.

"Good, good. And please, call me Cyril." He brought his right ankle to his left knee, leaning forward. "Your musical scores have been called emotionally powerful, triumphant, and haunting. As I was preparing for this interview, I came across my favorite review of your work. I think it encapsulates the feel of your music perfectly." He reached down beside him and picked up a piece of paper. "Would you mind reading it to our guests?" he asked, handing it to Callen.

My pulse jumped, my heart picking up a staccato beat. Callen took the piece of paper, his smile faltering slightly before he handed it back, smiling bigger. "Please, Cyril, you do the honors. I find it embarrassing to read my own praise."

Cyril laughed, pushing the paper back toward Callen. "Nonsense. It's only two short lines."

Oh. My. God.

With a sick shudder, I realized what was going on here. I glanced to the place where Larry was standing, leaning against the wall, his arms crossed. *He didn't. Surely not.* He looked at me and smiled, winking. *No, no, no. You miserable bastard.* My throat burned as if I'd actually screamed the words.

Shaking, I looked back at Callen, forcing my breathing to calm. He could handle this. He'd been in sticky situations before. He knew how to change the subject so no one suspected.

Nick seemed to have frozen next to me. He was obviously tense as he waited for Callen to squeeze out of this uncomfortable situation. Only Nick didn't know that Cyril was most likely setting a trap, because his question hadn't innocently put Callen in the position he was in. It had been orchestrated. Purposeful.

"Sorry, Cyril, I left my reading glasses at home." He turned to the camera and smiled, boyish and sweet, as he shrugged his shoulders. Women everywhere—eighty percent of the viewing audience—were swooning and had completely forgotten what the question was.

Callen looked back at Cyril, and the expression on Cyril's face was suddenly wolfish, his eyes narrowed and his teeth showing in the semblance of a smile that somehow looked more like a growl. "Reading glasses? Why, Callen Hayes, isn't the real truth that you don't need *reading glasses*, because you can't read at all?"

For a brief moment Callen looked confused, but then his face went white, his lips lifting slightly but falling, as if he'd attempted to smile—to laugh off Cyril's question—but hadn't been able to. His eyes darted around, as if looking for an escape.

A very soft, strange groaning sound reverberated in my ears, and I realized it had come from me. Nick reached over and took my hand, squeezing it in his. I swallowed back the lump rising in my throat. "This is my fault," I choked so softly only Nick could hear.

Before Nick could reply, Callen said, "I'm not sure where you got your information, Cyril, but—"

Cyril laughed, a booming sound that startled me. "It's easy enough to disprove me. Just read the lines." He pointed at the piece of paper still clutched in Callen's hand and then chuckled again, leaning forward. "And if you can't, why not admit it here, among friends? France, and America of course, wants to know how a completely uneducated, illiterate man like yourself composes such renowned music. Why, it's inspirational!"

Callen looked as if he'd gone into some strange trance, staring at the camera, his eyes wide, his body rigid. I wanted to cry for him. To have his most protected secret broadcasted like this in front of... who knew how many watched the show?

Nick let go of my hand, turning toward me. "How is this your fault?"

I let out a small whimper. "I told Larry."

Nick swore softly and looked over at Larry. Callen suddenly looked away from the camera, right at Nick, and then followed Nick's gaze to Larry, who was smirking as he stood against the wall. Callen's eyes widened as if realization was dawning. But then a look of confusion moved across his face as he looked down, maybe considering how Larry had found out. *Oh God.* His eyes moved slowly to Nick, who was now looking at me, and then settled on my face. He must have been able to tell by my expression that I was the guilty party because a look of such blatant betrayal overtook his expression that I flinched.

"How could you?" Nick gritted out.

I didn't mean to. I didn't know if the words even came out. I felt dizzy with the horror of this situation, woozy with regret.

Callen stood up and tore his microphone off, his hands visibly shaking. He let it fall to the floor.

"Callen, don't be so quick to leave." Cyril stood up, too, putting a hand on Callen's shoulder. "You shouldn't be ashamed of being illiterate. We all want to know how you've managed as long as—"

Callen pushed at Cyril, and the talk show host fell backward, landing with a whoosh of breath into the chair he'd just been occupying. Callen walked past him, not sparing me or Nick a glance. He still looked stricken, his eyes wide with humiliation, his skin pasty except for the two high points of bright red color on his cheekbones. He wove out of the room as if he could barely control his own limbs.

The room burst into an uproar, people who had been staring in silent shock at what was going on in front of them suddenly turning to their neighbors and expressing their surprise. Others were scrawling in their notepads, reporters who would now spread the story even before Cyril's show aired. *Oh God. Oh God.*

Nick stood, moving to go after Callen, and I wobbled to my

feet, too, grabbing on to Nick's shirt. He turned, glaring at me. "It was a mistake, Nick, please..."

"Tell it to him. He's the one who has a knife sticking out of his back."

I sank back in my chair as if my bones had suddenly turned to liquid.

But when I spotted Larry smiling and talking to Cyril in whispered tones near the front, the rage that overtook me was swift and severe, reanimating my body and giving me the strength to stand again, to move toward them with single-minded pursuit.

"You're a disgusting snake."

Larry turned, his expression unsurprised, one side of his mouth lifting in a mocking smile. "It's just fair play, Jessica. One good turn deserves another. Did you really think I wouldn't use it?"

"A game? Is that what that was?" I couldn't fathom these people.

Larry shrugged. "A game? Sure. Do you think Callen thought fucking my wife was anything more than that?"

I flinched. I truly didn't know. And yet I believed in him. I believed that the man who had involved himself in those games was not the true Callen Hayes.

I shook my head. "What you've done... you've potentially ruined his career, and your own in the process."

He laughed. "*My* career? Do you think *he's* my only client? *My* career has nothing to do with this. It wasn't me who outed Callen as an illiterate fraud. It was Cyril Sauvage. Where he gets his information is anyone's guess. Maybe he got it from *you*. But don't worry—he won't expose his source." His smile grew. "As for Callen's career, who knows? I was going to cut him loose anyway. He was becoming a washed-up drunk who couldn't write a jingle to save his ass."

God, he was vile. I was shaking again. "You're detestable. I pity you," I said, and turned and walked away as fast as my feet could carry me. I had to get to Callen. I had to try to explain and beg his forgiveness.

I barely remembered the trip upstairs, my mind reeling with the best thing to say, the right words to use. When I rounded the corner into the corridor where his room was, I took a deep breath, knocking loudly on his door. I waited, my heart racing, but there was no answer, no sound from within. I knocked one more time, stepping back and peering under the door. The door was almost completely flush with the carpet, but I thought I'd see a light from within if he was there. Had he not come back here? Where else would he have gone? Nick's room, maybe? Only I didn't know which one that was.

I pulled my phone out of my evening bag and dialed Callen's number, but it went straight to voice mail. Sighing, I knocked on his door one last time, listening closely for any sounds. When I was met only with silence, I turned and headed back toward my room.

For a little while I sat in the chair by my window, staring at the wall, reliving what had happened in my head. I called Callen's phone several more times only to be sent straight to voice mail again and again. Maybe he *was* in Nick's room. Or maybe Nick had taken him out somewhere. That would be for the best, probably. A friend to lend support, to make Callen laugh, help him see the bright side of this.

The bright side.

What was that? No more hiding. I almost laughed. I'd suggested it myself and then unthinkingly made it happen against his will. He must hate me.

It was going to be hard enough to part as it was, but now...to part this way. I couldn't bear it. I put my head in my hands, but the tears wouldn't come. I felt hollow, racked with self-loathing.

Finally, unable to sit for even a second longer, I left my room, walking through the château. The meeting room was empty now, the chairs put away, and though there were people in the bar, Callen wasn't there. I walked outside the front doors of the château and took the path around the building, walking slowly past the courtyard where Ben and I usually ate lunch.

I could hear people at the pool, talking, glasses clinking, a few shrieks of feminine laughter. Those people had something to laugh about. Callen wouldn't be there.

I meandered through the garden, getting lost a few times but not caring. I remembered the rose garden and choked back a sob. When I was back on the main path, I picked up my pace, following the cobblestones to a back door.

There were signs that pointed toward the main lobby, so I followed them, winded when I finally stepped into the familiar lobby area, moving quickly toward the elevators. Up, up, to the top floor, where I stepped off and again made my way toward Callen's room.

This time I saw a beam of light under his door and blew out a relieved breath. I knocked, my heart hammering again as I waited. The walk had calmed me, but standing here, my nerves were buzzing and my hands felt clammy. I ran them down my hips, realizing I was still wearing the cocktail dress I'd put on earlier. A lifetime ago, or so it seemed.

The door swung open and Callen was standing there, his hair wet, as if he'd just gotten out of the shower. His expression was blank, devoid of any warmth, and his eyes looked slightly glassy, as if he'd been drinking. "Callen," I breathed. "I've been calling you. I—"

"This isn't a good time, Jessie."

"We have to talk, Callen. I have to explain what happened earlier and—"

"Jessie," he said, the tone of his voice startling me so that I jumped. "I have company." *Company?* For a moment I didn't process his words, and then a blonde stepped from the bedroom into the sitting room behind him, craning her neck to see me. She was wearing a white bikini and a towel tied around her hips, as if they'd just come from the pool. *The pool.* The laughter.

Oh. Oh God.

My stomach dropped to my feet, and I brought my arms around my waist, hugging myself.

"Callen?" the girl called. I recognized her now. She was the same woman he'd been sitting next to in the bar the other night, the same woman I'd seen him with the first night I'd arrived here. The one who'd whined about him not joining her in the hot tub. Seemed she'd gotten some water time with him after all.

"Don't do this," I whispered, my voice full of all the anguish I felt, my heart aching.

"Sorry." He started closing the door, and desperation raced through me. I raised my hand, pushing at the smooth wood.

"Please! *Please* don't do this!" I repeated on a desperate cry, banging my hand on the door one more time.

For a moment he looked startled, but then he smiled coldly. "Turning into your mother already?"

I stumbled backward as if he'd hit me. It felt like he had. I shook my head, a denial, but of what?

I hurt everywhere,
My skin.
My bones.
My soul.
Callen closed the door in my face and my heart shattered.

CHAPTER TWENTY-TWO

CALLEN

The door clicked shut and the world fell out from under me. I clenched my eyes closed, taking a moment to get my bearings before turning to the girl—I still didn't know her fucking name—who smiled and began approaching me. But whatever was on my face caused her to halt, her smile slipping.

"You need to go."

A flash of irritation lit her eyes. "*Go?* I just got here. I thought you got rid of *her* for a reason."

Her.

"Yeah, well…" I narrowed my eyes in concentration, trying to remember the girl's name so I could use it. *Laura? Lulu?*

She must have realized what I was doing because she bit out, "Layla."

"Right, Layla. I changed my mind. I want to be alone."

I want to get drunk and pass out.

I want to be numb.

Layla put her hands on her hips and glared. "Think hard before you throw me out, Callen Hayes."

I massaged my head. A wicked headache was pounding in my skull. "I'm not throwing you out, Layla. I'm asking you to leave."

Get out of here.

As much as I hadn't wanted to be alone earlier, I now craved it badly. I was tempted to pick her up and chuck her out the door. The restraint I was hanging on to was the last bit of patience I had left in my body.

"Fine," she growled. "But this is it! If I see you around the hotel tomorrow, I'm going to ignore you."

Promise? "It's the best thing to do, trust me."

"I see that now."

She marched to where she'd dropped her pool bag on the floor next to the love seat and picked it up, swinging it onto her shoulder. Without a word, she walked toward the door, bumping me as she passed by. I took a step backward and then watched her open the door and slam it behind her. *Thank God.*

I walked the few steps to the love seat and sank down onto it, leaning my head back and gripping the hair at the front of my scalp. I stared at the ceiling, unseeing. Now that I was alone, in the quiet of my room, the alcohol buzz beginning to fade, the anguish crept back in like a prowler slipping through an open basement window.

I clenched my eyes shut as the memories of the interview assaulted me, the humiliation and shame I'd felt at being exposed in front of a roomful of strangers, in front of the world eventually. And there was nothing I could do. "Sue that man!" Nick had said as he'd followed me from the room. But for what?

Defamation? What he'd said was true. And what did it matter now anyway? I'd seen the reporters in the front row, scribbling furiously on their notepads, writing down each detail of my stupidity, my now very public shame. I'd spotted the cell phones held discreetly as guests recorded the moment. I could try to sue Cyril Sauvage not to air the interview, but what would that achieve? *More press. More attention. More humiliation.*

Why did you do it, Jessie? Had she confided my secret to Larry because it was a way to force me to address it? Had she seen *him* as an ally in her efforts to make me try again to learn to read? And did it even matter? Whatever her reason, I had been able to tell she hadn't wanted it revealed that way. The look on her face...she'd been almost as horrified as I was. Almost. She hadn't meant to hurt me publicly, and yet that had been the result. Tonight, because of her, in front of a roomful of strangers, I'd been that same little boy sitting at the kitchen table, being told to read—*just read*—when I couldn't...*I couldn't.*

She'd told fucking Larry I was illiterate. *Larry* of all people. She'd stood in this very room and seen the hatred in his eyes toward me. Was *that* why? Did she feel some sort of warped connection to Larry, the betrayed spouse? Did he represent her mother in that scenario, and I, her father? Yes, I'd been the villain that day—even I admitted it—but Larry was no prince.

But neither was I, and really, wasn't that what it *kept* coming back to with me and Jessie?

I'd watched her from my balcony this past week as she'd sat in the sunshine with that guy she worked with. They'd laughed and talked as they ate lunch, sometimes flipping through a book and reading aloud to each other as my gut clenched with jealousy and the despondency of knowing I'd never have that with her no matter how hard I tried. And then today it'd looked as if she was crying (over me?) and he'd taken her in his arms for a moment. It'd made me sick, and I'd turned away. And yet still...*still,* I'd held on to the morsel of hope that maybe we could work something out. But what? In reality, *what?* She wanted more from me than I could give, and she was *right* to want more.

Maybe what she'd done hadn't been entirely purposeful, but the wound was deep and excruciating and it would bleed for a long, long time. It had told me exactly what it would feel like to saddle Jessie with a fraud like me, to place her in what would now be a public spotlight surrounding my illiteracy. And so I'd made a *point* to be cruel and vicious, and there was no turning back from the way I'd dismissed her tonight.

Jessie and I were over.

I couldn't stay here another day. I sat up and pulled my phone from my pocket, tapping the phone icon next to Nick's picture.

"Hey, Cal." Nick sounded grim, tired.

"Would you be against checking out tonight?"

There was a beat of silence. "If that's what you need, buddy."

"Yeah, I...It's probably not a good idea to be in a place where the press know how to find me. I wouldn't be surprised if there was a horde of them in the lobby tomorrow morning."

"You're probably right."

Of course, they'd know how to find me in L.A., too. I wanted to dig a hole and burrow deep into the darkness like a frightened squirrel. "We could bum around Paris for a few days."

"I'm with you, man, anywhere I can get Internet access."

The emotion I'd suppressed for the last couple of hours flooded into my chest, clogging my throat. "I don't want to take advantage of you, Nick. I—"

"You're not, Cal. I'll tell you if I need to get back, okay? I'll call for a car. See you downstairs in half an hour?"

"Yeah, okay." I let out a shaky breath. "See you then."

After a few minutes I peeled myself off the couch and went to pack my suitcase, throwing things in with no concern whatsoever, even the damp swim trunks I'd taken off and left lying on the bathroom floor when I'd changed only a little while ago. It didn't matter. Nothing mattered. I felt like an empty shell that somehow still had the ability to ache.

I stared at the bed for a long moment, the memory of Jessie's sleeping form causing a sharp blade of pain to slice at the raw wound inside. I flinched, wanting to curl in on myself but forcing my body to turn instead and head for the door.

My half-written composition was on the desk, and I stuffed that into the front of my suitcase, wondering if I'd ever want to write music again, if there was anything left. Wondering if I had a career at all after today. Did I want one? I had enough money to survive for quite a while.

I made my way to the lobby, where Nick was waiting, and after a quick checkout, we got in the car Nick had arranged. As the driver pulled away from the curb. I didn't look back, not once.

"Where to, gentlemen?" the driver asked.

"Paris," Nick replied, giving me a wan smile. "Take us to la Ville Lumière."

I stared out the window. Yes, we were headed to the City of Light, and all I felt inside was darkness.

CHAPTER TWENTY-THREE

JESSICA

In the year of our Lord 1431, on the fourteenth day of May

I am numb as I walk through these days. My heart is broken, my soul shattered. I know not whether my beloved Olivier is alive or dead, and inside, my soul screams with misery, with the agony not knowing brings.

My father arranged for a kindly widow in the town of Compiègne to take me in, and here I have resided while waiting for Jehanne's trial. I know my father wanted me to stay as a final show of loyalty to the court and the favors that will be bestowed upon our family, including the arranged marriage to some titled stranger I do not love; however, this is where I belong. My father knows not of Olivier and I dare not tell him, nor ask for his assistance in garnering information on Olivier's status, for fear of what my father's reprisal might be. I yearn with every fiber of my being to search for Olivier, and pray that he is injured, but not dead, unable to come to me as I am unable to come to him. I find comfort in knowing that, for now, I am where I am meant to be, that it is with Jehanne I must stay. I know in my heart Olivier would want it thus and would advise that I do my duty, as promised, to serve Jehanne. But it is not only obligation that keeps me near to her, nor my father's directive, but friendship and love and a desire to alleviate her terror.

I meet with her as often as the guards will allow, and she is so frightened that I must be strong for her. Under threat of death she signed a confession and denied that she had ever received divine guidance. I must profess that the relief I felt was vast, but when I saw her and witnessed the way in which the denial tore at her heart, her very soul, I questioned whether I should feel any solace at all.

"Does not a lie of the soul cause more despair than death itself?" she asked me, and I could not disagree. She says she will retract her confession, that she let her fear guide her rather than God.

"But following God will get you killed," I declared.

Her face was pale and her hands shook as she answered, "Then that is what I was meant for." Before I could respond, she took my hands in hers and said, "Make me a promise. Live your life with joy and laughter. Do not take one second of it for granted. Live fiercely and without regret. For me."

"Maybe God wants me dead, too," I cried, filled with aching sorrow.

But Jehanne smiled in that soft way of hers and said, "No. God has other plans for you. Find your battle and fight it. Be brave and he will not desert you. Listen for him, though his voice be but a whisper on the wind, a birdsong, the deep feeling of rightness in your heart. Don't stop listening, my dear Adélaïde, and you will never, ever be alone."

I know not of God's reasoning, though I try to accept his will as she has taught me I must. But oh Lord in heaven, if she retracts as she says she will, they will burn her at the stake. A girl of only nineteen springs. My friend. And I cannot bear to watch it happen, though she says it is the only thing now that will free her from the chains.

The faint mustiness of my building's lobby combined with the sweet, yeasty smell of baking bread wafting from Mrs. Bertrand's apartment welcomed me home. I climbed the stairs slowly, hefting my suitcase behind me, and before I'd even reached the upstairs landing, our apartment door burst open and Frankie was there, squealing and holding her arms out.

I grinned, but once I'd dropped my suitcase and walked into her arms, the tears began to flow, and I was laughing and crying, a mixture of happiness and grief pouring from my body so swiftly I could barely control it.

I'd held myself together these last weeks at the château, working so long and so hard that I could only fall into bed at the end of the day. I'd been severely disappointed to learn that for me Adélaïde's story would end as she fearfully waited for her friend to face execution—an execution that history told me had most definitely been carried out. We had translated all the papers that had been found, and there were no more to indicate Adélaïde's fate. I wouldn't get the closure of knowing Adélaïde went on to live a happy life, would never know if she reunited with Captain Durand and whether or not their love story continued, or whether she was forced to marry another. It was another loss for me to grapple with. But life, I supposed, didn't always offer closure. I'd taken comfort in rereading Adélaïde's words, in experiencing once again the lessons she had to teach, as we'd gone over all the writings a second time, verifying and correcting where necessary. I'd let myself disappear into Adélaïde's world, into her words, shutting out the despair I felt at how my own love story had ended, the intense pain I felt whenever I recalled Callen's final cruel words. But now, in the security of my best friend's sympathetic arms, I finally allowed myself to feel.

"Oh, Jess," she crooned, squeezing me tighter and rocking us both back and forth. "My poor, sweet cabbage."

I sniffled and wiped at my tears, gathering myself enough to be led into our apartment. I sank down onto the couch, and Frankie went back into the hallway and grabbed the suitcase I'd completely forgotten about and brought it inside. "Water?" she asked.

I shook my head, wiping at my tear-streaked face. "No. I drank a bottle in the cab from the train station."

Frankie nodded, handing me a tissue so I could wipe my nose. "How was it, wrapping up the project?"

I nodded. "Good. Fine. I didn't really have to say goodbye to anyone since I'll see them all at the banquet dinner on Saturday."

"Only two days to find you the perfect dress."

I offered a small tip of my lips. "These are researchers and scientists, Frankie. They won't notice if I wear a grain sack."

Frankie raised a brow. "You doubt the genius of Clémence yet again."

I chuckled. "Never. I just think her genius might be wasted on them." Plus, I didn't know if I ever wanted to wear a Clémence Maillard dress again. They reminded me too much of Callen.

Callen.

After that night, that awful, awful night, my heartache and misery were buried under a layer of anger at his cruelty, at disgust for what he'd done. I hated myself for what I'd done to him, and I felt deeply ashamed at my error. But my mistake had been unintentional, and the second we'd had hurt and misunderstanding between us, Callen had turned directly to old habits: drinking and women. He had good reason for being unable to answer me when I'd asked about whether he was trustworthy or not. He'd proven to me what I feared most—I couldn't trust him.

And yet...despite my best efforts at lecturing my heart, it insisted on loving him anyway. Stupid, stupid, irrational heart.

Frankie was looking at me worriedly, as if she had followed my thoughts. "He's in Paris, you know," she said softly.

My heart twisted. "Who?" I whispered, though I knew from her tone she was talking about Callen.

"Callen," she confirmed.

My shoulders deflated. "Oh." I purposefully hadn't turned on the television, looked at the Internet on my phone, or picked up a publication of any sort. Frankie had told me the interview of Callen and Cyril Sauvage had been replayed continuously since it happened and written about in publications around the world. I didn't want to see any of it. Just the thought alone hurt and shamed me, and I could only imagine what it was doing to

Callen. Despite my anger and pain, I still managed to feel compassion for what he must be suffering.

Frankie pressed her lips together. "I thought you should know. He's been in all the newspapers, on the gossip sites..." She paused. "Looks like he's partying it up."

My eyes widened as I stared at her. He was...partying? *Oh.* A renewed burst of anger invigorated me, and I sat up. "Well, I'm glad to hear he's not taking what happened too hard."

Frankie's brow furrowed, and she shrugged. "He looks drunk in most pictures."

"Women hanging off him, I suppose," I muttered.

She bit her lip and nodded. "Yeah."

A spear of sorrow pierced my heart, but I gathered my inner strength—*my inner Adélaïde*—vowing not to crumble. If Adélaïde could remain strong through all she'd experienced, I could, too. I *would*.

* * *

"Wow," Frankie said as she came up behind me, where I stood before the mirror. "If those crusty researchers don't notice you in this, there's truly no hope for them."

I laughed, running my hands down the handmade, champagne-colored lace dress interwoven with gold beading. The lace pattern featured hundreds of roses, all intertwined, from the floor to the bodice, and there was a delicate gold belt at my waist. It was beyond stunning—a true work of art—and it hugged my body as if it had been made just for me.

When Frankie had first brought it home, I'd noticed the roses—they were subtle, and you had to look closely to discern the flower pattern at all—and I'd been tempted to reject it for that alone. But the longer I'd stared at it, something inside me had warmed. The roses…that weekend…it was a good memory, and despite how Callen and I ended, I wanted to hold that part of us close. Roses had scented that weekend, and now I would wear roses as I officially said goodbye to the Loire Valley *and* to him.

I would be brave despite my heartache. Though I would never learn the final pieces of her story, Adélaïde had taught me that. Jehanne herself had taught me that.

Frankie looked at me thoughtfully in the mirror, her eyes traveling from my gold strappy heels to my makeup to my twisted updo. "Something's missing."

I frowned, glancing back at the mirror. The only jewelry I had on was a pair of gold teardrop earrings. The neckline of the dress was too high to wear anything around my neck. "What?"

"Stay there." She turned and walked quickly out of the room, and I heard our apartment door open and close. I waited, confused, until she came back a minute later, breathing heavily from apparently running up the stairs, with a white rose in her hand. "Mrs. Bertrand's garden," she offered in explanation before bringing the rose to the back of my hair and clipping it in.

I turned, looking at the white flower pinned neatly in my hair.

"Perfect," she said.

The doorbell rang. "That must be Ben," I muttered, glancing at the clock and heading toward the door. Ben stood on the other side, handsome in a black tux.

"Wow," he said, his eyes sweeping over me. "You look incredible."

Frankie laughed from behind me, nudging my shoulder. "Told you." She stepped forward. "I'm Frankie."

Ben grinned. "Nice to meet you."

"Will you be up when I get back?" I asked as I walked into the hallway.

"God, I hope not. Have some fun," she said, smiling and winking.

I released a breath. "Okay. Night, Frankie."

Frankie waved, shutting the door.

Down on the street, a limo was waiting for us. "Ben. You didn't have to do this."

"I wanted to. We were in a dusty basement for a month. We deserve one night in high style, don't you think?"

I smiled. "Good point, and thank you."

Sparing no expense, the banquet dinner was held at one of the most luxurious hotels in Paris. Not only would the team I'd worked with in the Loire Valley be in attendance, but many top administrative staff members from the Louvre, as well as donors who had helped fund the project, would be there as well. Maybe I'd even make a connection that could lead to a permanent position.

The ride was relatively short, and when our limo pulled up in front of the hotel, I had to admit how decadent it felt when a doorman opened the door and took my hand to help me out.

Ben and I followed the line of people dressed in elegant evening wear entering the building and stepped into the massive foyer, resplendent in gold and marble, with glittering chandeliers hanging from the high ceilings and enormous vases of fragrant flowers everywhere. Roses, of course. *Naturally* the place would be decked out in roses. I sighed, a soft sound that I hoped Ben couldn't hear, and forced a smile to my lips.

Ben led me up the stairs to the ballroom, which was even more beautifully decorated, with draping white tablecloths on the long tables, candles set on mirrors to reflect the light, and tall, clear-bottomed vases that overflowed with roses and ivy. Everywhere I looked, soft lights glowed and sparkled, bouncing off the paneled walls. The entire space appeared magical. "It's beautiful," I breathed.

Ben nodded. "It is." He pointed toward the bar. "Do you want a drink?"

"Just water for now. I haven't eaten anything since breakfast, and I'll be drunk if I drink a glass of wine before dinner," I said on a laugh.

Once we had our drinks, we wandered out a side door that led to a sweeping balcony. A few people were milling about, but I didn't see anyone I knew.

As we moved to the edge of the balcony, Ben pointed off into the distance. "Look."

I turned my head and spotted the Eiffel Tower, just lighting up. I sighed with pleasure. "That sight will never get old."

He smiled, leaning on the balcony ledge and looking at me. "There's no city in the world more beautiful than Paris."

I nodded my agreement as I gazed at the sight of that famous tower, sparkling against the nighttime sky. "Do you ever consider moving here?" While we'd been working, I'd learned that Ben lived in Marseille, a city in southern France. He'd been recommended to Dr. Moreau because of his specialty, but he had a permanent job waiting for him at home.

His gaze lingered on me for a moment. "Sometimes. But I like living near my family, my brothers and sister and all their kids. I'd miss watching them grow up."

"You're close to them."

"Yes, very."

I nodded. How wonderful to have that kind of loving support. "You're lucky."

He considered me for a second. "I know. I don't take them for granted. What about you? Is your family still in California?"

"My dad and his new wife and my brother are, yes. But we're not...close." I did talk to my brother occasionally, but mostly about superficial things. Both of us had sought to be anywhere but at our house for most of our childhoods and then our teen years. Our absence from home didn't exactly lead to a close relationship.

Sometimes the beginning of love is just a simple matter of proximity.

The words Madame Leclaire had said as Callen and I had left her inn that rainy weekend caused a sharp ache to spear my gut. I took a sip of water to keep from grimacing.

"You look so sad, Jessica," Ben said, putting his hand over mine on the railing and taking a step closer. I glanced up, seeing the nervousness in his eyes, the concentration on his face. He was going to kiss me.

I blinked, going still as he leaned in and pressed his lips to mine. The kiss was sweet, mostly chaste, as he simply held his mouth over mine, brushing our lips together and then retreating.

I brought my fingers to my lips. "Ben..."

He shook his head, grimacing. "You don't feel anything for me, do you?"

I turned my hand over and squeezed his. "I feel so much for you. I respect your mind. I admire your kindness and your humor. I think you're one of the nicest men I've ever met."

"Nice. Ugh, the kiss of death." But he smiled kindly, if not a little bit sadly.

I shook my head. "No. I didn't mean—"

"It's okay, Jessica. I know you just broke up with someone. I'd still hoped..." He sighed, letting go of my hand. "Well, I hope we can be friends. I value that."

"Me, too, Ben. So much."

He nodded, giving me another smile. "I think I'm going to go get another drink and lick my wounds at the bar. Will you be okay out here?"

"Yeah. I'll be just fine."

With one last squeeze of my hand, he turned and moved toward the doors we'd entered through. There was another couple standing near the doorway, but other than them, I was alone. I wanted to groan aloud. I'd had no idea Ben had any romantic interest in me. He'd never even hinted that he'd felt more than a friendly, coworker respect. Maybe he'd just been waiting for our project to end so that if I was interested, too, there wouldn't be any worry of impropriety.

I simply wasn't attracted to Ben as more than a friend. *Did Callen ruin me for other men? Or rather, will he continue to ruin me?*

A soft, tinkling sound caught my attention, and I turned, drawing in a sharp breath and freezing.

Callen. One hip leaned in the doorway of a second entrance near the end of the patio. He had a glass of amber liquid in his hand, and when he swirled it casually, the tinkling of the ice sounded again.

I backed up against the railing, my hands latching on to the edge behind me, and watched him. He pushed himself off the doorway and walked slowly to where I stood, my heart galloping in my chest at his approach.

He was wearing a tuxedo, but something about him looked far from formal. His jaw was dark with stubble, his hair was tousled and a little too long, and his bow tie was crooked and a bit loose, as if he'd recently pulled at it.

"We meet again on a rooftop in Paris," he said, his voice slightly slurred. *He's drunk.* He stepped right up to me, boxing me in.

"What are you doing?" I whispered, my pulse jumping. I could smell his cologne mixed with the singular scent of his skin, and though he *looked* worse for wear, he smelled the same. It caused my heart to ache with longing. *No, no, no.*

He inclined his head toward the door where Ben had exited just a few minutes earlier. "I see you haven't wasted any time. Looking to find a daddy for junior?"

I frowned in confusion. *"What?"*

He tilted but caught himself. "I came here tonight to see if you had some news for me, Jessie." He ran his hand over my stomach and then glanced at my water sitting on the balcony ledge next to my hand.

I let out a short, incredulous bark of laughter and pushed at him. He stumbled back a step, smiling as if in amusement. "Are you *kidding* me? First of all, I'm not pregnant, and if you wanted to know that, you didn't have to crash my work party...*drunk*. You could have just called. Second of all, how *dare* you question me about who I spend my time with. *You* headline every tabloid. *You* dismissed me from your room so you could spend the night with another woman." A small sob choked me, and my last word cut off abruptly, but I swallowed down my tears, refusing to appear weak in front of him. I took a shaky breath, lifting my chin. I was heartbroken, but I was angry, too. "I don't want any part of your games, Callen. Just leave."

For the briefest of moments, I swore I saw the shadow of pain blow across his expression, but then he replaced it with a drunken smirk. He took a quick sip of his drink. "You used to like games, Jessie. Adventures."

"Yeah. I also used to like you." Defeat was in my voice. I sounded tired. I *felt* tired. Exhausted, in fact. I shook my head. "I'm sorry, Callen. For what I did. It was a mistake, and I regret it deeply. I'd do anything to change it, but I can't. I'd never hurt you on purpose, and I think deep inside you know that." I paused. He was watching me closely, though his expression was neatly blank. "But what you did to me was purposeful. And even worse, what you're doing to yourself is purposeful." I looked pointedly at his drink.

He laughed, and it sounded cold. I resisted cringing and squared my shoulders. He brought his glass to his lips again, and I saw, though his expression was a vacant half smile, his hand was shaking. Despite my resolve, tenderness welled inside me. "I saw you. I know who you are. I saw you as a boy, and I saw you as a man one beautiful weekend. You didn't hide from me then. You didn't hide from yourself."

The amused smile on his face slipped. "Goddamn it, Jessie, that wasn't even *real*. That weekend was as much a fantasy as the fairy tales we used to come up with together."

"Is that what you've been telling yourself?" I shook my head. "No. It was real, Callen, and you know it as well as I do. It doesn't matter, though, because you're too afraid to admit it. You're too busy making a mess of your life and throwing away the gifts God gave you."

He did laugh then, a harsh sound that contained more pain than anything else. "God? *God?* I'm bored of all your God talk. Take your writings and your stories and your questions to someone who cares. Joan of Arc was a crazy loon who heard voices, that's all. There's no God. And if there is, he's never spared a second of time for me. Should I pray to him now, Jessie? Should I get down on my knees and beg for guidance?"

I shrugged. "There's a saying about the best prayer being gratitude. You could thank him for the treasures bestowed upon you. You could thank him for the gift of your talent, for the means not only to change *your* life for the better but the ability to help others in so many innumerable ways, most especially with the way your music makes people *feel*. For the way it transforms and lifts and inspires. But what do you do instead? You *waste* it. You squander it." I shook my head. "You're a disgrace."

His lips tipped up in a mocking smile, and he raised his glass. "That's what he always said, too."

"So *you* picked up right where he left off." I sighed. "At some point you're going to have to take responsibility for your own life, Callen, instead of blaming everyone else. At some point you're going to have to stop being a coward. I sincerely hope you do." I scooted away from the balcony ledge, turning my back on him and walking away. He didn't call my name, and I didn't look back.

I left him there to fight his battle...*or not*.

Because I understood now.

Some battles could only be fought alone.

CHAPTER TWENTY-FOUR

JESSICA

Monday morning dawned warm and sultry; summer was in the air. The myriad scents of the Paris streets greeted me as I made my way from the train station to the Louvre: warm pavement, exhaust, fresh-baked croissants, and rich-brewing coffee.

Dr. Moreau had asked to meet with me this morning, and nervous butterflies swarmed in my belly. Ben and I had worked with him more closely during our final weeks in the Loire Valley, and he'd praised my work when we'd wrapped up at the château, so I had my fingers crossed that this meeting pertained to a job, or maybe even another temporary project. Otherwise, I'd be sending out résumés again tomorrow. I hardly had the emotional energy to job search, but a girl had to eat, and I'd do what I had to do because I didn't have much choice.

Callen's face flashed in my mind, the way he'd looked on

the balcony of the hotel a couple of nights ago in his wrinkled tux, but I pushed it away. I couldn't dwell on him right now. I wouldn't. And anyway, I still felt crushed but was glad I'd said my piece to him. My heart was broken, but I'd meant what I said: he had to take responsibility for his own life. There was nothing I could do short of begging. And that wouldn't work either. I knew from experience that people didn't change because they were begged to do so. People changed only when they made the choice to change on their own.

I took the elevator down to Dr. Moreau's office and rapped lightly on his door. "*Entrez*," he called, and I opened the heavy, wooden door slowly.

His office was just as untidy as it'd been the first time I was there, and something about the disorderliness made me smile.

"Ah, Jessica, *ma chérie*, do come in." He stood and rounded his desk, kissing me kindly on each cheek before returning to his chair. I smoothed my skirt and took a seat in front of him.

"How did you enjoy the banquet dinner? I'm sorry we only got a chance to chat briefly."

"It was lovely. I met several of the donors and most of the Louvre staff."

"Good, good. It's what I want to talk to you about." He smiled, and I sat forward. "An offer." I released the breath I'd been holding, and Dr. Moreau chuckled. "Good news?"

"Yes, very."

"Good. Your work, Jessica, is wonderful. The way you interpreted Adélaïde's voice was not only technically accurate, but contained a level of intuition that not every translator has. Words are so"—he rubbed his fingers together as if he was thinking of them as a tangible thing—"powerful. And language, if not translated properly, never perfectly conveys the meaning of the writer. It does not speak from their heart as they meant it to do. It does not give us the *essence* of them. You, Jessica, helped to bare Adélaïde's heart, and in turn, a small part of Jehanne's as well. For a moment in time, you brought them back to life."

His compliment made my heart thrum with joy, and I let out a soggy-sounding laugh. "Thank you, Dr. Moreau."

"You're very welcome. Now, about the offer. There is a position in our ancient documents department I believe would be perfect for you. I've recommended you for it, but you'll have to meet with the head of the department as a formality. If you're interested, of course."

"Interested?" I sputtered. "Yes."

Dr. Moreau laughed. "I hoped for as much. Here is her card. She's expecting you tomorrow morning at nine."

"Thank you, Dr. Moreau. I...really, I can't thank you enough. For everything."

"The feeling is mutual." I started to stand, when Dr. Moreau smiled in a way I thought was just a bit mischievous. "Oh, just one more small thing." I sat back down and looked inquiringly at him as he took a folder from his desk drawer. "Two of the writings you were meant to work on were misfiled at the field." He shook his head. "An unfortunate mistake, though they were written on a different type of parchment and used a different color ink, so they were assumed to belong to a different project. These are copies. I've only glanced over them briefly. I know how disappointed you were not to have the completion of the story, and I would love for you to do the honors and translate them as you've so skillfully translated the others. But please send them to me the minute they're completed."

Oh my God. I released a startled breath as I met Dr. Moreau's eyes. My heart thumped with surprised elation. *"Oui,"* I breathed as I took the manila folder and opened it to peek inside. I immediately recognized Adélaïde's beautifully formal script, and my heart leapt as if spotting an old friend coming toward me on the street. *Oh.* "Thank you, Dr. Moreau." I struggled not to tear up. "Thank you so much. I'll e-mail the first one tomorrow," I said, my voice breathless with the surge of emotions filling my chest.

Dr. Moreau stood. "*Très bien.* And remember to attach an invoice for the work." He came around the desk and took my hand in both of his, kissing me on each cheek once again. "*Bonne journée*, Jessica."

* * *

I saved my excited squeal until I'd made it halfway from the Louvre to the train station, stopping on a street corner and releasing the joyful sound. A permanent job. At the Louvre. I leaned back against the building behind me, the warmth of the stone seeping into my blouse and heating my skin. I turned my face toward the sun and felt the warm rays on my face. "Thank you," I whispered. I clutched the smooth manila folder tightly to my chest, hugging it as if it were Adélaïde herself and she were experiencing this moment with me. I was dying to read what was inside, but I wanted to sit by myself in a quiet room so I could absorb every word. So I could return to the fields in the Loire Valley. *To my heart.*

I felt more at peace than I had since I'd left the château. It would take time to move on from the pain of losing Callen, but eventually I would. I'd taken a chance on love and I'd lost. Despite how it had ended, I wouldn't regret the time we'd spent together. That, too, had been a gift, and I would try to ensure the loss changed me for the better. I had no idea what that meant at the moment, but it was a goal and goals were vital. *Dreams were vital.*

The half-hour trip home seemed to take longer than usual. Frankie was at work, and I normally wouldn't relish spending the rest of the afternoon alone, but I had Adélaïde to keep me company and knew her familiar voice would bring me comfort.

When I rounded the corner of my street and looked up, the sight of a man walking directly toward me caused me to halt. I gulped in a breath.

My heart clamored with fear as Nick approached me slowly. "Is he okay?" I asked, rushing to him, my first thought that Callen was hurt and Nick had come to deliver the bad news.

"What? Oh yeah, he's fine."

I put my hand over my heart, and Nick grimaced. "Sorry. I didn't consider you'd think I was here to bring bad news."

"His lifestyle doesn't exactly inspire confidence in the state of his health."

"No, it doesn't, does it?"

I looked at him in silence for a moment. He was wearing jeans and a short-sleeved T-shirt with some website design company logo on it—*his* probably, though the T-shirt design was faded and I couldn't make out the exact company name. He looked good, not like Callen had when I'd seen him. "I'm surprised to see you."

"Yeah...I know. I'm sorry I walked off on bad terms that day after the interview."

"I don't blame you for that, Nick. I deserved it."

Nick shook his head. "No, Jessica. You said it was an accident, and I believe you. Whatever happened, I don't think you meant to hurt Callen, especially publicly."

"No. I didn't." My apartment was at the end of the block,

and I gestured toward it. "Do you want to sit down and talk?" I asked.

"I really only have a short time. Callen and I are flying back to California this afternoon."

"Oh, I see," I said softly.

"But, um, I saw a coffee shop a block over, if you wouldn't mind joining me for a cup? I spotted some delicious-looking cake in the window."

I smiled. "Sure."

We walked the block over to the coffee shop I knew well, entering and taking a seat at a small table. The scents of rich coffee and sweet desserts hit my nose and made my stomach roil. Nick's visit had obviously shaken up my system. "Can I get you something?" Nick asked.

I shook my head and waited while he ordered a cup of coffee and a piece of decadent chocolate cake.

"Does Callen know you're here?" I asked after he'd polished off half the dessert in two bites.

He sat back. "No. I just…I don't even know exactly why I came." He let out a small, embarrassed chuckle and scrubbed a hand down his face. "I've worried about Callen for a long time, and I guess I've come to the conclusion that he has to start worrying about himself if he's going to move on. What happened at that interview—awful as it was—maybe it will be the thing that will finally make that happen. They say you've gotta hit rock bottom before you start to climb out." He picked up his cup and took a sip of coffee.

I breathed out a huff of air. "I came to the same conclusion, Nick, and I hope you're right about Callen figuring out how to move forward." *But it's none of my business anymore, as much as that hurts.*

He tilted his head, watching me for a moment, then setting his cup down and crossing his arms. "He used to go to this boxing ring in L.A. where they let amateurs spar. I went once to watch. Wasn't my thing. It reminded me of my past, and unlike Callen, I'd never liked being hit."

Oh. Both parts of that statement filled me with sadness, but Nick didn't seem to be there to talk about himself, and I didn't know him well enough to ask more. "Callen enjoyed it."

He looked thoughtful for a moment. "I don't know if *enjoyed* is the right word, but yeah, he sought it out. He *wants* to hurt himself, Jessica. The drinking, the women, it accomplishes two things at once—it numbs him for a while, and it hurts him because he hates himself for it."

"It hurt me, too."

"I know."

I looked at him, saw the grief etched in his eyes. Yes, he did know. Only not in the same way. But he cared about Callen as a brother would, and so watching Callen ruin his own life must bring him pain as well. "He's very lucky to have you," I murmured. "I hope he realizes it."

He gave me a wan smile and then studied me for a moment. "Callen told me what he did to you when you went to his room that night." *That night.* The ill-fated night when I'd tried to tell him the truth. The truth he hadn't wanted to hear.

I flinched, looking away, not wanting to think about that night at all. "Yeah."

He took another sip of coffee and then toyed with the cardboard cup for a moment, seeming to be considering something. "It's not really my place to tell you this, but...nothing happened between Callen and that girl. She left right after you did, Jessica. Callen and I checked out thirty minutes later. He hurt you on purpose, but he didn't have sex with her. I just thought you should know the truth about that."

I blinked at him, furrowing my brow. "Then why...?"

"To hurt you, and to hurt himself. He's spent these last weeks in Paris trying to get into the lifestyle he led before, but it's not working for him. He comes back to the hotel alone every night and sits out on the balcony looking pathetic and completely miserable." He smiled brightly. "It's giving me hope."

I couldn't help the confused laugh that bubbled up from my chest as I simultaneously shook my head.

"He's sick with jealousy over who you might be with, and he's never been jealous before. I think it's making him just a bit crazy. He's a mess, but maybe... maybe in a good way for the first time ever. Only time will tell."

I sighed, watching him polish off the last of his cake. "Nick, I hope he makes a turn for the better, but I can't invest in hoping. And even if he pulls himself together, there's no future for us. I'm here, he's in L.A., and our lives are a thousand miles apart in other ways as well."

He nodded. "I know. I hope me coming here didn't upset you. I meant it as an act of goodwill between two people who care about him. We might be the only people on earth who really do."

God, that was a sad thought. And even sadder was that while I still loved Callen, I couldn't be part of his life anymore without driving a stake through my heart every day.

"I don't suppose you'd have any interest in keeping in touch?"

I shook my head slowly. "That wouldn't be good for me, Nick. I hope you understand why."

"Yeah." He breathed out the word, a sound of resignation. "I do."

"But I'm so thankful to you for coming to me today. I've

been...struggling, and now I think I can put some of that to rest."

"Good." He smiled, tilting his head. "I think fate knew what she was doing when she brought you and Callen together."

I smiled, a genuine one, as I picked up my things and stood. I agreed. No matter the outcome, I had faith that our time spent together was for a purpose, even if I wouldn't know that purpose for a long time to come. "I think so, too."

"Take care of yourself, Jessica."

"You too, Nick."

I turned and walked out of the coffee shop, heading toward my apartment while I pondered Nick's words. Callen hadn't slept with the girl who had been in his hotel room that night. Why, I wasn't sure, and maybe it shouldn't matter whether he had or he hadn't, because either way, he'd wanted me to believe he was going to. That he was capable of doing it. But it *did* matter to me, and the relief I felt was like a balm to my heart. It didn't change anything now, but the knowledge brought me a measure of peace.

I turned the corner to my street, leaving my past behind, grateful to be able to enter into Adélaïde's past instead. Inside my apartment, I sat on the couch and brought my legs up under me, taking out the top copy of Adélaïde's writing.

In the year of our Lord 1431, on the first day of June
It is over. Her spirit soars with the angels. I did not want to watch her suffering. My heart bled with agony, and I trembled with horror to see her body tied to the stake, a wooden cross clutched to her chest. I know not much, but I know that what happened to Jehanne to-day is an injustice of which the world will come to

grieve. *And so I forced myself to bear witness, to be as brave as she taught me to be, to watch as she met her earthly end with composure and courage. And I vow always to remember the truth she lived: that there is more than what we see with our human eyes, that God shows us our path and fate whispers her dreams for us, guiding with love and grace. It matters not who doubts us, only that we listen with our heart and are fearless enough to look with the vision of faith. In the end, my only hope is that it brought her some small comfort to know that as the flames licked higher, she was watched with celestial eyes of love.*

Live fiercely and without regret, I promise to remind myself when I am afraid or uncertain, repeating the words Jehanne first said to me in that quiet stream what seems so long ago. The same words she whispered to Charles the Seventh, the phrase the wise and kindly priest who gave Charles comfort in his father's desertion said to him as he passed from this world to the next, words Charles had never repeated to another living soul. But they were more than words. They were the very thing that secured Jehanne an army, won an abandoned king a throne, and gifted France a heroine.

And I myself shall live by them all the days of my life.

Now I sit here at the edge of the sea looking out over God's masterpiece as the sun rises and casts the water in shades of gold. I did not board the carriage my father sent for me; nor will I return home to the life I once led, to the stranger I was promised to by those who do not know my heart.

The wind is blowing against me, plastering my dress

to my body and forcing me to turn my face north, and I swear I feel Jehanne beside me pointing the way. Facing me toward a cave in the Loire Valley where my beloved Olivier promised we'd find each other again if ever we were lost. Is he alive? Is he injured? Will he find his way back to me? Does he love me as I love him? With body and soul? I have no answers, and yet I have faith. I carry inside me the peace of knowing my life will be led fiercely and without regret. Please, dear Lord, dear beloved Jehanne, guide me where you would have me go and I will humbly follow.

PART THREE

I am not afraid. I was born to do this.

—*Joan of Arc*

CHAPTER TWENTY-FIVE

CALLEN

The California sunshine blazed through a gap in the blinds, hitting me like a spotlight, causing me to groan and bring my pillow over my eyes. We'd gotten in close to dawn and I'd slept for only four or five hours. Apparently, I hadn't made sure the shade was completely shut before I stumbled into bed last night.

I attempted to go back to sleep, but the damn light was too bright now that I'd woken up. I tossed the pillow aside and rolled over, opening one eye blearily to look at the clock: 12:17. I stared at the familiar ceiling of my bedroom, depression settling in around me like the unwelcome visitor it'd become. Would a drink help? It was only noon here, but it was nighttime in Paris.

Paris.

Jessie.

My gut clenched at the reminder that an ocean now separated us. That was good, but still, it fucking hurt. Everything hurt, and I had no idea what to do about that other than what I'd always done. Except that hadn't worked in Paris, and it no longer sounded appealing, either. Nothing did.

My mind returned to that balcony in Paris, the way Jessie had looked in the gown of golden roses. *Roses.* Shimmery and elegant. A beacon of light. So incredibly beautiful it'd clawed at my heart. I'd seen a poster for the gala and gone to find out if she was pregnant, knowing inside that I was hoping for it, praying even, because I still wanted her—so fucking badly—and the agony of missing her had made me selfish enough to cling to any reason she might want me back. Selfish enough to show up uninvited where I knew she'd be, but not before a few shots of liquid courage.

And then I'd seen *him* kiss her, touch her. I'd been jealous and hurt and angry, and so I'd been cruel—again.

You're a disgrace.

God, I knew I was. I knew.

My cell phone rang from somewhere across the room, and I lay there, letting it go to voice mail. But when it began ringing again, just a few seconds later, I sat up, swinging my legs off the bed. "Jesus."

I followed the sound and located my phone in the pocket of the jeans I'd tossed aside last night before falling into bed. "Hello?" My voice sounded rough and filled with the sleep I hadn't gotten enough of.

"Callen, dear?"

"Hi, Myrtle."

She sighed softly. "I'm sorry to be the bearer of bad news, dear, but your father...he passed away."

I walked back toward the bed and sat, letting out a puff of air. "My father?"

"Yes. A man who worked at the VA hospital called you. He found your business number in your father's records. He left his information so you could call him back. But I thought you'd rather hear the news from me than a stranger."

"Okay. Thanks, Myrtle."

There was a pause. "I'm here for you, dear. Do you need me to come over and help with any arrangements—"

"No, thank you. I'm okay. My father and I, we were…estranged."

"Oh, I see. I'm sorry to hear that. That's not easy either."

"No," I murmured. I felt as if I were in a daze. Myrtle gave me the number of the man who'd called and then she rattled on for another minute. I didn't grasp all her words, but her calm tone soothed me.

After I hung up, I sat staring at the wall for a very long time.

* * *

The old house was abandoned. I wasn't surprised. It'd been a shithole when we'd lived here eleven years ago, and another decade's worth of renters had sealed its fate. Even the owner had apparently walked away. The sign on what passed for a lawn showed the logo of a large California bank. They must own it now.

I wasn't sure why I'd even driven by. But my dad had moved back to my hometown of Santa Lucinda at some point—I didn't even know exactly when—and his small, sad funeral had been held up the street. I'd paid for a headstone for him and shown up. I didn't think he would expect more from me than that, if he even would have wanted me there at all. He'd apparently had a few old friends, army buddies who'd shown up looking like something the cat had dragged in and then stood around in a group afterward, smoking cigarettes and trading stories, on what topic I couldn't say.

My father hadn't moved back to this house when he'd moved back to town, if it'd even been available for rent at the time. But this was where I was drawn. If my pain resided anywhere physical, this was it.

The front door had been locked, but I'd been able to push a side window up enough that I could squeeze through.

What am I doing?

My footsteps echoed through the empty rooms as I sidestepped animal droppings and garbage that had been left behind.

There was a large hole in the floorboard in the hallway, likely where animals got in.

My old room...the closet where I'd hidden the keyboard—that beloved keyboard—only to take it out when my dad wasn't home, losing myself in the music that I could miraculously read. That was a good memory. The bathroom...my dad's room...and then the kitchen. I stood in the open space looking around. All the lower cabinets had been removed, along with the light fixtures, even the baseboards. The upper cabinets hung precariously, most of the doors tilted and hanging by a single rusted hinge. The linoleum on the floor was cracked and peeling, and rusty pipes where the sink had once been were exposed.

Worthless idiot! Read! Read this line. Just this one fucking letter!

My gut rolled with the echo of my father's words as my eyes moved slowly to the place the table had been, the location of my misery, my shame and humiliation. I pictured myself there now, a book open in front of me, praying to God to help me read.

Please. I'll do anything. Just help me. Help me, please.

And suddenly a wave of anger overcame me so violently that I let out a fierce yell of rage, ripping one of the already-loose cabinet doors from its remaining hinge and hurling it at the wall. The door splintered, and plaster flew from the place the door had hit, the wood clattering to the floor. My chest heaved as I sucked in air. It wasn't enough. "I needed you!" I screamed. "I needed *help*!" I wrestled with a whole section of cabinet, finally tearing it from the wall and hurling that as well. "You never helped me! You never helped me! Why? *Why?*"

You're stupid. You're so fucking stupid.

Another door ripped away, another piece of cabinet. Wood splintered, plaster exploded, my muscles burned, and blood splattered on the floor from some injury I couldn't even feel. "Why couldn't you love me?" I yelled. It sounded desperate, animalistic.

Why did you have to be my son? Why did I have to get you?

There were no more cabinets left, so I went for the pipes, shaking and twisting them until those, too, came loose in a burst of black water that bubbled up and then disappeared back into the floor. I used the pipes like a club, bashing the wall closest to me until I'd busted through the drywall, growling and panting with the effort. "Why couldn't you love me? I just wanted you to love me."

I continued to swing the pipe, but my arms were shaking with fatigue and the wetness splattering on my bare arms wasn't blood, but tears. I let out another yell, but it ended on a sob, and I dropped the pipe, hanging my head as tears coursed down my cheeks. I fell to my knees and then to my side on the cold, dirty floor. "I wanted you to love me. I needed you," I gasped. "I didn't have anyone else. I needed you, and you never helped me."

I didn't know if I was talking to God or my father, or maybe both. All I knew was the agonizing pain that had come up from deep inside my soul and was demanding to be set free. It was beating at my bones, ripping through my muscles, clawing at the inside of my skin.

I sobbed as I surrendered, letting it pour out of me, shaking with the pain and shame I'd held close to my heart for so very long. I cried for the feeling of worthlessness that I'd held tight to, owning it because I believed it was rightfully mine. I cried for the desperate longing to be loved by the one person who refused to offer it. "I needed you," I choked again, my chest heaving. "I needed you to help me."

I'm here to save you.

My eyes flew open, and I swiped at the blurriness, sitting up and looking for the child who'd just spoken near my ear. I scooted backward quickly, pressing my spine against the wall as I attempted to catch my breath. I used both hands to swipe away the tears on my cheeks. There was no child. The voice had come from my memory. But it'd been sweet and clear, and I'd swear she'd spoken right in my ear.

Jessie.

It'd been Jessie's voice. The voice of that eleven-year-old, freckle-faced princess.

I'm here to save you.

I drew in another long, shaky breath, my heart slowing, a trickle of calm beginning to move through me as my shoulders relaxed. I brought my knees to my chest, sitting against the wall in the same way I'd once sat in that boxcar. I rested my forearms on my knees, noting the state of my scratched-up, bloody hands, and closed my eyes, leaning my head back against the wall.

I'm here to save you, she'd said, not once, but twice.

I'm here to save you.

It echoed in my head like the ringing of bells. Was…was *that* how God worked? Did he send *people* to save us when we needed saving? Signs? Small guides? Had I been too blind to see that I'd asked him for help and he'd *answered* again and again? My heart thumped with hope, a sweep of wonder rushing through me. I'd asked him to help me, begged him to save me, and he'd sent *Jessie*, not only to provide friendship and laughter when I needed it most, but to gift me the joy of music. She'd delivered it straight into my arms, like a messenger bearing miracles, and I hadn't once recognized her for what she was. *My gift. My fate. My love.*

Oh, Jessie.

I pictured her eager face peering into the boxcar that day, pictured her grasping my hand and leading me through fields and over train tracks, transforming the miserable world I knew into a magical land filled with happiness and *hope.* I pictured her reading to me, engaging my imagination, and teaching me how to dream. I saw her going over musical notes, her finger touching on each one as she taught me the language I'd been meant to know, the language that flowed through my blood—my marrow, my very soul—as if it were the mother tongue learned in some distant place that I could no longer remember but still somehow carried inside.

It was like every good and beautiful thing in the world came together all at once and you'd found a way to express it in one single song.

I wasn't useless. I wasn't. Jessie had tried to teach me that. And yet I hadn't been able to trust anyone to love me, even someone kind like Jessie, when my own father hadn't been able to.

I sat for a long time in the desolate shack, my tears drying, the blood hardening. I stared at the ruined wall as my heartbeat became a steady *thump, thump, thump.*

Oh God, I was a fool. I hadn't seen. I hadn't realized.

I held my head in my hands, so many visions flowing through my mind, not just Jessie. Not just the second time she'd shown up to save me on a rooftop in Paris, not only the third, in a French château in the Loire Valley. But Nick, how he'd arrived in my life when I'd needed a friend the most, how I'd protected him and how he'd unfailingly had my back. Even Myrtle. Even crazy-ass Myrtle. I gasped, gripping my hair.

Maybe I had been loved all along...by something...or someone. By a loving hand that sought to guide me if only I'd listened. The feeling that something immense was happening danced across my skin, through my veins, and settled inside. It felt warm and shimmery, like a light. It felt like love.

You're a disgrace, Jessie had said. I let go of my head, laughing out loud, not with self-mocking, but with the truth of her words and the realization that she was right. *Of course she was.* But the *greater* realization was that I didn't want to be a disgrace any longer, and I needed to find the strength not to be.

I'd spent my life rejecting miracles. I'd spent my life snubbing fate. I'd spent my life sending boats away. One after the other.

Fate hadn't given up on me, though. Fate had sent Jessie over and over again, and, God, I wanted to be worthy of the gift.

A scratching sound caught my attention, and I pulled myself to my feet. The last thing I needed was a run-in with some rabid raccoon that was squatting in the abandoned house. But when I peeked around the corner into the short hallway, I spotted a medium-sized brown and white dog, its expression moving between a grin and a pant. I backed up and the dog came forward, rounding the doorway into the kitchen where I now stood, moaning softly.

"Whoa," I said, holding up my hand. The dog sat down,

dropping its eyes. I paused. It seemed to have remarkably good manners for a stray. I could see the outline of its rib bones beneath its matted fur, so it was clearly hungry and homeless.

I shifted on my feet. "I should take you to the pound," I murmured. The dog, seeming to know the word *pound*, dropped onto its stomach and covered its eyes with its paws. I laughed in surprise at the clear intelligence of this mangy animal. "Been there before, huh?" I sighed. "Well, I can't take you. I live in an apartment in Los Angeles. No yard. No pets allowed."

The dog continued to stare at me as if waiting for something. *You could move.* I let out a ragged breath, leaning back against the wall behind me. "Where am I gonna move to? France?" The dog's ears perked up, and it lifted its head, letting out a moan. *Of course.* I wasn't sure exactly where the thought had even come from other than that maybe…maybe it'd been swirling around in my head for weeks now. Perhaps I'd just been too scared to even ponder it and all the other risks I'd have to consider if I took that leap.

I pressed my lips together, still looking at the dog. "If we moved to France, I'd name you Pierre. It's a really stupid name and you'd have to put up with it." The dog leapt up, barking softly. I laughed. "It figures."

I sighed again. I'd have to think about moving, really think about it, but it seemed that for now I had a dog. "Come on, Pierre. Let's go get you a hamburger." The dog moaned happily and then started panting, joining me where I stood and looking up at me solemnly. "I know. I didn't expect you either. I think that's the point."

Pierre followed along behind me, and I unlocked the latch of the front door. Before I opened it, I looked back into the kitchen, picturing that small boy sitting at a table, scared, sad, filled with shame for who he was and what he couldn't do.

"You were wrong about me," I whispered, and then I opened the door, Pierre running ahead of me as we walked away.

* * *

"What do you think, Monsieur Hayes? Very nice?"

I turned, giving the modern kitchen a once-over. It was all shiny stainless steel and sharp edges. "It's nice, I guess, but...do you have anything with a little more...history?"

The Realtor raised his eyebrow. "History? Monsieur, Giverny is rich in history. But in real estate that often translates to...needs work."

I chuckled. "That's okay. Within reason."

The agent, Monsieur Voclain, brought his phone out and swiped through a couple of screens, stopping on one. He glanced at me. "I do have one you might like to see. If you like...history." He smiled.

"Yes." *Or rather, someone special to me does.*

"Okay. If you'd like to follow behind me, I will show you the way."

I followed Monsieur Voclain's car for several miles and pulled up next to him in front of a stone cottage, overgrown with ivy, white shutters falling from the hinges. I stood at the open car door for a moment, looking at it, a feeling of...rightness settling in. Pierre barked, sliding past me and jumping out the open door. "Hey. You're supposed to stay in the car," I said. The damn dog ignored me, trotting toward the house, where she lay down in a patch of sunlight on the stone pathway and put her head on her paws.

I looked around, taking in the overgrown yard fenced in by a stone wall that still looked sturdy. Massive trees shaded the property, and flowers and vines grew rampant and wild. It needed some taming, but the natural, unbound beauty of it caught at something inside me.

There was a familiar quality about the light here. The way it glowed so softly behind the house and then diffused gently away into the trees and the sky beyond. It brought to mind the way the light had looked behind Jessie that day as she'd stood in front of the window at the inn.

And as I tipped my head back and inhaled the breeze, I swore I could smell the sweet, spicy scent of roses wafting from somewhere beyond.

Monsieur Voclain approached. "It's a fixer-upper, no doubt. But it has a lovely private garden in the back, and the fireplaces inside are still working. It has all the original beams and wood floors." We started walking toward the front door. "You know that Monet's house is nearby? When he moved here in 1883, the beauty of Giverny became a source of great inspiration for him. He painted several of his most famous paintings here. It is…a special place for artists."

"Hmm," I hummed. I'd heard Monet's home and gardens were nearby. *She would love that.*

Monsieur Voclain chuckled as he looked at Pierre, who had made herself right at home already. "Your dog will like it here, too. There are beautiful places to walk, a river with an old bridge just that way." He pointed to the left. "And above the trees, you can see the steeple of an eleventh-century church."

A melody pinged inside me: soft, sweet, lonely, speaking of things I'd always longed for but never had the courage to try to make my own.

Love.

Home.

"Monsieur Voclain, I'll take it."

He laughed, turning from the front door he was just unlocking. "You haven't even seen the inside."

I grinned. "All right, let's walk through, just to make it official."

CHAPTER TWENTY-SIX

JESSICA

"Jess?" I turned from the stove where I was heating up some soup as Frankie entered our apartment.

"Hey," I greeted, giving her a smile.

"Hey. How was your day?"

"It was good."

She came in the kitchen, looking over my shoulder into the pot of vegetable soup and wrinkling her nose. She tossed some mail on the counter, holding up a magazine that had been on top. "Look." She grinned. "It's the published article about how my brilliant friend helped uncover one of history's great mysteries."

I sucked in a breath, setting the wooden spoon I'd been using on the counter. I took the magazine from Frankie and leafed to the page where the article about the words Joan of Arc had said to Charles the Seventh to get him to give her an army was located. I'd already read the piece, but to see it in print sent a thrill through me. I was still so proud of the work we'd accomplished and overjoyed about the information that had been contained in the misfiled writing.

Frankie looked over my shoulder as I glanced through the article. "We're framing that, you know."

I laughed, setting the magazine down on the counter and spotting a large, padded envelope on top of the pile of mail Frankie had set down. "What's that?" I nodded to the pile.

Frankie grabbed an apple from the fruit bowl, bringing it to her mouth. "I don't know. It's for you," she said around a bite of the fruit.

I picked up the envelope. It had a label with my name and address on it but no return information, except the postmark that indicated it was posted in France. I frowned, pulling open the seal and peering inside. I removed a music CD case with a blank cover. "What the...?" Pulling the cover open, I saw a CD with JESSIE's SONG written in bold, black letters. "Oh my God," I whispered, leaning back against the counter for support, my hands beginning to shake.

"What is it?" Frankie asked, taking it from my hand and staring at it for a moment. "It's from Callen?" she asked, blinking at me.

"It—it has to be." I shook my head. I hadn't heard a word from or about him for more than two months, not since Nick had stopped by unexpectedly the day they were leaving for the States. I'd asked Frankie for verification that he'd actually left, that there was no news on him in the tabloids, and she'd told me that she'd searched online and there wasn't a whisper of him anywhere. It was as if he'd just disappeared.

And now...he'd sent me a song. "Jessie's Song." What did it mean?

"I think you need to go in your room and listen to that," Frankie said softly.

I looked up at her. My heart was suddenly beating so rapidly, I could hardly catch my breath. "O-okay."

She nodded, looking concerned. "I'll be here when you're done listening. And stop gripping that so tightly. You're going to crack it."

I let out a strangled laugh, releasing my grip on the CD. I walked on wooden legs into my room and closed the door behind me, going to my desk, where I plugged in my headphones and slipped the disk into my computer.

As the first notes played, I clenched my eyes shut, the tune that he'd hummed constantly while we were in the Loire Valley filling my ears, filling my heart. A singular violin, beautiful, but the notes...*bleeding* somehow. It had been only the soft sound of his voice then, humming the melody, and then later, the harmonies, but now they all came together, an entire orchestra, and it was unbelievably beautiful. I put my hand over my heart as if to keep it from bursting from my chest at the story this music told. Of longing, of despair, of loneliness, of love and joy. He had named the song for me, but this was Callen's story, being told through notes that had drifted straight from his soul. His heart was here, being laid bare on a thin, silver disk. He had given it to me.

When "Jessie's Song" ended, another began to play. And then another. Each one told a story, some I thought I understood and others beautiful but mysterious to me. Perhaps speaking of things he had never told me. Maybe of things he hadn't even told himself—until now.

If heartache and redemption mixed together to form a soundtrack, this would be it. And I understood his pain even more poignantly. *Oh, Callen.* I listened to each song, tears streaming down my face, sitting in my room as the sun slipped away, *waiting* with bated breath for the way in which he had chosen to end the final song. And when it came, my heart squeezed so tightly I let out a gasp. The music lifted gently, the sound of a singular violin again, the notes soaring, my heart following.

Callen... Callen.

He'd written an ending filled with happiness. With hope. With love.

* * *

In the year of our Lord 1431, on the seventh day of October

There is a chill in the air today as I sit in the mouth of our cave, the Loire Valley beautiful in all the shades of autumn splendor. Olivier wanders the field below, exercising his leg, and I can see from where I sit that his limp is less noticeable. I can't help smiling as I recall the day several months ago when we met again under the light of a new moon, the way he swung from his horse, limping toward me as I ran, colliding in a heap of tears and kisses, love and laughter. His words, "You're here, my love, you're here," and the way he shook as he said them, will stay with me forever.

Olivier promises we will make a good life, a peace-filled life, in a distant part of France, growing apples perchance, or maybe grapes. No war, no fear, no rules or strictures, our hearts governed only by God. And I know, with all the faith in my heart, that it will be so, for my destiny has led me here, and it is not only Olivier's promise that brings me solace, but the knowledge that it is also a promise written on the wind.

I feel certain that we will not return here, that today is goodbye to this wondrous place where Olivier's and my heart became one. He is my family now. Him and the child that grows in my womb. A tiny speck of hope, of love. Proof that though life takes, so does it give back.

I shall leave my story here, that and the pieces of Jehanne that she lovingly offered. The parts of her that did not belong only to France, but to me, her friend and confidante. Perhaps someday fate will decide it is time for this story to be shared. I cannot help but feel a kinship for the unknown person who will first read these writings, a connection that, if it comes to be, destiny herself will surely orchestrate. In this way, though perhaps through decades of time, we are bonded together. And so my message to you, reader of my words, knower of my heart, is this: I questioned once whether the winds of fate are benevolent or merciless. I know now—believe—with every fiber of my being, that they are only good. For it was Jehanne who taught me so until the moment of her final breath. I hope, dear unknown friend, that you believe it, too. With love, Adélaïde Durand

CHAPTER TWENTY-SEVEN

JESSICA

It was fall in Paris. The temperature had dropped, and with the tourists mostly gone, Parisians took back their beloved city.

Stepping from the train tunnel and beginning the walk to my apartment, I tugged my jacket around myself, trying to manage the buttons while stuffing files I'd been reading on the train into my briefcase, and failing with the buttons. "Oh, for God's sake," I muttered, as a swirl of dancing leaves crossed the sidewalk in front of me.

The first drop of rain splattered on my nose, and I blinked at the sky, letting out a tiny squeak when another drop fell straight into my eye. I swiped at it, picking up my pace. There hadn't been rain in the forecast, so I hadn't brought an umbrella.

The rain picked up, falling steadily now as I ducked my head and fast-walked, not daring to run in the work heels I wore. I used my briefcase to protect me from the rain, holding it above my head. I must have forgotten to zip it closed in my haste to stuff the files inside, though, because suddenly the folder fell out in front of me, causing me to let out a scream as I came up short, squatting and attempting to stop the papers from flying away.

Someone bent down next to me, putting his foot on top of a loose piece of paper. The shadow of an umbrella fell over me, and the rain, mercifully, was blocked. I laughed, shaking my head. *"Merci beaucoup—"* I looked up, dropping the papers I'd just gathered, my heart leaping in my chest.

Callen.

Breath whooshed from my lungs, and I almost fell backward.

"Whoa," he said softly, wrapping his hands around my forearms and guiding me to my feet. "I'm here to save you," he said, his voice slightly throaty. He tried to hold on to the tilt of his lips, but the smile wobbled and slipped as our gazes locked, his eyes full of gravity.

Oh.

I just stared. The shock of seeing his face, of having him right there in front of me so unexpectedly, had stolen my voice and all my wits, too, it seemed.

He glanced at the papers I'd dropped, moving to gather them, but I reached my hand out, stopping him. "It's okay. They're just…uh…" *Copies of something, nothing important.* "I mean, they can be replaced."

He bent anyway, gathering up the drenched pile, unmoving now, made heavy by the water and stuck to the pavement. "Still probably shouldn't litter," he said as he stood.

"No," I said, my eyes moving over his face as if he might not be real. "I mean, yes." I shook my head, trying desperately to clear it. It'd been so fuzzy lately. "Yes, littering is bad."

His smile widened, and it was so beautiful. He was so beautiful, I almost began to cry. Someone brushed past his back and he stepped forward, guiding me closer to the wall of a building, out of the way of people walking on the sidewalk. He still held the umbrella over our heads, creating an intimate space perfect for two. It made me picture that small room we'd shared in the Loire Valley and a wave of emotion washed through me. Hope, both tentative and strong. "What are you doing here?"

He used the hand not holding the umbrella to run through his damp hair, slicking it back, and then ran his hand down his thigh to dry whatever wetness it had come away with. "I was on my way to your apartment. To see you."

"You were?"

He nodded, staring at me for a moment, so much longing in his eyes that my heart jumped again. He patted the pocket of his jacket as if he'd just remembered something, and then reached inside, pulling out a folded piece of paper. When he held it toward me, I could see that his hand was trembling. He cleared his throat. "This is for you. I, uh, wrote it for you."

"Music?"

He shook his head. "No, ah, no. A letter. Just a short one."

I sucked in a breath. *A letter.* "You—you *wrote* it?" *Oh my God. Oh, Callen.*

He nodded, the expression on his face filled with such raw vulnerability that tears burned in my eyes. "Please don't laugh at it, Jessie."

I let out a tiny sob, taking the paper. "I would never laugh at you."

He shook his head, grimacing. "I know. I'm sorry. It's just…It's just a start. I'm not very good yet. But Madame Pelletier says I will be."

"Madame Pelletier?"

"My tutor."

"Oh, Callen," I breathed, swallowing down the lump in my throat that threatened to choke me.

He nodded toward the note, putting his hand in his pocket as he watched me.

I unfolded the piece of plain white paper, my own hands shaking as his had a moment before. Inside, in childish-looking blocky letters, the ink bleeding in several spots where it looked as if he'd stopped and then started again in great concentration, read:

> Dear Jessie,
>   I'm sorry and I love you.
>   Callen

The most gorgeous love letter ever written in the history of life on earth.

The tears broke free, a sobbing moan rising in my throat as the love in my heart burst forth, mixing with my pride in him, the aching loneliness of the past four months, the worry, the doubts, the pain, and the fear.

"Jessie," he croaked. "You're not supposed to cry." He moved forward, brushing the tears from my face.

I shook my head. "I'm just so proud of you. And y-you wrote this for me. And the songs," I gasped, "the beautiful, gorgeous songs."

Callen had moved in even closer and was kissing the tears from my cheeks now. "Jessie," he murmured. "I have so much to explain to you. That day in my hotel room, I—"

"I know about that," I whispered. "Nick came to see me."

He nodded. "I know. He told me." He smoothed back a piece of hair that had stuck to my damp cheek. "But I'd still like to explain myself to you in my own words. I want to undo the hurt I caused you. I want to earn your forgiveness."

"I do forgive you, Callen. And I want you to forgive me, too. I never meant—"

He put his fingers over my lips, halting my words. "There's nothing to forgive. You can tell me how it happened, but I know you didn't mean to hurt me. You've only ever brought me gifts." He paused. "And in a way, that was one, too, Jessie. Funny as it seems. You saved me once, and then again, but I needed to save myself." He ran his knuckle down my cheek, and I leaned into his touch. "You were right about that. You were right about so many things."

I smiled. "Oh, Callen, I—" A gust of wind blew straight at me, causing me to step backward as my coat flew open, my dress plastering itself to my body. I turned my head against the gust, and when it changed direction, I opened my mouth to continue the sentence I'd started. When I looked back to Callen, he was staring down, his eyes wide, his mouth slightly parted.

His eyes flew to mine, his forehead creasing. "Jessie?" He reached down, running his palm over my swollen belly, just beginning to round with his growing baby.

"I tried to call you," I said, nerves assaulting me. "But your number was changed."

He blinked, still staring, as if in shock. "I changed my number when I moved to France," he murmured.

France? "Oh. Um, well, I didn't know how to reach you, and I didn't have anyone else to call. I tried to look Nick up, but I didn't have his last name, and Los Angeles is a big city…lots of, ah, website design companies. And then I thought after I received your music that you'd get in touch with me...I was waiting...I've played your songs so many times." I let out a strangled laugh. That was an understatement. I had the entire soundtrack memorized, every note, every chord. "I've played them all to the baby, too," I whispered. "I wanted he or she to know you right from the beginning...and...I felt your heart there. I..." *Oh God, say something. Anything.*

Something seemed to break inside him as he let out a breath, his shoulders relaxing and a slow smile overtaking his face. "We made a baby that weekend in that tiny attic room, in that tiny bed." His grin widened even more, and he laughed, a sound full of joy.

"Yes. I...You're...happy?"

"Jessie." He laughed again, dropping the umbrella on the street and reaching for me, pulling me into his arms. "I'm happy. It's a miracle." He brought his lips to mine, laughing as we kissed, and he spun me around in the dwindling rain. Elation gripped me, a relief so intense that it felt like my knees might buckle. But Callen held me tightly, not allowing me to fall. *Rescuing me.*

After we'd kissed for a few more minutes, he pulled back. "You told me you weren't pregnant, that night at your work dinner."

"I didn't know. It had only been two weeks since that weekend. And I guess I just figured I wasn't. Maybe I...maybe I even hoped I wasn't. I didn't know how to feel. Things were so—"

"I know. I'm sorry. I'm so sorry." Callen kissed me again, holding me close.

After a minute I tilted my head, his words from earlier penetrating. "Wait, you moved to France? When?"

He smiled. "Yep. A few months ago. I bought a house in

Giverny. It's really old, has tons of history, and a beautiful private garden in the back with so many rosebushes you can smell them in the air when you step outside." His expression sobered. "It has plenty of extra bedrooms. There's a small one next to the master that would make a perfect nursery. It has this window seat and lots of light…"

I let out a sound that was half laugh, half sob, not sure whether I wanted to laugh with joy or cry with unspent emotion. Maybe both. I cupped his cheek in my hand, running my thumb over his cheekbone. "You've been there all these months by yourself?"

He shook his head. "No. I mean, yes. I mean, I have a dog now. Pierre. She's good company."

I raised a brow. *Pierre?* "She?"

He laughed. "Yeah. I didn't look closely enough before I named her. By that time she was already answering to it. I'll tell you all about how I found her later." He leaned in, resting his forehead on mine. "We have so much to talk about, Jessie. I have so much to tell you."

"I have so much to tell you, too," I whispered, smiling. "But tell me again."

"What?"

"What you wrote in your letter."

"That I'm sorry?"

"No, not that part. The other part."

His smile was filled with tenderness. "I love you, Jessie. Only you. I've loved you for a long, long time, forever I think. I want to make a life with you and our baby. I want to write you love letters with my music. I want to feed you French chocolate." His smile increased, and I let out a soggy-sounding laugh before we both went serious again, my breath suspended at the look of adoration on his handsome face. "I want to hear the passion in your voice when you talk about your work. I want to take walks, and sit in front of fires, and make love, and raise children, and grow old together. I want to be your prince."

I was crying again, silent tears that coursed down my face, but I smiled through them, so much happiness in my heart.

"I love you, too," I said, pulling him to me again, touching my lips to his as the last of the raindrops fell and the whole of Paris seemed to pause, just for a moment, just for us.

EPILOGUE

CALLEN

The little boy toddled unsteadily through the wildflowers, the faint vibration of sound emanating from his throat and floating to me on the mild spring breeze. He was humming. My heart caught, squeezing with love, and just a little bit of fear, before resuming its calm, steady pace. Music lived inside him, too—I'd passed on that gift. Perhaps I'd passed on my struggles as well, and maybe it was what the music did: fill our brains so completely that there was little room for other things. Then again, I'd learned to read. I would never grasp written words and phrases, sentences and language structure the way Jessie did, but I could read menus now. I could read signs and directions, product information, text messages, and e-mails. The world had opened up to me, but most of all, I felt a renewed sense of my own capabilities, the pride that came with putting my mind to something and

accomplishing it, the self-respect that accompanied a new willingness to *try*, even when I was afraid.

And in any case, I would be proud of my son for whoever he
was. The words that would ring in his head when he thought of
me would be words of love and admiration, pride, and joy. He
would always know that when I looked at him, I saw a miracle.

"It's a beautiful day, isn't it?" Jessie asked, coming up next to
me and wrapping her arms around my waist, her head resting
on my shoulder. I put my arm around her and pulled her closer,
kissing the top of her head as we watched our son laugh and
change direction, following after a romping Pierre.

"It's perfect," I said. We had come to the field next to the cave
where Adélaïde's letters had been found and had a picnic lunch,
enjoying the gorgeous Loire Valley as spring burst forth and
basking in the sweet memories of the place where we'd fallen in
love. The place where our family had begun.

Maybe that wasn't totally accurate. Perhaps our family had
actually begun its story many years ago, in an abandoned boxcar
on a summer evening in California. Maybe fate had waited all
this time for us to see the path she'd so lovingly laid out for us.
She seemed to be patient that way.

"I feel them here," Jessie murmured, turning to the cave behind us. "I can still hear Adélaïde's voice in my head sometimes.
I imagine the things she might say, the advice she'd give."

I looked into her dream-filled eyes, my gaze moving over her
beautiful face, those large hazel eyes, those sweet, full lips that
I'd never tire of kissing. *Thank you*, I whispered inside myself.
Thank you for her. For them. The sun had brought out Jessie's
freckles, and I leaned down and kissed one, unable to resist. She
laughed and I smiled. "What does she say?"

Close to where we stood, Austin lost his balance and went

down on his well-padded, diapered butt. Pierre was at his side in an instant, licking his face as our eighteen-month-old son pulled himself to his feet, continuing the exploration they'd been on.

"She tells me to listen to my heart, to notice all the gifts I'm given, even the seemingly small ones, and to have patience when you leave your cereal bowl in the sink without rinsing it out."

I laughed. "She's a wise soul."

Her smile became pensive. "She is. Mostly, she reminds me to be grateful for it all." I pulled her closer, feeling just that.

The year before, to create a more complete picture of the writings that had been translated, Dr. Moreau and Jessie tracked down information on Captain Olivier Durand, who had served in the French army during the Hundred Years' War. They searched through ancient French archives and finally found records that showed that Captain Durand had married Adélaïde Beauvais, the disowned daughter of a French aristocrat, the same year Joan of Arc was burned at the stake for heresy. Captain Durand had retired from the army, and together they'd raised five children. They'd lived out their days in a village in France, where Olivier and Adélaïde farmed the land, tending their orchards until their deaths. Olivier passed first and Adélaïde followed three weeks later.

There was no information that could be found on where they'd been buried, if the gravestones even still existed, and so we came here to pay homage. It felt right. Here they had lived. Here they had expressed their love for the first time, and here was where they'd been brought back together.

And it was the same for us.

Jessie had given her notice at the Louvre the week before and was going to venture out on her own as a freelance translator. She'd been the lead on several big projects since she'd worked there, but she'd get more variety of work if she was a free agent. And she'd be able to work according to her own schedule and travel if she wanted. She'd already been contacted by a museum in the French Riviera that had come across buried writings from an old French prison and a family on the coast of Normandy who had found a box of letters that they believed incriminated a distant relative who had been a duchess of murdering her husband the duke.

And so we'd go on adventures together once again, Jessie and me, at least while Austin was young. She'd learn to cook, she said, and continue to fix up our French cottage, which she'd fallen madly in love with. And she'd tend the roses in our garden. Roses, to remind us of the weekend that changed everything, the weekend that fate brought us to an inn with a room that provided very close...proximity. The room where I handed over my heart and had been happily ruined for anyone else forever. The room where we'd unknowingly created our beloved little boy.

And, of course, I would continue to write Jessie love letters with my music.

The soundtrack I'd written, with the title song for Jessie, had become a success beyond any of my wildest dreams. I'd even won several Academy Awards, which had brought my career into a whole new realm. The security the money brought was nice, but the fame didn't fill me anymore. I cherished my quiet life in Giverny, venturing to Paris only once in a while for the occasional business meeting with my new agent or to wine and dine my wife. Jessie went a little more often, to visit Frankie and have lunch with friends and old colleagues.

After that disastrous interview with Cyril Sauvage, I'd spoken of my illiteracy and how I'd subsequently learned to read only once, at the Oscars. As I received my first award, I read my speech to the audience, the one I'd painstakingly written out in my own hand, dedicating the words to my wife. The media replayed it ad nauseam, including the tear-streaked faces of almost everyone in the theater. Jessie never had enough of replaying it. I only laughed, still slightly embarrassed by the attention for something I'd hidden all my life as a secret shame. But like Jessie often said, there was no real bravery without fear.

"Should we head home?" I asked. The afternoon was dwindling toward early evening and the sun was lowering. "If we leave now we can be home by sunset."

She nodded, dropping her arms from my waist.

I whistled for Pierre as I walked to my son, scooping him up into my arms and tossing him into the air, and he shrieked with laughter. I caught him easily, laughing along with him. Then I perched him on my shoulders and returned to Jessie.

We gathered our things and began the walk through the meadow to our car, our fingers linked, Pierre running ahead of us. Jessie's thumb ran over the back of my hand, her touch as soft as the brush of a feather. Austin hummed happily, something I could feel with his chin propped on my head. And in my mind's eye, I saw the shadows of two long-ago lovers who had once walked right where we now tread. Who, like us, had walked toward their destiny with love and conviction.

The music swelled around me, within me, filling my heart with hope, the notes my own personal guide down the path fate had set before me. My father's words no longer had the power to wound me. They had been replaced with words of truth and courage. But I also knew now that life was *more* than words. It was laughter and love, faith and joy. And mostly, it was the deep peace that came from living life fiercely and without regret.

ACKNOWLEDGMENTS

I am so lucky to work with such amazing, talented people. Without them this story would be a mere shadow of itself.

To Marion Archer for helping me structure and organize, rearrange, and streamline. And thank you for not only being my editor, but for being my friend. You have a heart of gold and I value you so very, very much.

Thank you to Karen Lawson for your eagle eyes and your huge heart.

Gratitude to Tessa Shapcott for your thoughtful notes and helpful insight.

Massive appreciation for my beta readers, Elena Eckmeyer, Cat Bracht, Ashley Brinkman, Denise Coy, Holly Michelle Downs, JoAnna Koller, Rachel Morgenthal, and Shauna Waldleitner Rogers.

Thank you to Patricia Varange for staying up far too late translating my words into French, editing my French references, mapping distances in the Loire Valley so I didn't look like an idiot, and giving me information only someone who lives in France could give. Thank you for the wonderful discussions about Joan of Arc, telling me what Paris smells like in the fall, and for correcting me when I tried to end every French character's sentence with *oui?* Somehow this crazy book business brought you to me from across the globe and I have been blessed.

Heartfelt gratitude to Amy Pierpont. I truly feel as if you worked on this book as hard as I did. Editing can be a very personal experience as both the editor and the author spend an incredible amount of time in each other's brains. Thank you for having such a pleasant, sensitive, extremely astute brain to be in. You helped elevate my storyline, deepen my characters, and strengthen my voice. If I am a better writer going forward, it's because of you.

Thank you to Penina Lopez for your immense amount of knowledge and for going through my manuscript so thoroughly. I always love this step of the process because I learn so much!

Thank you to the entire Forever family for making this feel like such a team effort.

To Kimberly Brower who is a true heroine and the best agent there is. I don't know what I ever did before I had you. Flail, I think. I remember a lot of flailing.

To you, the beloved reader, thank you for choosing me.

Thank you to Mia's Mafia for your love and devotion.

To all the bloggers, tweeters, Instagrammers, and book groups who work long hours to support us authors. It is so often because of you that readers find our work and you deserve all the gratitude in the world.

And to Kevin for arriving on a breath of fate.

ABOUT THE AUTHOR

Mia Sheridan is a *New York Times*, *USA Today*, and *Wall Street Journal* bestselling author. Her passion is weaving true love stories about people destined to be together. Mia lives in Cincinnati, Ohio, with her husband. They have four children here on earth and one in heaven.

Learn more at:

MiaSheridan.com

Twitter, @MSheridanAuthor

Instagram, @MiaSheridanAuthor

Facebook.com/MiaSheridanAuthor